A TABLE ROCK MYSTERY

A TABLE ROCK MYSTERY

Tom Wood

To one who knew it should never end.
I am grateful beyond words.

Contents

1

The fib that lit the fuse

Monday, August 5th, 2024, 10:30 A.M.

THE MAILROOM AT THE LAW firm of Bronson Cummings is the first office where visitors, lawyers, secretaries, or employees would approach after coming through the firm's reception area. Sixty-two attorneys occupy offices of assorted sizes, determined by their rank in the firm, and they each receive various amounts of mail which must be sorted to the individual lawyer after being delivered by the post office.

Because of the importance of the mail, the boss in the mailroom had the responsibility for sorting the mail into what would become the delivery sequence based on each lawyer's particular office location. Carl Schultz, the mailroom's original manager from the time that the firm began, known then as Stone, Bass, and Taylor, was almost let go when it became Bronson Cummings five years ago. When the firm merged and Bronson Cummings became the firm's identity, Carl's age worked against him. At age sixty-four and almost deaf, it was logical to push him into retirement. Carl convinced the partners to keep him at least until he qualified for social security.

Even with all the duties properly defined and delegated as to who should do what, things can still happen and go wrong. That is what occurred the morning during the previous week as a letter boldly marked with the words, Certified Mail, was being delivered by a Special Delivery Messenger and required a signature when it was delivered. The receptionist signed it just as Carl Schultz reported to work and handed it to him. Carl saw the addressee was none other than Bronson Cummings.

He went into the mailroom and placed the letter on his desk before taking off his coat, when suddenly he felt dizzy and slumped over, pushing the letter off onto the floor where it slid into a two-inch space between the desk and a filing cabinet.

Carl was rushed to the hospital where they discovered he had suffered a stroke. He remained in the hospital for the next four days, one day less than it took for the important certified letter to be found. The custodian, who only vacuums the mailroom on Sundays when no one is working there, found the letter and put it with the mail that would be delivered the next business day to Mr. Cummings's personal secretary, Elsa Pemberton. It was only after she opened it and saw it concerned Lucas Juliano, the letter received the urgent treatment that the sender intended for it, albeit later than when it would have been useful to do anything that could avoid the outcome that was warned of inside it.

The letter that was lost when Carl Schultz fell ill and slid into that hidden crevice in the mailroom was endorsed Personal and Confidential. The return address shown was a law firm Bronson Cummings recognized immediately. Tomas Cullerton, who sent it, was a classmate of his at John Marshall Law School.

The letter began by explaining that his firm was handling a divorce case for Emily Flynn Paladino. During the Discovery process it was learned that her husband started a new business and borrowed $350,000 from Lucas Juliano who was represented by the Bronson Cummings Law Firm. He pledged 100% ownership of his three Taverns, known as Mickey Flynn's for collateral. Cullerton was writing to inform all interested parties that the amount pledged was fraudulent in that his client, Emily Paladino, owned fifty percent outright in her own name and that she did not sign the note used by Mickey Paladino to secure the loan. As a courtesy, Cullerton would wait for a response until 5:00 P.M. Monday, August 26, 2024, before notifying the District Attorney's office.

Bronson was aware that his former classmate most certainly knew of the friction between himself and District Attorney Howard Wills. Should the D.A. get hold of information that the loan application papers were drawn up by the Bronson Cummings Law Firm and that they contained false information to support the loan, it would be all that was necessary to open an investigation to bring charges of malpractice against him to the Illinois Bar Association.

It would not matter that the loan applicant, Mickey Paladino, lied, since it was the responsibility of his firm, which prepared the documents, to validate the collateral entries on the application. What concerned Bronson most was having the real source of the loan discovered, knowing that Lucas Juliano was merely a front for the mob-run group that provided the money for that loan. Juliano's silent partner was better known as La Cosa Nostra.

Cullerton's deadline meant that less than three weeks remained before Bronson Cummings could unravel the series of errors that would, at a minimum, damage the reputation of his law firm, and even worse, place him on the losing side of a conflict with La Cosa Nostra.

"Mrs. Pemberton," Bronson spoke softly while calling her back to his desk. Then, in a firmer tone he added, "Call Lucas Juliano."

2

A Silent Partnership

Monday, August 5th

Bronson Cummings began his career in law twenty-five years earlier as a criminal defense lawyer in Cicero, Illinois. He did not like the fact that this line of work meant that he was often associated with people charged with breaking laws. Those were people that often thought laws were not meant for them... until they needed someone like himself who followed the laws, and had studied the laws, and now could explain to a judge or a jury why there were parts of the laws which were vague and that some otherwise illegal conduct could be explained in ways resulting in acquittals.

Bronson was remarkably successful in securing for his many clients their desired outcome in court. His reputation flourished exponentially in pace with his wealth. Eventually his resources were sufficient to obtain financing that he used to merge and purchase majority interest in one of the most respected law firms on LaSalle Street. The money needed arrived through the connections his client, Lucas Juliano, had with the mob, but it did everything he hoped for regarding his reputation. It was not just that Stone, Bass, and Taylor had become Bronson Cummings. It was that Bronson Cummings had become Stone, Bass, and Taylor.

His new firm had a client portfolio of super-rich, crème de la crème, pillars of Chicago society. His firm was now known for handling estates, taxes, divorces, patent litigations, and antitrust cases. Ordinary criminals did not even think of calling on him anymore. At last, most of those types understood they were in his past. Most of them moved on, and except for one, Bronson had escaped from that more sordid life.

*   *   *

Lucas Juliano began his career running a numbers game in Berwyn that made all kinds of money and two types of enemies, the law… and La Cosa Nostra. The police wanted to get him out of the numbers racket by arresting him. The Cosa Nostra thought they owned that racket and wanted to get him out of it… in a less temporary way. But Lucas continued and even expanded his "business." The police were no trouble thanks to his lawyer, Bronson Cummings, who knew more about the nuances in law than any of those just-out-of-law school assistant district attorneys.

"Procedures have a purpose" was the most frequent way Bronson began each defense, whether solely before a judge or in opening statements to a jury. Then he always proceeded with a litany of ways in which the procedures were violated either during the arrest, or in the preparation of the statement of charges. When all else failed, he found mistakes made in the production of evidence against his client that allowed for doubt concerning its authenticity.

"You cost me a fortune," Juliano complained once to the lawyer. "But a hundred percent is a heck of a batting average so keep up the good pitching," he added, unaware of the mixed metaphor.

However, having an organization such as La Cosa Nostra line up as the other enemy was something Lucas had to worry about. The Mob sent one of their soldiers, Piles Beck, to persuade Juliano that that there was no business like show business unless that business was the kind his bosses liked to call their own. In the instant case, the show business was the Numbers game.

The Mob's territory covered everything south of Twelfth Street from Lake Michigan on the east to DeKalb on the west and all the way to Peoria for their southernmost boundary.

"Like map reading was not my favorite course at Taft high school," Piles explained. "Still, it's easy to see that Berwyn lies smack in that circle somewhere."

The whole time Piles was speaking he kept trying to hold his mouth at an angle as he talked just like he saw Hollywood actors did in the old gangster movies he watched on Turner Classic Movies. It was comical, but Lucas was smart enough to know that as twisted and tangled the words spoken by Piles were, at their core, they were the same message he was sent to deliver. Juliano told Piles that he could return to his bosses and tell them that all he was asking for was a meeting to see if they could resolve things.

Lucas heard nothing for a whole month. Then, out of nowhere, he got a call from Piles telling him to be at the West Side Sportsman Club on Laramie Avenue within the hour. When he pulled into the gravel parking lot behind the club, as were the instructions he received, he wondered if the right time might be now to make that Perfect Act of Contrition he learned at Help of Christians Elementary many years ago.

Turned out that the question of ownership of the Berwyn Numbers Game was not on the agenda that day. The man who called for the meeting did not look like someone from La Cosa Nostra. This guy looked more like a banker. His accent was

French when he introduced himself to be Guy Chevron, and then, pretending as if he was truly a gentleman, thanked Lucas for coming in.

"Lucas, I'll come straight to the point," he began. "We could take Berwyn away from you before the tears you might be tempted to shed would fall upon your chin."

Lucas was now a bit confused. He could tell that this Mister Guy Chevron was leading up to telling him that something else that he was going to have to give them was the something they wanted more than his Business-in-Berwyn.

Chevron walked towards the bar as he spoke, waving for Lucas to follow. After he told the bartender to fix him a Scotch, he asked if Lucas wanted something.

Juliano smiled as he looked up at the shelves behind the bar where there were fifty different choices. Just as the bartender poured a Johnny Walker Black over two ice cubes for Guy Chevron, Lucas made his choice.

"I'll have what Mr. Chevron is having," he said. "But make mine without the JWB, just two ice cubes, and some club soda… if you got that handy."

Both Chevron and the bartender looked puzzled. Was this guy wising off? Or was something else going on?

With their drinks in hand the two men settled in a booth by the juke box. Two men who appeared to be there only if any trouble occurred were in an adjacent booth. They stumbled out and went to the bar so as not to be thought of as listening in to someone's business that was not their own.

"Mr. Juliano, we have a mutual obstacle to our preferred types of business, not just in Berwyn but throughout southwest Cook County," he said after taking a polite sip from his drink. "We know that you have had any number of troubles thrown your way by this same obstacle, Mr. Assistant District Attorney, Howard Wills, right?"

Juliano said nothing but kept his eyes focused directly on Guy Chevron's eyes. Chevron took that gesture as being affirmative and continued with what he was saying.

"We have been watching how you have been able to keep your business going strong, even with all that trouble that Wills causes. It left us wondering, just who does Lucas Juliano own in Berwyn or in Cook County? The mayor? the City Council?... the politicians that support the D.A.?" He paused at that point searching for any clues he might observe in Juliano's expression.

"Actually, you see, we finally figured it out," Chevron smiled. "That lawyer you got. You go to that fella Bronson Cummings and... **Whoosh!** away goes the troubles with the law."

The little mouse that spins the wheel that fires up those axons and dendrites that turns sparks of thoughts inside the brain of Lucas Juliano were by this time making way too much noise to allow him to continue playing like he had no idea what the purpose for this meeting was.

"You want to get my lawyer to be your lawyer. Okay, I get it," he said. "But why do you all need me? Why not just pay the retainer and get on with it?"

Chevron leaned forward in the booth indicating he wanted Lucas to talk more quietly.

"You see," he said in an almost whisper, "Mr. Bronson Cummings thinks he has a reputation problem. He just does not want more clients like..."

"Yeah, I know," Lucas laughed. "Like me is what he must have told you. So, cutting this to the sharpest point," Lucas continued. "You guys want me to talk to Bronson and see if I can change his mind, right?"

Lucas Juliano knew that he would not have any trouble arranging the legal services that were being sought by Guy Chevron. He was not sure how their interests could be homogenized with something he might want to receive for making that arrangement, other than it would get the mob off his back. He decided not to ask any questions. That way they would not have the chance to ask what it was that made him and Bronson Cummings so close.

That thought brought back some good memories of how it came to be that the lawyer and he were such "good friends."

"We're partners for life," was what he told Bronson Cummings on that sunny day they met at Hawthorne Racetrack in secret five years earlier.

Bronson seemed uneasy with that assertion but understood its meaning after Juliano "arranged" to change the government's star witness's planned testimony. That help from Lucas led to the Illinois Racing Board's decision to acquit Cummings in the scandal that involved knowing the outcome of races before the horses entered the starting gate. It was back when his law practice was struggling financially and a horse trainer by the unfortunate name of Frank Schade, pronounced Shady, paid his legal debt off by giving Bronson inside tips when fellow trainers took money to hold back favorites in certain races.

"Partners for life, you say?" Bronson responded to the implied contract being declared by Lucas Juliano. "Change that to… let's see," he said before offering a handshake. "Make that Silent Partners and we have a deal."

3

Come to Chicago

Monday, August 12th, 10:00 A.M.

THERE WERE TWO OBJECTIONS that Mickey Paladino had about traveling away from his home in the Ozarks. The first one was that for too much of the time you were stuck in either a plane or an automobile, usually for six to eight hours straight. The other complaint dealt with hotels. Mickey did not like sleeping in beds that who-knew-who slept there just before he arrived. But when he received the telephone call from Lucas Juliano's attorney, Bronson Cummings, during which was mentioned that his presence in Chicago would be "appreciated," well… that dropped those objections too far down his list of priorities to leave room for any further concern.

All Mickey told his girlfriend Kylie Cooper was to pack up because they would be on their way to Chicago as soon as she completed that task. He knew that, unlike how he felt about traveling, Kylie was "ants-on sugar bread excited" just at the suggestion that they were leaving Southwest Missouri. When she found out they would stay at the Palmer House Hilton, within walking distance of the Magnificent Mile with the stores and beautiful people along the Gold Coast, all she could think to do was throw her arms around his neck and give him a big wet kiss.

* * *

The Palmer House was only a short four block walk to the Ronson Building on LaSalle Street where Bronson Cummings's law firm was located on the twenty-first and twenty-second floors. The lawyer never gave a reason for holding the meeting, or if Juliano would even be there. But that word, "appreciated" was meant to be understood more like a command. Be There... or else!

The only thing that Mickey could think of might be a reason concerned the money he borrowed through Juliano to use for the purchase of Ozark Lake Leisure Boats. He speculated that the attorney wanted an update on the financial conditions, stuff like current revenues, competition, things that could affect the viability of the loan. Since each of these items looked solid, and if that WAS all that this was about, the meeting would not take too long, and he could get back to his "Vacation in the City" with Kylie.

The lobby at the Ronson Office Building was impressive with shiny marble finished walls and floors and a building directory with digital touchscreen features. Noting that the receptionist for the Bronson Cummings Law Firm was on the twenty-first floor, Mickey moved quickly to catch an elevator that was in the process of closing its door. The elevator had only four other people using it, but Mickey had to wait until it stopped and let off someone on the fourth floor to push the button next to the number twenty-one. He was surprised to discover that in his rush to catch this elevator he failed to notice that this one went only to the twelfth floor. He would have to wait until it stopped going up and stay on it while it returned all the way back to the lobby. A feeling of irritation crept into his thoughts and prompted a concern about what else he had failed to notice in his haste preparing for the meeting.

When Mickey finally reached the twenty-first floor, he stepped out of the elevator directly into the Bronson Cummings Law firm Reception area. The walls were covered along the lower half in wainscoting made of a dark wood while the upper half was wallpapered in a rich gold pattern. He caught sight right away of the blonde attractive receptionist who smiled as he approached and gave his name.

"Good morning, Mr. Paladino," she greeted him. "Yes, I see that you have a meeting with Mr. Cummings. If you take a seat, I will call for someone who will escort you."

Mickey thanked her and stepped back to where a leather sofa was located behind a round glass coffee table. He sat down and noticed that among the reading material on the coffee table was a copy of The Wall Street Journal, the Chicago Law Bulletin, and the Chicago Sun Times. He reached for the Sun Times just as the employee she called entered and asked Mickey to follow him to Mr. Cummings's office.

The receptionist turned abruptly towards the guide after hearing what he said. "David," she began, "The meeting was changed from Mr. Cummings's office to the small conference room upstairs on 22." Turning back to Mickey she added, "Mr. Cummings asks that you wait for him there as he has a few items he wants to complete before your meeting." Mickey said nothing but the guide acknowledged his understanding of the change and led them back to the elevator.

"If this is the small conference room," Mickey thought to himself while waiting for his meeting to begin with Bronson Cummings, "the one they call the large conference room must be one massive son-of-a-bitch."

The guide pulled out a chair for Mickey next to the end of the conference table. "Probably where the lawyer intended to be seated," Mickey suspected. As far as he knew, there was only going to be himself and the lawyer at the meeting. Nonetheless, there were four chairs along the table on the side where Mickey sat and five more across from them. Counting the ones at each end there was room for ten more people. Mickey hoped that was not the case. He wondered just what was going to happen next.

Almost thirty minutes after Mickey arrived in the conference room, he heard someone talking just out of sight in the hallway. Unable to hear everything, he was able to make out that it was a man's voice, and he was telling someone else that something was "not a very wise… something… something and don't worry about… something." Then the voice lowered to a whisper and Mickey thought he heard someone else talking but not loud enough for him to understand what was being spoken. He thought about getting up and sneaking closer to the conference room door when in stepped a man who greeted him and then introduced himself.

Bronson Cummings impressed Mickey as being exactly how he thought he would find him. Tall, a bit over six feet, and trim… something like one hundred and ninety or so. His hair, what there was of it, was dark with indications that it was in the initial stages of changing to gray.

But it was the suit that he wore that really left the impression that he was far too successful to worry about such things as shopping for any clothes off the rack. "This one had to set him back at least a couple of grand," Mickey thought silently as he reached out and accepted the handshake Cummings offered him. Bronson Cummings stepped back and took a seat at the farther end of the conference table.

A nice-looking woman in her early forties next entered the room carrying a thick file and set it in front of the lawyer.

Cummings opened and inspected the first few items and then looked up and nodded showing that it was what he had told her to bring to him. She gave a timid smile back and then left the room, closing the conference door as she left.

The lawyer said nothing more as he culled through the file, occasionally removing an item and laying it either in front or on his left or right side. Mickey watched in silence, not wanting to interrupt anything going on, but wondering what those papers had written on them and how did they apply to what he thought this meeting was about.

Waiting all this time in silence and having no idea why this important man was taking all this time solely for something involving him brought an unwanted feeling of tension. Mickey grew impatient while at the same time began feeling progressively more intimidated. Still, he wisely retained his poise waiting for the lawyer to say why the meeting was called.

Finally, Bronson Cummings stood up and set what remained in the file on the chair alongside him. He left that location and walked and stood directly across from Mickey before he began talking.

"Mickey," he smiled, "Do you remember who it was that arranged for you to come to Lucas Juliano when you needed that loan to buy Ozark Lake Leisure Boats?"

For a few seconds Mickey stayed silent, wondering if the lawyer was going to pull out a chair and sit across from him or should he, himself, stand up?

"Uh, yes, I remember that one of my employees at the clubs we own set us up… uh, Frankie Valenti was… uh, is his name."

The lawyer remained standing across from Mickey. It was becoming evident that he was holding all the cards in this game, and he might as well maintain the dominant posture too.

"That is right. Valenti was working at those bars that you own… What are their names…??

Mickey sat up more straight in the well cushioned high back conference chair but remained seated in it. "Yes, we opened up the first one in Branson… and it went so well that we opened another in St. Louis and one in Chicago."

"Yes, I know there are three of them. But my question was… what are they named?"

"Oh?" Mickey stuttered an apology. "We called the first one Mickey Flynn's, you know, sounds like that drink… a Mickey… Mickey Finn??"

"And when your accountant persuaded you to open more you named them all the same way. Right?"

"Yeah… sure. It was catchy and people took to it… the name. And then too, the food and the bar stuff. Oh, you do know we also have cabaret licenses for each of them so that we can include live entertainment…"

The lawyer had moved back to where he left the file contents. "I understand all that Mr. Paladino. But I am curious about that name… Mickey Flynn's…"

"Like I just told you, sounds just like Mickey Finn. The drink was a knockout, just like what we promised our customers… a knockout of an enjoyable time…" His response trailed into an implied question, "Get it?"

"Let me change the subject for a minute now. I understand that you are in the middle of a divorce proceeding, right?

Mickey nodded but said nothing aloud in response.

"You are being divorced by a woman named Emily Paladino… Emily **Flynn** Paladino, true?"

Once again, Mickey only nodded his affirmative response.

"So then," his voice picking up an edge. "You picked the names for your restaurants using your first name and… your wife's maiden name."

Mickey stayed quiet, almost pushing his interrogator to hurry up and get to his point.

"Mickey... And... Flynn," Bronson Cumming's voice went up on Mickey and back down on Flynn... in song. "Even... steven"

The lawyer moved to the right side of the conference table and picked up what looked like copies of a contract. "When you borrowed three hundred and fifty-thousand dollars through my client, Lucas Juliano, you used that to purchase the Ozark Lake Leisure Boats from a company in Lampe, Missouri that goes by the name of Worldwide Lake Boat Sales. As collateral you signed a contract that put up one hundred percent of your three establishments known as Mickey Flynn's. Isn't all of that correct?"

Mickey leaned forward and rested his elbows on the table. His breathing was noticeable, going at a faster pace than just moments earlier. This time he answered the lawyer's last question with a weak, "yes... right... all true!" He recognized how his inexperience at dealing with a lawyer had him at a severe disadvantage.

Bronson Cummings then walked the length of the table back to where Mickey sat and put in front of him the loan contract that he just referred to a minute ago. "Take a look at the signatures on that contract. One by you and the other by your wife."

Mickey merely glanced down at the papers.

The lawyer decided that enough ground had been covered and he began drawing things to their conclusion. "Mickey, the lawyer for your wife in the divorce proceeding has informed me that Emily Flynn Paladino has not signed over those three Mickey Flynn's as collateral... and that she will retain her full fifty percent ownership regardless of how successful you are at paying back your loan to Lucas Juliano."

Mickey sat stoically numbed at the discovery of the forged signature. "What does this all mean?" he asked. "What's next?"

Bronson Cummings began reassembling the contents of the file. Before leaving the room, he turned and looked sternly back at Mickey, now slouched into the back of the conference chair.

"The loan you received is being recalled. I have been told by my client, Lucas Juliano, to inform you that you have until Friday… THIS coming Friday… to make full repayment. With interest and appropriate penalties applied, my client expects a sum of five hundred thousand dollars. If you are successful in meeting that deadline you are to bring that amount to my office no later than 5:00 P.M. on Friday, August 16th and I will hand back to you the contract that you signed, for yourself, and for your wife."

Bronson Cummings then left Mickey Paladino sitting by himself in the large conference room… at the end of the long conference table. In all his life Mickey Paladino never felt any more all alone.

4

So much to do.
So little time.

Monday, August 12th, 11:30 A.M.

MICKEY FELT LIKE A 'DEAD MAN WALKING' after leaving the offices of Bronson Cummings. The sidewalks were much less populated than when he used them to walk from the Palmer House earlier to the meeting with Lucas Juliano's lawyer. Mickey took little notice of that difference except that it was adding to his growing feeling that the entire world was changing and coming to an end.

Waves of worrying thoughts kept crashing against each other in his mind jumping from what just happened, to how do I explain any of this to Kylie, back to what can be done to… gulp, get out of this jam??? By the time he was back inside the lobby of the Palmer House his focus was forced to center on Kylie Cooper. She came with him expecting that his business meeting would take only a few hours away from their plans to enjoy the sights and sounds of the Windy City.

Now, none of that was going to be possible. He had been

given a deadline to figure out something that would allow him to remain alive afterwards.

The next two hours were spent trying to explain why it was necessary to cancel their plans together in Chicago followed by many futile attempts to console the bitterly disappointed woman whom he had brought into the mess that he had now made of his life. In between the unwanted repacking chores that Kylie left for him to do alone after leaving the room to think everything over, Mickey tried to make reservations for a return flight to Branson, Missouri, only to discover that all were completely booked. Other than to wait another full day he learned that the best option left was to grab reservations for a flight to St. Louis that would depart from O'Hare in less than three hours. Mickey, knowing that time had become more valuable than money to him now, booked himself and Kylie into First Class, the last two seats available. Finally, he called Hertz and reserved a Dodge Nitro that they would use to drive from the St. Louis airport to where they had been living at Kylie's condominium in Branson.

They lost some time at the Hertz Rental location waiting for the clerk there to find the Dodge Nitro Mickey reserved. Eventually, things worked out and they began the four-and-a-half-hour drive to their destination in Branson. Kylie was silent during the flight as she fought back the hurt from the abrupt change of plans. But by the time they were in the rental car she began to realize the danger that caused Mickey to make that decision. They had almost reached Rolla, almost half-way to her luxury condominium at Indian Point before she let go of her own sadness and expressed how frightened she had become for his safety.

"I won't fib-ya," Mickey said, happy that Kylie was returning to her normal self. "Those bums play hardball and leave nothing to chance when someone screws with them."

"But you didn't really screw with them," Kylie said. "You were paying off the loan and you weren't behind on payments…"

Mickey kept his eyes on the road ahead but turned slightly to let her know he was paying attention. He recalled Kylie's frequent complaints since the time they became a couple that she felt he just took her for granted, that whatever she thought was "cute" but not much more valuable than that. He had not yet told her exactly what it was that drove the wedge between him and Juliano. But time was running out and sharing it all with her might lead to some kind of plan.

"Baby, Emily's lawyer got a look at the collateral I put up for that loan from Juliano."

"So what?" she asked looking directly at him. "Juliano loaned you the money you needed for the Ozark Lake Leisure Boats, and you put up your half of...,"

Mickey could see that she just did not get it. "I just told you it was Emily's lawyer who blew the whistle... damn-it."

Kylie turned away from him, looking instead out the passenger door window. "You don't have to get so mad," she softly complained."

Mickey knew that the panic that was rushing through him was blocking his ability to think logically. He removed his right hand from the steering wheel and searched for her hand, hoping to express how important he felt she was to him now.

"Baby, those lawyers... Emily's, and now Juliano's, they think I forged Emily's name on the loan collateral papers and now they are calling back not only the whole $350,000..."

"But why?" she asked. "Why would they think you needed her signature?"

Mickey sighed, not wanting to shut her out, just not feeling there was any benefit in continuing this conversation.

"Let me finish what I was just saying," his voice still reflecting the fear building within himself. "They gave me until this Friday to pay off the whole loan. Plus, they want another $150 Gs for interest and penalties… and… I do not have squat… notta… no way! You understand?"

They did not resume conversation until they left route 44 and turned south onto route 65 towards Branson.

Kylie understood that she did not have all the facts that were involved in making this such a horrifyingly awful problem. But, looking across at the man driving, all she could think to do was to let him know she was there for him now. She reached across the compartment that separated the bucket seat she was sitting in from his and put her hand on Mickey's lap.

"I was thinking," she began. "Why not go back to Jari and tell him what this is all about?"

"What?? So, he can do… WHAT??" Mickey shouted.

Kylie was getting used to these outbursts, just not what was causing them from the man she was in love with. She knew enough about him that if she would just continue talking, in a nice, soft voice, he would be listening.

"We both know Jari Abdou," she resumed. "I dated him for better than a year and you and Emily doubled with us to enough places and enough times that you got to know something of him yourself… enough to become convinced you wanted to buy the luxury catamarans and other yachts he had at Worldwide Boat Sales."

Mickey had calmed down just as Kylie knew he would and was listening.

"So, I know him, not like you do, uh did, while you two were a couple.. But get to your point."

Kylie smiled, proud that she might have something that could be of help. "Why not see if he will take back one of the boats that he sold to you? You have enough equity in either the Horizon P52 or the Belize Lake Yacht."

It was not an idea that Mickey imagined that Kylie could produce. Yet, it was something that he could massage into a plan.

"Why do you think our Jari Abdou friend would want to just buy back some things he sold to me three years ago?

Kylie was happy that Mickey did not dismiss her suggestion out of hand. "Well, sweetie, since you have owned them, the business of leasing them has almost doubled in customer traffic. Let Jari buy back the ownership of however many are needed to pay off the loan. You will guarantee the lease income for him. Wouldn't an offer like that make it a bit attractive to him now?"

Once again Kylie surprised him. Mickey knew that his fatigue and anxiety had him in such a state that he was not capable just now of thinking things through in a logical step-by-step process. But what Kylie just said made some sense. He let his thoughts wonder to half-hoping that Jari could see it in the same way Kylie just outlined. He might even get the whole $500,000 that was needed to soothe Lucas Juliano's anger problem with him. He could once again put up his half of the loan… or combine them with the Ozark Lake Leisure Boats franchise as collateral for borrowing the full $500,000 from either a bank or whoever has that sum available.

By the time they finally got back to Kylie's luxury condominium at Indian Point in Branson it was midnight and that left Mickey less than forty-eight hours to produce the money. As short as time was for him now Mickey knew he needed nonetheless to squeeze in a few hours' sleep. He was dog-tired and just finding the strength to think was more of an effort than he had the energy left in him.

Kylie, who agreed to leave the unpacking for later, had slipped away long enough to get out of the clothes she had worn all day long and into that Nirvana French Terry pajama top that Mickey loved on her. She poured a glass of Cabernet for herself and brought it and a Jack Daniels on ice for her man.

For now, at least, Mickey's troubles found a hiding place and a smile was released on his worried face as he watched her setting the drinks on the coffee table in front of him.

"Ah," he sighed. "The French Terry Pajama top, sans the rest, shows my baby still loves me."

Kylie was happy to see him finally relax a bit.

"Who would ask for anything more…?"

5

A Plan and a back-up

Tuesday, August 13th, 7:00 A.M.

MICKEY WAS SURPRISED UPON waking to find that it was already 7:00 A.M. Somehow, with all the troubles he had, he hoped that he might manage to get five or six hours of sleep before calling Frankie Valenti and getting Plan A into action. He expected to awaken at sunrise, a habit that began for him when he was a child delivering the morning Tribunes and Sun Times along his neighborhood route on Chicago's northwest side.

Even as precious as time had become for him since that meeting in Bronson Cummings' office, those extra hours of sleep he enjoyed found him refreshed and possessing clear thinking. Both were qualities that he would treasure soon.

He turned his head and saw that Kylie was still asleep. Still wearing only the pajama top, she looked so beautiful to him that he turned and got out of bed rather than yield to the strong impulse he was feeling to kiss her. Of course, that was how it all started things off last night.

They had both retired to the bedroom after a few drinks that were sipped while planning various alternatives that they might seek to get out of the jam with Juliano. He was quite exhausted and thought that he would fall sound asleep as soon as his head hit the pillow. But Kylie had something else in mind.

It began with a simple kiss good night, then he took notice again that she was wearing only her Nirvana French Terry Pajama top, 'rien d'autre,' and the sleep he mere seconds earlier so desperately wanted took a distant second place along with everything else that struggled to find space in his conscious thoughts.

Kylie woke up hearing the shower and had the coffee started by the time Mickey finished and got dressed. They exchanged brief good morning greetings as Kylie passed by him to begin her own morning bathroom routine. Mickey picked up his cell phone along with the cup of coffee she prepared for him and went outside. He loved this spot outside her rear patio sliding doors where her property ran down to the edge of beautiful Table Rock Lake. It was especially peaceful at this early hour since the tourists and other vacationers had not yet cluttered the lake scenery with their power boats, sail boats, and occasionally, small houseboats.

He finished his call to Valenti before Kylie came out to join him by the lake. Their moods were much improved compared to the previous day. Each was back to being playful and naughty and thoughts of how wonderful their lives were, still were, filled them with quiet joy. They had no way of knowing if the plans they discussed and finalized while enjoying the drinks Kylie prepared the previous night were going to prove successful. But by this time tomorrow afternoon all those questions would have their answers.

Two plans: Either Mickey would be successful in convincing Emily to call her lawyer saying that she had authorized Mickey to sign her name on the loan collateral and the deadline demand he imposed would be withdrawn. Or Kylie would be able to charm her ex-boyfriend, Jari Abdou, to buy back one or all their luxury cruise yachts using the Worldwide Lake Boat Sales business he owns.

Mickey, standing with Kylie at his side, silently recalled an old quote from his Saint Ignatius high school Latin studies that never had more significance than now in their lives… "Alea iacta est"… The die is cast.

6

Tricked!

Tuesday, August 13ᵗʰ, 11:30 A.M.

EMILY PALADINO'S MIND WONDERED while diving to the last stop on the regular Friday tour of Open Houses for the newest Multiple Real Estate listings. She had none of her own listings scheduled for this week's tours and none of the four she just went through inspired any excitement for a quick sale. Today's tour contained nothing of interest to anyone she knew who was looking for something to buy, but out of courtesy to her fellow agents she had decided to come along.

When she pulled up to the last planned stop on the tour, a condominium unit that fronted on Table Rock Lake in Kimberling City, her cell phone buzzed indicating a message was waiting. The office manager at My Missouri Home, Twyla Turner, texted a message that a Mr. Valenti called and asked to have Emily show him a house that she had listed for sale near Cassville.

Emily knew Frankie Valenti back when he was a bouncer at one of the Mickey Flynn bars and restaurants she and Mickey owned in Branson. She lost track of him when she and her husband split up but heard recently that her soon-to-be ex hired him subsequently as a mechanic at a business he started called Ozark Lake Leisure Boats.

Before getting out of her Lexus she called Twyla back and found out that Valenti was going to be at the Cassville house and hoped that Emily could meet him there around noon. After checking Emily's desk planner, Twyla said she told him that she thought that could be arranged. Valenti thanked her and then hung up without providing a phone number she could call back to and confirm the appointment.

Emily sighed. That did seem just like the Frankie Valenti she knew, someone who would automatically assume that because he worked with Mickey Paladino, Emily would drop everything else she was doing and meet him at the time he arranged. But, since Twyla did mention that Emily's schedule looked open, she decided that she would skip this final stop on the new listings tour and drive there to meet him.

During the hour drive to Cassville, Emily's thoughts were on Twyla and how anxious she always became if the schedules she drew up for the twelve real estate agents at My Missouri Home needed adjustments. She was that way, in fact, for anything that fell within her responsibility as the office manager. Once, when Emily asked why she always seemed on edge, Twyla snapped at her saying that she worried... so that her boss, Armand Locke would not.

Emily always suspected that Twyla had a schoolchild crush on the Managing Partner at the My Missouri Home Real Estate office. Twyla had an expensive wardrobe and always came to work wearing dresses or business suits that complimented her best features while distracting attention from her figure which would be called stout in polite company. At five feet, two inches in height and two hundred ten pounds, which she admitted to weighing, stout seemed a much nicer way of describing her.

Emily recalled the way Twyla dressed for the office this morning. The Jessica Howard Plus Size Printed Dress with the faux-suede jacket she wore made her easily the best dressed person at work. Emily smiled remembering how Twyla made every effort to be noticed by her boss while achieving only a casual glance from him. Emily could think of no apparent reason that Twyla should own any reasonable expectation that there could be any chance in the future for the intimate relationship with him that she so obviously desired.

Armand Locke became the Managing partner after marrying Estelle Caldwell. Her wealth, coming from inheritance and twice-widowed marriages, made up for her stern ultra-Christian personality and was enough to put the hook into Armand who was until then just another real estate agent. Yet it was her that showed the most frequent indications of being the jealous and the insecure one in their marriage.

The people working at My Missouri Home formed a tightly knitted group over the years, going to 4th of July picnics and attending baptisms, birthday parties, and many Christmas office parties, often with their spouses. Armand always managed to find a way to get Emily aside from the others and whisper compliments about how attractive she looked. It began playfully but over time, as it became something else, Emily did everything she could to avoid being caught alone with just him, away from the others. She found that the most effective strategy was to always be around either his wife Estelle, or Twyla, whom Armand was himself trying to avoid.

Her listing in Cassville was a nice affordable one but left her wondering why Frankie Valenti might be as interested as he seemed. If he were still employed as a mechanic at Mickey's company, Ozark Lake Leisure Boats, there would have been many similar houses for sale closer to his job, such as that condominium she was earlier going to see on the new listings tour over at Kimberling City. However, she had been in the real estate business long enough to know that her reasons never sold houses as well as the ones buyers had for wanting them. If he liked this one, she was confident it was something he would consider being in his price range.

When she turned on to Sunset Heights Street, she saw that a black 2024 Chevrolet Traverse was parked in the driveway. Emily wondered if he realized that parking there in this narrow driveway meant that she would need to park her car on the street. But then, that is how she remembered Frankie Valenti… always taking care of number one!

As she walked up the driveway she wondered if he was even in the car parked there. The windshield, side and rear windows, were tinted making it difficult if not impossible to see inside it. When she was next to the driver's side door, she was about to get close enough to the window to peek inside when suddenly the door swung open. Emily stumbled back, tripping, and out stepped Frankie Valenti.

It was warm, almost 80 degrees, but he wore a leather motorcycle jacket over a crisp, white t-shirt, dark Levis, and black leather boots. His appearance was almost frightening but as Emily regained her balance and stood next to him, he seemed more like a kid in high school than the Marlon Brando he was imitating. Emily forgot that Frankie was that short. With her heels she was almost 5'5 in height, yet Frankie was barely eye-level with her.

After they greeted each other, Emily stepped around Valenti and began walking towards the house when she heard her name being called by someone stepping out from the back seat on the passenger's side of Valenti's car. She recognized immediately that voice. It was coming from her husband, Mickey Paladino. A chill went through her entire body as she realized that Mickey had arranged all of this. But for what reason, she wondered.

Emily froze in place hearing the gravel crunching behind her as Mickey approached. All that she could think to say when she turned around was one word, "Why?"

7

A sit-down special

Tuesday, August 13th, 4:00 P.M.

LUCAS JULIANO LIKED MANY TYPES of music ranging from Classical Rock and Roll of the 60s to any of whom he called the great Italian singers such as Dean Martin, Frank Sinatra, Tony Bennett… up to and including an occasional Pavarotti song. The juke box at the Westside Sportsman's Club had some of these and similar selections usually being played and made it seem a bit more pleasant for him whenever he was called in for a meeting there with Guy Chevron. Though as much as he liked the music it was the opposite of the thoughts that he had for Monsieur Chevron, as he was referred to by those who did any business with him.

Lucas wondered silently to himself how the bosses in La Cosa Nostra found anything of value in this Frenchman. Guy Chevron dressed unlike any of the other regulars, mostly second-generation Italians, who found companionship at the long bar inside the club. Always wearing expensive tailor-made suits or sports coats often an ISAIA Micro plaid-pattern two button suit or a Herringbone Twill Double Breasted with a Maison Martin Margiela label, he seemed completely away from his "types."

The ties he wore were just as expensive, either Brioni solid satins or one of his Saint Laurents. He preferred shoes that came with price tags north of $1500 and always wore Betanin & Venturi with laces.

And for Lucas the worst part of Guy Chevron was his accent. He arrived with his parents from Europe forty years ago and attended elementary, secondary, and university in America. There seemed no excuse to have not lost that accent after all that time unless it was for impressing every one of the nobilities that his family name still owned. Guy Chevron was soft spoken and always polite, even as some have pointed out, he made decisions on who lived… or not.

In any case Lucas understood that Guy Chevron was the point man for the Mob and to play rough with him meant you were planning on a permanent move from the planet earth. Lucas hoped that the trouble he was now having with that loan to Paladino, which was the stated purpose for him being told to meet with the little French dandy, could be worked out without any such result.

Lucas was met at the back entrance door by an old acquaintance, Piles Beck, who told him that Monsieur Chevron was waiting for him in his upstairs office. After climbing the circular stairs to the second floor Lucas felt something pulling inside his chest. He wondered if his shortness of breath was from the difficulty he had walking up the twisting staircase or was something going on with his heart… or his nerves.

"Come right in, Lucas my friend," Guy Chevron greeted him when he reached the open doorway to his office.

"Yes, come into my pretty little web" the spider coaxed his unsuspecting prey, Lucas thought to himself.

Juliano towered over the smaller man who somehow had managed to become the mob's consigliere and thus the far more powerful of the two of them. At six-two and weighing more than three hundred pounds, Lucas was always bigger than most of his contemporaries, which explained in some ways the self-confidence he had in his disposition for dealings with friends or foes alike. But his knowledge of the Mafia structure and how the Capo in any Borgata is the only one outranking the consigliere left little doubt of who deserved to be respected and who's role was required to be compliant.

Not wanting to engage in conversation standing up facing the much larger man, Chevron pointed to the chair across from his desk for Lucas to sit as he returned to his own seat.

"Lucas," he began in his usual quiet way of speaking. "I know that you understand what is meant by the term a Sit Down, isn't that correct?"

Juliano nodded showing he did. "It refers to a meeting that is ordered from up high to settle on something that has gone wrong, I believe…"

Chevron smiled. "Yes, that is the meaning of that term. I have been called by our Capofamiglia to reside over one of those Sit Downs whose purpose will be to decide on the merits of that loan you made to Paladino."

Lucas squirmed upon hearing how high and how fast the news of the Paladino loan being in trouble travelled so that now it had the attention of the Bosses.

"Well, perhaps I can bring you up to date on all that stuff," Lucas said finding his own voice a bit on the softer side. "I just heard from Bronson Cummings, and he said the deadline to pay off the loan was fast approaching without any word from Paladino. When I asked if that meant we would begin foreclosure and take over ownership of the three Mickey Flynn's restaurants he suggested it might not be so easy."

Chevron's eyebrows raised as if this news surprised him.

"Oh?" Chevron sounded as if he was not anticipating that

kind of information. "When you proposed this loan, I asked you two things," he pressed forward. "One was how secure the collateral was and the second wondered was it sufficient if the loan went unpaid."

"I know. I remember that discussion," Lucas said. "I told you that I had looked into both of those concerns and was absolutely certain that the collateral was sufficient and that I knew that much because the Central States Bar Management business that we own has been under contract to run the business at those restaurants and therefore, gave me… us… first hand assurances."

Now it was Chevron's turn to refer to the conversation that preceded the loan approval process.

"Lucas, you seem to be leaving out the part that we talked about if the loan went unpaid."

"Well, to tell you the truth, I was focused on the interest we were pretty sure would be coming in on the loan… and if not, those restaurants were making tons of dough… and not the baking kind."

Chevron laughed at the small joke. But just as fast his expression returned to its usual business-first countenance.

"To tell you the truth, when I went to get the loan approved the Don seemed to be most interested in those restaurants. He asked about who our Shylock was for this loan and when I said it was you, Lucas Juliano, the Don relaxed. He okayed the loan and suggested that when—not if—the loan collateral needed to be foreclosed upon that you were the right goombah for the job."

Both men sat quiet until Lucas realized that he had just been told that the Don expressed a level of confidence in him.

"Seems the Don kind of wanted the loan to fail."

"Well, he did and now it has," Chevron noted. "Did Bronson Cummings say when the takeover could proceed?"

Lucas did not respond immediately. Instead, he stood up so he could remove a handkerchief from his back pocket and wiped some perspiration that had suddenly sprouted along his hairline and above his upper lip.

"Turns out that much has happened along that line, all in the last five or so hours," Lucas said hoping to sound more casual than alarming."

Chevron's eyebrows pulled closer together. After indicating for Lucas to sit back down again, he stood up and walked toward the only window in his office.

"Please explain," was all he said without turning to look at Lucas. But in his mind, he was tying that piece of surprising news to when he received the call for the 'Sit Down" from the Don. That call came within those same "last five or six hours" ago when Lucas said that much had changed. Chevron wondered silently if the Bosses heard about that news before Lucas had.

"Well, Cummings said that he received a phone call from Emily Paladino's lawyer who informed him that Mickey Paladino forged her signature on the collateral papers and that meant that the loan was made on false pretenses and that in any case his client's fifty percent ownership was not something that could be foreclosed upon."

"How was it that we... meaning you... failed to verify the signatures?"

Lucas leaned forward. "When Mickey applied for the loan, things were still okay with his marriage and there was nothing to lead towards any suspicion of even any need to forge her signature. The problem evolved when the asshole started making it with their mutual friend, a singer at the Branson restaurant, and Emily found out and filed for the divorce... months after we gave the loan to them... to him, anyway."

"So... now all we have is the fifty percent that the husband owned?" Chevron sounded as frustrated as Lucas ever recalled him being.

Lucas needed the handkerchief again. Wiping it across his

forehead he turned to face Chevron who had walked behind him during the discussion.

"Uh… Well, it gets worse than even that," he said in a hesitating, unsure response.

Chevron froze.

"Worse than…?"

"Bronson explained to me that when he played hardball with Emily's lawyer and suggested that she damn well did not want you and me as her new fifty percent partners the lawyer laughed and told Cummings to read over the Limited Partnership Agreement he had drawn up when they went into the restaurant business. According to Emily's lawyer the terms of the Limited Partnership gave each partner the ability to prohibit any encumbrance against any mutually owned part(s) of the business that was not purchased in the mutual interest of the Limited Partners. Another clause gives the right of first refusal to the other partner if one of them decides to sell his or her interest."

"What did all that mean as far as what we want to do now" Chevron asked, sounding very irritated. "Do we foreclose only on Mickey's fifty percent and become co-owners with his wife?"

"Actually, according to Emily's lawyer the collateral is legally deficient because Mickey forged Emily's signature and cannot be presented in court seeking a foreclosure remedy."

For the next few moments neither said anything. Lucas kept looking at Chevron who kept looking into space. Finally, Chevron returned to his desk chair and sat down. A look in his eyes unnerved Juliano. It indicated that the cagey Frenchman was inspired by an idea he just had and was close to a solution.

"Mon Cher Ami," he began. "I intend to meet with the Don and to have the news that he wants to hear from us. That is that the loan payments cannot be made and that there will not be anyone disputing the rights we have as the loan makers to foreclose on the collateral and take possession of the restaurants."

Lucas was aghast at hearing this.

"How can that be even remotely possible," he asked. I just told you that…

Chevron held up his right-hand palm facing Lucas.

"If there are no more living owners of the restaurants and the loan payments are going unpaid… I think you can see what needs now to be done."

Lucas stood up and followed slowly behind Guy Chevron to his office door.

"I will need help," Lucas explained.

"What you need will be provided," Guy Chevron said. "Just keep me completely informed… at all times."

8

Lost

Saturday, August 17th

Elizabeth Lane's heart began pounding the moment she answered her cell phone and saw that the call was coming from the real estate office where her missing sister Emily worked. Finally, she thought, either Emily had shown up there or at least they knew more about where she may have gone.

Eight days had passed since either Elizabeth, or her sister Frances, had any contact with their younger sibling. For them such a duration of time without being in touch with one or the other was unusual. The three were remarkably close and, although each now lived in a different state, they stayed in touch either with emails or phone calls at least once or twice weekly. Then, without any known reason, contact with Emily stopped. Recently, emails received no replies. Phone call messages left on Emily's answering machine received no response.

This was not the first time Emily left and gone missing during her rocky marriage to Mickey Paladino. From the start their marriage seemed to be a series of struggles, fights that were up to now limited to threats and abusive language. Then, six months ago when Emily learned of his affair with their mutual friend, Kylie Cooper, she filed for divorce and kicked him out of their house in Kimberling City.

When he continued to harass her about their different thoughts toward working out a settlement, her attorney got the judge to issue an Order of Protection to keep Mickey away from her. Now that she was missing, Elizabeth worried that Mickey had done something that was the cause.

When Elizabeth called earlier and spoke with Emily's secretary, she learned they too were trying to find her. Emily had not been at work at My Missouri Home Real Estate Agency during the previous four days. After Emily missed the closing on the most recent house she sold, the office manager at My Missouri Home became alarmed and called the Stone County Police seeking help in locating her.

The secretary called Elizabeth now merely to let her know that the police were reluctant to open a full-scale investigation citing the fact that Emily was a thirty-three-year-old adult. If there were no threats that had been made then there was, at this time, no reason to suspect that simply not returning phone calls was sufficient reason for police to get involved.

* * *

Sunday, August 18th

Elizabeth had just left the church after attending Sunday Mass when she switched back on her cell phone and saw that the text message from Frances read "Urgent." Her heart began racing and caused her fingers to tremble so badly that she had difficulty clicking on her sister's phone number.

"So, you said you were not going to turn off your cell phone for any reason?" Frances's voice carried the familiar guilt shifting nuance that the older sister often used with her younger sisters.

"No, I mean, yes… I had to turn it off while I was in church," Elizabeth told her. "I didn't expect to hear from you unless…"

"Unless Emily has been found," Frances interrupted.

Elizabeth let out a loud hallelujah and then sheepishly looked around to see if she was heard by the few others who, like she had done, left Mass early immediately after receiving Communion.

"Where did they find her… Where was she… Where is she?" Elizabeth fired off her questions, unconcerned about any order in priority.

Frances waited until her sister stopped for a breath before telling her what was known so far. "I don't know very much yet but either she has been found or they have finally agreed to declare her a Missing Person… or they know something…"

"What's something?" Elizabeth shouted, disappointed as this was not the news she expected from her sister. "Emily has been missing since she showed a house for sale in Lampe to someone who it turns out was just recently released from prison… And all you know is that either she has been found… or someone now knows something??

Once again Frances stayed briefly silent showing some understanding for the reason her sister was so excited.

"No sweetie," she began, "this is all I know. I was called by her secretary when she was not able to reach you less than an hour ago. She said that the police called their office trying to find a way to contact a member of Emily's family and that she gave them our two phone numbers."

Before ending their conversation Frances gave Emily the telephone number of the Stone County Sheriff's office and suggested she might call them if she preferred not to wait until either of them heard anything. Frances pointed out that since she lived the farthest away in Tampa and that Elizabeth, being in Tulsa, less than a three hours' drive to Emily's house, was the person that the police would choose to contact.

By coincidence, as soon as she clicked off from the conversation with Frances, her cell phone buzzed and showed that a new call was coming from Stone County Police. Hoping that this was the good news that she had been waiting for, Elizabeth was taken aback almost immediately after the conversation began, sensing there was something else that was the purpose of the call. The detective's voice sounded vague, almost unsure if he wanted to tell her anything more about Emily until they met in his office.

Elizabeth guessed now that it was something that related to some rule, something they had regarding just who could report a person missing. The detective told her that he called Emily's employer and was informed that Elizabeth or Frances was listed as the next of kin. He asked if it would be convenient for her to meet in his office around 1:00 P.M. tomorrow. She agreed to the meeting but before she could ask for more information regarding Emily the detective said a quick good-bye and hung up.

Elizabeth called Frances back and told her about the call from the Stone County Detective. "I never even had a chance to ask him why he wanted to see me."

"I'm wondering the same thing," Frances said. "But the crazy thing is…"

"Is what?" Elizabeth asked, waiting impatiently for her sister to finish her thoughts.

"I was just wondering why he set the meeting almost 24 hours from now. It does not make me feel that there is any urgency."

9

News and weather together

Monday, August 19th, 7:00 A.M.

THE SKY BEGAN LOOKING VERY ominous as Elizabeth drove past the exits for Joplin along route 44 on her way to Galena. The cloud cover hid the morning sun and with each mile marker she passed it became darker until she finally had to put on her headlights. The weather reports she caught listening to KIX Radio warned of heavy rain and strong wind gusts for the next hour in the Joplin area and she considered pulling into a rest area to wait it out.

She saw no signs that anything like that was coming up soon, so when she reached the last exit for Joplin, she made up her mind that she would be better off to brave it and continue towards Springfield, only a short drive away from her appointment at the Stone County Sheriff's office in Galena. She estimated she was only an hour or so away.

The one good thing that the horrible weather provided was something for Elizabeth to focus on other than her concerns for

Emily. But as lightning flashes that shocked the darkness increased in frightening numbers, Elizabeth decided to turn off the radio and its frequent weather updates that only managed to add to her growing anxiety. She let her mind drift on to thoughts of Emily, Frances, and herself growing up in Royal Oaks, Michigan. Elizabeth was two years younger than Frances and almost two years older than Emily. She smiled, remembering how Emily objected to being called the baby in the family. She was, she protested, old enough to be attending the same elementary school as them.

"And it is well known babies can't go to elementary school," Emily, then in the first grade, argued with an air of certain triumph.

Frances was the "straw boss" in the bedroom the girls shared growing up. Being the oldest she was the first to do anything of importance. She was the first to attend school; first of them to get a two-wheel bike to ride around the neighborhood; and years ahead of her younger sisters for having her own diary which she kept locked away. Elizabeth never minded being second as it offered her a guide of what to expect when she got to be that same age that her sister had already attained.

It never mattered either that the only person under her in terms of sibling seniority was her younger sister. Emily would not listen or obey anything Elizabeth instructed her to do anyway. But for Elizabeth it was only important to try to fill the mentoring expectations and responsibilities in her relationship with Emily. Even when she failed in those efforts it still allowed her the freedom to move on unencumbered by any guilt and to become involved in doing whatever she really preferred to be doing. Often, just being by herself, re-reading a favorite book or drawing trees or horses in her sketchbook was more likely the favorite way she chose to use her free time growing up.

A bolt of lightning followed quickly by an explosive clash of thunder shook her awareness back to the storm. It began raining harder with frequent lightning flashes. The weather had turned much more ominous during the last fifteen minutes and frightened her. Wondering if there were warnings being announced about severe weather, Elizabeth turned back on the radio. The news was just coming on and she wished they would hurry it along and get straight to the weather. Then she heard something being said about a body found near Lampe, Missouri.

Just as fast as she was made aware of this report a weather bulletin interrupted saying that conditions were right for tornados to form, and that particular care should be taken by everyone in the Joplin metropolitan area. Up ahead she saw that much of the traffic was exiting at a truck stop. Elizabeth decided that as shaken as her nerves were that it would be wise to follow them off the highway.

The lights from the restaurant showed eerily bright against the pitch-black darkness that had descended from the storm clouds contributing to the almost scary sense of pending doom. Elizabeth pulled as close to the building as possible. After parking in a space near the entrance she quickly turned her attention back to the radio hoping to hear what that news was about the body that was found. A loud clash of thunder frightened her so much she almost peed. She was about to head into the restaurant and use the bathroom when once again the news mentioned the body found near Baxter Boat Dock.

Elizabeth listened as a reporter interviewed a young couple who said they had been at a concert at the Black Oak Mountain Amphitheater and were walking with their dog along Highway H back to where they had their Airstream Touring Coach parked in the Baxter Boat Dock parking lot.

"A passing car that must not have been expecting to see anyone walking in the dark along the two-lane road had to swerve and barely missed hitting us," the man said. "We decided to continue walking, but much farther away from the roadway. When we neared the lighted area of the parking lot at Baxter our dog, Archie, pulled on his leash and led us to where a rowboat sat half in and half out of the water as if it had drifted from the lake onto the small clearing along the shore."

"Archie began barking and could not be persuaded to leave until we went down and inspected the deserted rowboat," the woman anxiously interrupted. "That was when we saw a body lying face up along the bottom of the boat squeezed under the middle seat. I immediately used my cell phone and called 9-1-1."

The interview ended with the woman saying that when the Stone County police came, they mentioned that there was a woman from the Table Rock Lake area who had been reported as a missing person and they suspected this could be her......

Elizabeth switched off the ignition and fell back weeping. Was this why she was being summoned by the Stone County Sheriff's Department... just so that she would... identify the body??

10

It takes a team to pull the sled

Monday, August 19th, 7:00 A.M.

"MONDAY—MONDAY, CAN'T TRUST THAT DAY…"
Sheriff Lambert sat back as the Administration Deputy, Alison Monroe, brought in his order from Starbucks; two chocolate croissants and a large black coffee. He pulled back the report he was reading from the task force known as COMET.

After setting the breakfast down she asked about that song he was humming when she came into his office.

"Oh? Just something that was popular back in the day," he replied. "Ever hear Mama Cass sing anything?"

"Mama Cass?" Her voice gave evidence that she had never heard of her. "Was she one of the Plummer Family that used to perform over at Cedar Lodge?"

The Sheriff groaned. "I guess that you were still running around barefoot and in diapers when she…," he paused after considering that Alison was only twenty-eight years old. "I mean your folks must have still been babies when her group came to

Springfield for a concert." He looked up and saw only a blank stare coming from the deputy.

Just as he was pulling back the tab on the lid on his large coffee the intercom buzzed.

"I think Miss Helen has a sixth sense when she suspects I might be taking a sip of coffee," he sneered looking up from his swivel chair. "I know she was my mommas' closest friend but why I let that persuade me to hire her and put her out in the public lobby at the business window selling those passports and fishing licenses was just plain old stoopid!"

The voice coming through the intercom sounded scratchy and way too loud. "Sheriff, there is someone here from the F.B.I. and he wants to see you, okay?"

Sheriff Lambert sighed and looking at Alison asked if she knew anything that would prompt a visit from an F.B.I. agent.

The blank stare that was still present after she was asked who Mama Cass was grew ever more intense.

The voice on the intercom came back on, "He says he is here on that case about the young lady that was in the boat… I mean the lady that they reported missing… or something."

The sheriff hurriedly put the croissants back in the bag and shoved it into the empty bottom drawer of his desk. He handed the cup to Alison and told her to take it back to her desk before showing the F.B.I. agent to the staff conference room where he would be waiting for him. He followed her out of his office after retrieving the file labeled Missing Persons Reports.

Upon entering the conference room Sheriff Lambert stopped abruptly.

"I didn't expect to see our Homeland Security Special Agent in Charge when our Miss Helen said my visitor was from the F.B.I.," he laughed while offering a handshake. "How are you, Horace… and what the fuck brings you down to Galena this morning?"

Horace Haywood smiled and then pulled out a chair across the conference table from where the Sheriff was preparing to sit.

"Bull, what I'm going to talk with you about has got to be private… and remain private between just you and me and perhaps whoever you name… and who I agree with… that will be required to become involved in this."

The sheriff sat up taller and looked across the table into his visitor's eyes. "You know that I am good with that, Horace. Just tell me what you are talking about, okay?"

"Bull, that body that you have stored in the coroner's freezer is someone that we think paid the price for knowing just too much to be allowed kept alive."

Bull Lambert was showing signs of becoming impatient. "Are you saying that you've been investigating someone or something here in Stone County and you're finally getting around to informing the Sheriff of said county?"

The Special Agent looked surprised by the implied criticism. "Bull, you know that I… that anyone with Homeland Security would not ever open a case that falls under the authority of your department without you knowing all about it. But this one was not such a case… until that woman's body was discovered over by Baxter Boat Dock."

"So, what is it… was it… that made her so interesting to you guys?"

"Bull, that poor woman was more than a local. She was once the girlfriend of someone we have reason to believe is involved in something so big… huge… that our national security is under threat."

Now it was the sheriff's turn to express surprise. The somber expression on the Special Agent's face was all the proof needed to persuade him that he was about to hear something that could become the most important case in his lengthy career in law enforcement.

Without knowing any more than he learned so far, Bull Lambert's adrenaline rush told him this is the moment he dreamed might never come for him. Whatever it was, the top Homeland Security man in the entire southwest Missouri area had found that he needed something from Bull Lambert, just when things had become a bit too quiet for him to hold back thoughts of retirement.

11

Meet Captain Travis Holden, C.I.D.

Monday, August 19th, 7:00 A.M.

Each morning when Travis Holden reported to his job at the Stone County Police Department he felt joy. It was that way from the very start, eight years ago, when he began his career as a deputy assigned to the traffic division. That feeling of joy only grew stronger with every new assignment that coincidentally led to each new promotion.

This morning was a special one as it marked the second anniversary of his promotion to Captain in the most desired section, the Criminal Investigation Department. He knew that being the Captain at C.I.D. put him in the running for consideration for an array of higher paying and more important positions in law enforcement at either the county or the state police levels. And, if ever he would be willing to locate elsewhere, his rank in the C.I.D. with the Stone County Sheriff's Police would put him ahead of other applicants seeking one of those jobs in either the FBI or even Homeland Security.

Driving to work this morning Travis thought back to how his career began after he was hired in 2016 and was assigned to the Traffic section. He decided fast that his real interest in law enforcement was not so much in catching offenders but rather solving crimes once they were committed.

Less than two short years later he was promoted to the rank of Detective and assigned to the drug task force known by the acronym COMET, the Combined Ozark Mutual-jurisdiction Enforcement Team. While waiting in line to pick up his breakfast order at the Starbucks drive-up window he remembered two occasions when he went under cover and infiltrated rings of drug dealers that led to arrests and convictions. A year later his application to be reassigned to C.I.D. was approved and he was slotted on the team headed by Lieutenant Ernie Mize. The team subsequently began making great progress with successful investigations in four Cold Cases that drew a lot of news coverage.

While driving through Galena's downtown business section only a few blocks from the Stone County Sheriff's Office, Travis recalled how fate must have meant for him to become the Top Cop in the C.I.D. unit. Lt. Mize was on vacation enjoying a Riverboat Leisure trip in Europe when the team arrested a suspect in a case involving the rape and robbery of a woman at the Kimberling Hotel. In the absence of Lt. Mize, Travis became the Team Leader for that investigation and received the most attention from the press.

When Mize returned from his vacation, he appeared jealous to learn of the unit's success without him. His negative attitude became more apparent with each of Travis's successful investigations in the Cold Case unit. Travis heard whispers in the squad room that Mize had been grumbling that his subordinate was working to fill his own resume hoping to become a serious rival to him for future openings for advancement to the rank of Captain. Lt. Mize soon acted on his suspicions and assigned Travis to partner with a newcomer, Deputy Honey Holcomb.

Initially, Travis was pissed off about that roster move since he guessed that Lt. Mize was planning to eventually succeed Captain Kerwin who headed up the C.I.D. unit at that time and had been frequently discussing his pending retirement. It was widely speculated that Mize was in line for the top job leaving his lieutenant's position open. Travis's actual plan was to follow Lt. Mize up the career ladder by succeeding him as the lieutenant in the C.I.D. unit. That required that his success in the Cold Case section continued for him to earn top consideration to take Mize's place.

Placing him with a pure novice and unproven newcomer as his partner could severely dampen Travis's prospects. For reasons that made no sense to him he knew that Mize seemed bent on making things difficult for him and left the definite impression that Mize's personal recommendation for his replacement when he received the promotion would be anybody but Travis.

The two new partners got off to a smoother beginning than Travis expected. It helped some that she was good looking. In fact, Honey Holcomb was the sexiest police person he had ever come across. In only a brief time Honey was up to speed on all C.I.D. procedures and was contributing in unusual ways to Travis's investigations.

During his time in the C.I.D. Travis gained valuable experience assembling facts in criminal cases and he hoped to teach those traits to his new partner. Often, to his surprise, Honey would interrupt him with an "off-the-wall" observation of those facts that led to what he called "a light switch moment." Cases that were assigned to them moved quickly to successful conclusions.

As more time passed their work together investigating the highest profile crimes was also successful. Travis discovered that Honey Holcomb proved to be quite an asset in his career advancement hopes. Besides those reasons, her detail to work with him, he later learned, had come straight from Sheriff Cole "Bull" Lambert.

Travis pulled into the Parking area marked "Reserved for C.I.D. personnel" as he recalled how that imaginary relationship of him being Mize's rival soon played out. When the longtime leader of the Stone County C.I.D. unit, Captain Wally Kerwin did retire, Ernie Mize's suspicions proved to be one hundred percent correct. Detective Travis Holden won the promotion, advancing two pay grade levels, and leaving Lt. Ernie Mize's career on hold. Being right all along in his suspicions regarding Travis offered little solace and instead rewarded Ernie Mize with nothing more than adding extra pace to his growing feelings of betrayal.

There was only one Deputy and six detectives that were assigned to the CID section under Travis's command but with his management and organization skills, that proved to be sufficient. It helped that the workload was quite a bit less than it was for police departments in Springfield or Kansas City which needed four times the size of their staff to handle the criminal investigations for which they were relied upon.

There were such crimes as armed robberies, rapes, and child abuse cases requiring sometimes lengthy and even dangerous investigative work. But they were frequently committed repeatedly by the same people, or their relatives, and were swiftly solved by Travis or the senior detectives assigned to him.

Less than six months after he was passed up for promotion, Mize was put in for a transfer to the COMET unit. He kept his rank of lieutenant but, as it was a lateral reassignment, there was no increase in his paychecks. The only thing that seemed to increase was his contempt for the person who beat him out of something he wanted badly and was certain was his due.

Travis promoted Honey to fill the position Ernie Mize left which some thought was meant to say that even a novice could do as well as Mize did there. That did set tongues to wagging and morale did suffer a setback. But that did not last, at least in the open, and things got down to business again soon.

It is all so strange!

Monday, August 19th, 8:30 A.M.

"Do you know why you are here?" the detective asked. "Here? Do you mean here in this police station… or here in… where am I?" Emily was seated at an uncovered table after being escorted through the Stone County Sheriff Police headquarters into a room with no windows, three cement block walls and the other with what might seem like a large mirror framed in it.

The detective moved her chair so that she was seated almost next to, rather than across from Emily.

"My name is Lieutenant Holcomb, Emily. We brought you in because you have been away, missing from your business, and missed by your family. Do you think you want to talk about your reasons for going away?"

Emily was puzzled, not as much by the questions, but that way the lieutenant was speaking… like how people talk to a child… or someone who has a mental concern.

"I am not sure why… why you… are interrogating me," Emily replied. Her mind was racing over everything that exploded out of nowhere almost a week ago and escalated to uncontrollable moments of horror ever since.

Lt. Holcomb reached across the table not touching Emily's hands which were held prayer-like in front of her face.

"Emily, this is not a police interrogation. "We have no suspicion that you've done anything that is a crime," she said in a soft reassuring tone. "This is what police refer to as an interview," she continued.

Emily continued to stare through her hands. Her eyes had a blank look displaying the confusion swirling in her mind.

"Uh… I haven't had any sleep for… I don't remember… days, I guess," she said. "I do not think I even know if I can explain why I had to go to that place…" Her expression changed suddenly to appear as one about to experience a panic attack.

Lt. Holcomb moved closer to Emily in case the weakness in her voice was an indication that she was about to faint.

"Emily, let me help you. You were reported to us as a missing person by the manager at My Missouri Homes Real Estate Agency. Can you remember his name for me now?"

Emily's hands tightened into fists hearing again the sound in that voice… that almost condescending way of talking. The irritation she felt was prompting a welcome stirring feeling of being awake for Emily. She investigated the face of the detective and for the first time realized it belonged to a woman. Strange, she wondered silently to herself, that she had not taken notice of that fact until that moment.

"Uh… Oh yes, his name. "The manager at where I work is Mr. Locke."

Lt. Holcomb was pleased to see that Emily's memory was shaking off some of the effects of sleep loss.

"Locke," she repeated. "Do you always call him Mr. Locke… or sometimes by his other name?" The detective hoped to push Emily's focus on something familiar, and later getting her to complete that thing she had hesitated to say when trying to explain why she went to that place… (What place)?

"Oh? No, I almost never call him Mr. Locke. I always use his first name."

Lt. Holcomb remained quiet, waiting for Emily to realize that something more was expected in her answer.

Emily turned then and blurted out…" I call Armand by his first name."

Two knocks and the door opened, and Emily saw a man peeking inside and giving a wave to the lieutenant to come outside of the room. Lt. Holcomb excused herself after offering to bring Emily something to drink, "coffee… water?" she asked, without getting a response.

When Lt. Holcomb stepped out, she walked to where Captain Travis Holden stood looking through the one-way glass at the woman sitting inside.

"Travis?" Lt. Holcomb asked as she moved next to him. "What do you think?"

"Well, I've decided to stop this interview for now, Honey," he said without taking his eyes away from the glass. "I have just received word from Branson P.D. that Mickey Paladino has been found murdered."

Honey Holcomb took a step back upon hearing this news. "Mickey Paladino?" The lieutenant's voice displayed her complete surprise. "Isn't that the name of Emily's husband?"

Travis turned away from the one-way glass and began walking toward his office a few steps down the hallway. Lt. Holcomb followed along his side.

"Yes, Mickey is… I mean, was her husband. They were going through a divorce. He moved out five, six months ago."

"So, why did you say you wanted to stop this interview?" Lt. Holcomb asked sounding more confused than she wanted to be with her boss.

"Honey," Travis said turning into his office, "What I saw during your interview with her is that she is in no condition to answer any of our questions tonight. She is obviously either dead tired or under some kind of medication… and I…" Travis stopped talking as he hurried into his office to answer the page coming from his intercom.

"Captain, an Elizabeth Lane is waiting to see you."

Though she was standing just outside Travis's office, Honey could hear the message coming from the intercom. "She said that you have information about her missing sister."

"Yes… Yes, I do want to see her," Travis interrupted. He beckoned for Honey to come inside his office.

"Elizabeth Lane?" the lieutenant asked.

"Honey, Elizabeth Lane is Emily Paladino's sister. I called her yesterday at her home in Tulsa and asked if she could come in today. Ernie Mize heard we opened a missing person case on Emily, and he told me that one of the drug-buster boys in his unit had an interest in her… something connected with a man they knew served a sentence on various drug charges and was back in the Branson area. Emily recently showed a house to him that was for sale over in Cassville."

"Did you want to know if Emily's sister knew if Emily was using…"

Travis made no response and instead clicked back on the intercom and told the deputy on the desk that Lt. Holcomb was coming out to the lobby and would escort Ms. Lane back to his office.

"This is becoming a whole lot more than I thought it could be when I arranged for Ms. Lane to come in. We had not yet found Emily and we knew nothing about Mickey Paladino being killed. We will have to go slow with this news…"

13

Could Emily be next?

Monday, August 19th, 10:00 P.M.

Eᴌɪᴢᴀʙᴇᴛʜ Lᴀɴᴇ ʀᴇꜰʟᴇᴄᴛᴇᴅ sɪʟᴇɴᴛʟʏ to herself how much had changed since she left her home just this morning. She had to drive through one of the worst storms she had ever been in, all the while thinking that she was only needed in Galena so that the Stone County detectives would open a Missing Person investigation regarding Emily's disappearance. Then, before even getting to the sheriff's office she heard that horrible news about the body found in Lampe.

It was night now as she reached route 44 for the return drive to Tulsa. Elizabeth's night vision, which from the time she turned thirty-three years old had progressively diminished over the last two years, was being tested by headlights from oncoming vehicles. She knew that soon she should expect to be suffering from the fatigue coming from being on the go since six in the morning. She would just have to tough it out, stay focused, and do whatever it might take to remain awake. They had been through so much already. No reason to compound everything that had gone so wrong with having an accident.

Perhaps turning the car radio on to the Rock and Roll station she listened to on her way through Springfield this morning would help, she thought. But then it might interrupt "Sleeping Beauty" next to her in the passenger's seat. That was something that would qualify as the last thing she wanted to happen right then.

Elizabeth remembered how overwhelmed with joy she felt after arriving at the Stone County police headquarters and learning that not only had they found her sister but that she was alive and in another part of the building. She had to wait for over an hour while detectives did something they called a de-briefing hoping to get information as to why she stayed away from her home and her job. Elizabeth also wanted that same information but her whole concern while waiting was just to see her younger sister and be sure she was well.

Then, suddenly came the surprises, one following another. A detective with the first name of Honey came back out to where she was waiting and explained that Emily would follow soon, but that she seemed tired and was suffering some confusion that may have been caused by something she took before she was found. She was happy that a family member was going to be with Emily through the rest of the evening.

Surprise number two caused an even bigger shock. Emily's husband, Mickey Paladino, had earlier that afternoon been discovered murdered in Branson. Detective Honey said that when they learned of that they worried how knowledge of it could affect Emily's already weakened emotional state, Captain Holden decided to stop the de-briefing session and said he was happy that Elizabeth was available to be with her.

Surprise number three came when she was reunited with her sister and discovered how she appeared so confused. The detective suggested that it might be best if Emily was taken to the emergency room at Ozarks Community Hospital in Springfield as soon as possible after they left the police station. After less than five minutes of trying to talk with her sister, Elizabeth was convinced of the urgency and took directions to the hospital.

Emily was quite groggy as she accompanied Elizabeth to her car but seemed to snap out of it once they started to drive away. Emily's mood was calm enough at first to answer a few of Elizabeth's questions regarding her current health. But as soon as Elizabeth mentioned that she wanted to have her checked out at the emergency room, Emily reacted in sheer panic.

"We cannot go there," she cried. "We can't go anywhere that I will be found by..." and then stopped talking in mid-sentence.

While driving towards Springfield, Elizabeth became aware of the sudden terror that ran through her own mind as she listened to her sister. Someone wanted to harm her, or so she feared. And just being with her meant Elizabeth was in danger too. The longer Emily talked about these mysterious problems, the more intense she became. At one point, when she was not convinced that Elizabeth believed her about being in danger, Emily unbuckled her seat belt and tried to get out of the car. Elizabeth felt a shiver remembering now that they were driving close to fifty miles per hour during those frightening moments.

It was not until she agreed that she would listen to her sister's warnings and rather than going to a hospital close by, they would keep driving until they reached Elizabeth's home in Tulsa, before Emily's panic seemed to lessen. Elizabeth noticed her sister taking something from a jacket pocket and putting it in her mouth but relaxed when Emily said it was a prescription that she had been taking to help her sleep while going through the divorce proceedings. It seemed less than five minutes later, the pill or pills took effect and Emily was sound asleep.

Once Emily was sleeping Elizabeth resumed her thoughts on many of the events that took place during the last twenty hours. The adrenaline spurt that shook her own drowsiness away while she was calming her sister was fading and more than once, she felt an increasing urge to close her eyes. Looking for somewhere it would be safe to pull off Route 44, she was jolted by the buzzing sound coming from her cell phone.

"Thank goodness you just called," she said to her sister Frances. "That cell phone is paying big dividends tonight."

"Forget that" came the abrupt reply. "I just called Stone County and was told you have Emily there with you. Just where are you two right now?"

"To answer that question first," Elizabeth said, "We are half-way home… to my home…"

Frances was never one to show any patience when her younger sister used more words than needed.

"Elizabeth," Frances said in a deliberate manner. "Put Emily on the phone… I want to talk to her myself. I need someone to tell me what is going on…"

Elizabeth just laughed. It was fun… her knowing something that her big sister did not.

"I can't give the phone to Emily just yet," she said. "And before you ask…"

"Elizabeth……???"

Elizabeth laughed again, reminded of how impatient Frances had always been with her growing up back in Royal Oak.

"Emily is sound asleep… and I do mean asleep," she said. "And thank God she is…"

"Meaning.?"

"I'll have to tell you all about it tomorrow but trust me…"

"Wait a minute," Frances said sounding genuinely concerned about something. "I just finished having quite a conversation with someone named Detective Holcomb…"

"Yes, I met her…"

"Listen," Frances demanded. "Did you give something to

Emily to help her fall asleep during your long drive back to your house?"

"No, I do not have anything like that. But now that you mention it…"

Frances interrupted, "So, she is sound asleep just from being so tired?"

Elizabeth paused…" Uh, Emily did take something out of her pocket and swallowed it… and I asked her about it…"

There was a brief silence as Frances recalled her conversation with the Stone County detective about the strange death of Kylie Cooper.

"Elizabeth, listen closely," Frances sounded worried and very deliberate. "Pull over somewhere as soon as possible… and wake up Emily."

"I hear you," she said. "But with all this loud conversation we have been having… and seeing her still as sound asleep as she was before you called…"

"Elizabeth, that lady they found in the boat at Baxter Boat Dock died from some strange combination of drugs. Our sister knew her… and hung around with her… before all that serious stuff happened with Mickey cheating…"

"Yes, I know…"

"Lieutenant Holcomb said that she was afraid that somehow Emily may have got access to some of those same drugs…"

Elizabeth's heart began pounding. "What do I do… I have no idea where to find a hospital… WAIT!"

Frances was just as shaken by this new worry as was Elizabeth. Suddenly she knew exactly what to do next.

"Call 9-1-1. Pull over and call 9-1-1"

A long silence. Too long… and then Elizabeth spoke. "I have pulled over. There is a Highway Patrol car with the red lights on… parked right behind me…"

14

It's murder, m-u-r-d-e-r, you say!

Monday, August 19th, 10:00 P.M.

BREAKING NEWS   OZRK24   BREAKING NEWS

Camera One is on the co-anchor, a round-faced man, 50ish, wearing a yellow blazer, brown shirt, and multi-colored bow tie.

"Good evening, Springfield! Today is Monday August 19th, 2024, my name is Steve Gardner. And there is Breaking news ahead on the Ten Tonight News on **OZRK24**".

The director switches to Camera Two which is focused on a woman close to the same age, wearing a high buttoned white blouse under a rose-colored vest with a red OZRK24 insignia.

"That's right, Steve. Hello everyone. I am Elaine Valley. OZRK24 just learned within the hour that the Stone County Police's Medical Examiner is calling it now... a murder. The young woman whose body was found lying in an abandoned rowboat over the weekend was the victim of a homicide made to look like a suicide. The Medical Examiner has identified her as being Kylie Cooper, 31 years old, and a lifelong resident of Lampe, Missouri. The Medical Examiner ruled out suicide after additional information regarding how the victim's body came to be found in an abandoned rowboat."

Back to Camera One: "I am looking now, Elaine, at a digital copy of the M.E.'s report. It states that her death was caused by a combination of alcohol and oxycodone overdose that poisoned her and caused her death by person and/or persons unknown."

Camera Two: "Thank you, Steve. Our Evening News team contacted Bull Lambert, the sheriff in Stone County, and found out only that he has scheduled a news conference for nine o'clock tomorrow morning but until then he said that the police need the help from any citizen who may have knowledge of Miss Cooper's whereabouts since last Wednesday."

Camera One: "Elaine, my sources at the sheriff's office told me off the record late this afternoon that a person of interest has been found and is in police custody. I want to emphasize the source did not refer to this person as a suspect."

Camera Two: "Did your source say whether the Person of Interest is a man or a woman? Or, in what way is there any relationship to the victim?"

The camera that was on Elaine shifts to Steve Gardner who looks like that last question was a pure curveball.

"Actually, … Elaine… uh… I do not think I asked… and, … uh… I'm sure he didn't say…"

Camera Two switches back to Elaine as the director worries aloud that this is causing a ping pong effect for the viewers. "That's okay, Steve. I imagine that question… as well as many others needing some answers will come up during the news conference tomorrow morning with Sheriff Bull Lambert. In other news today… huh?"

She turns to see that Steve has his hand pressed to the ear where he has an in-ear monitor. His face has become flushed, and he is bursting with excitement about something...

Camera One... back on Steve:

"Wait... Hey, Elaine?... Pardon me just a minute, our producer is just now telling me that the P.O.I. is a... She... a woman is a Person... of Interest!!! And... She is related to the victim as a (what? A farmer? Oh...) Steve turns and faces Elaine... She is a former something that the police think now is related to this case. There you have it folks. That is the complete up to the very minute news on this, what is now being called, an official murder case."

Camera Two... "Thank you, Steve. OZRK24 meteorologist LuAnn Biggins is up next. She has all the news and video updates of that huge storm that hit the area yesterday".

Camera One turns towards where the regular evening news weather map is located just as Meteorologist LuAnn Biggins steps in front of it. Now off camera, Steve Gardner slides closer to his co-anchor and gets her attention.

"You know, Elaine, I was excited and just plain happy that we had any news at all to add to that No-News-For-Now type news break that the sheriff was willing to give out."

"I agree. Thank goodness you have those sources and could fill us in on that Person of Interest."

Feeling reassured, Steve smiled and slid back to his assigned space behind the news desk. Elaine always knew the right words to say, he thought silently. A furrow suddenly creased his forehead as he remembered how she raised her eyebrows and produced a hint of a smile when she spoke prompting some doubt in his mind now of her sincerity. Was she complimenting him? Or was she putting him on?

15

Emily must die!

Tuesday, August 20th

L ATER, THE MEMORY OF THOSE events brought a shiver to her as she prepared to leave with Emily from the emergency unit at Ozark Community Hospital. In hindsight it caused Elizabeth to smile how being stopped for speeding proved to be the best thing that could have occurred at that time.

After she was able to convince the highway patrol officer of her sister's unexplained loss of consciousness, he reacted first by radioing in a request for an ambulance. The EMT's arrived, it seemed to her now, within a blink of an eye and had Emily in the ambulance on the way to the nearest hospital, Ozark Community Hospital, just off Route 44.

Elizabeth laughed now as she recounted these events to Emily, remembering how the police officer referred to the hospital as OUCH!

"He called it, ouch?" Emily asked.

"Yes, and he said it using the same inflection you would say that word if you hit your thumb with a hammer. It was only after I learned they had finished bringing you back to our world of the living that I was able to relax and see the humor in what he meant by that."

"I must be still a bit out of it… but… what's the joke?"

Elizabeth took her eyes off the road momentarily to look closely at her sister, looking to see if she could detect if Emily was suffering any relapse.

"Ozark Community Hospital has signs on the highway that just use their initials to refer to themselves as OCH. The officer mentioned that a person might have need of them if they had an o-u-c-h…"

Emily stared straight ahead showing no indication that she found that explanation humorous. After a few more miles of driving along Route 44 in silence, she turned to Elizabeth and said she was not sure if going to Tulsa was the safest thing they should be doing right now.

"Well, you definitely made it clear last night… and then again when we checked you out of the hospital this morning that for some reason you had to stay away from your own home."

Emily did not say anything except an acknowledging, "Uh-huh."

"Can't you tell me anything about this danger you feel you are in? Elizabeth asked. "You were missing for six full days and all you have explained to either Frances or me or those Stone County detectives is that you went somewhere for some unexplained reason with Mickey on August 13th and then lost all sense of time until you were picked up by the police at Indian Point on Monday, six days later."

Emily bristled at the recounting of the events in her life since that sunny afternoon in Cassville when Mickey Paladino showed up and surprised her. So much of what followed was still just a mist in her memory, but she was certain that she was in some serious trouble and that her life was, and remained, in danger. She had a vague recollection of Mickey pleading with her to sign over her shares in the restaurants… or was it… calling her lawyer to do something… a deadline or something?

Emily understood that Elizabeth needed answers to her questions about the missing seven days but told her that she hesitated only because of two reasons.

"One, I am not sure myself that I remember about all that is needed to know why or where I was then. And two, the one thing I am sure of is that someone needs me dead."

This was the first time her sister made even that little bit of a response to these questions. On the one hand it made Elizabeth feel that her sister's memory was beginning to show signs of improving. But, hearing now that the danger she only briefly mentioned as a reason for those lost ten days concerned life and death caused Elizabeth's anxiety thermometer to leap much higher.

Before Elizabeth could inquire further regarding what Emily had just told her the cell phone buzzed showing their sister Frances as the caller.

"Elizabeth, the hospital said that they released Emily an hour ago, right?"

Elizabeth handed the cell phone to Emily. "You take this one, little sister," she said handing the cell phone across to the passenger side.

"Good morning, Frances," Emily's voice was still weak, and she needed to pause and clear her throat. "We are heading to Elizabeth's home, and I wonder if there is any way you might join us there?"

"Oh?" Frances sounded surprised to hear Emily speaking. "They told me at the hospital that you had way too much of something… they suspect, Valium, in you and that you were…"

Emily interrupted her sister realizing that Frances's concern for her deserved all the information she could remember but that so much remained still too foggy for her at this time.

"I did take something to fight the panic I was feeling that knocked me out, but they took care of me in the emergency room at the hospital and I am beginning to feel better now," Emily tried to assure her. "But the reason I interrupted was because I am hoping that you can somehow get to Elizabeth's home by tomorrow so we can all talk this through. I need to decide… something… I need your guidance."

Frances wondered what it was that Emily had in mind. But, knowing that her sister now needed her enough to ask her to drop everything and drive all the way from Tampa to Tulsa was all the persuasion she required.

"Baby sister," she said swallowing hard. "I will be there… just as I always have been."

16

The investigation

Wednesday, August 28th, 7:30 A.M.

Deputy Alison Monroe liked the changes she noticed in her boss's mood ever since his meeting with Horace Haywood that took place nine days ago. Until then he seemed almost bored, and she worried that he was seriously considering retirement. Of course, being sixty-four years old, it would be quite normal for any man to look forward to taking life a bit easier. But she thought she knew Bull Lambert well and taking it easy was not anything she figured was in his DNA…

Whatever it was that occurred in his meeting with the Southwest Missouri Chief of Homeland Security was yet unknown to Alison. But what happened since that day her boss, The Bull, was his old self; angry and alert and acting more like he was planning to be reelected, using once again his familiar campaign slogan… 'Crime's Worst Enemy.'

Alison often thought of the sheriff as being more of a hero than her boss. Standing two inches over six feet tall and weighing just under two hundred fifty pounds, Bull Lambert commanded respect even from fellow church goers in the pews aside him at Sunday Services at Reed Springs First Baptist. But it took more than his size to impress people enough to keep voting him back as their sheriff. Alison knew all about his background and how it all was filled with accomplishments that led to where he came to be the sheriff.

Cole "Bull" Lambert left his daddy's home in Reed Springs when he was barely eighteen years old and joined the Army. He returned thirty years later a decorated hero, winning battle ribbons on two occasions for bravery and valor during the battles at Khe Sanh and at Hamburger Hill. After his tours in Vietnam, Lambert rose through the ranks in the Military Police, eventually achieving the pinnacle in his career, being promoted to Sergeant Major at the Military Police Training school at Ft. Leonard Wood.

It was during his stint at Fort Leonard Wood that he met and later married Carrie Rockland, the daughter of the Base Commander. The following year Carrie's father was transferred to Fort Jackson in South Carolina and the happy couple were on their own. For Bull, that period in his life was the happiest he had ever been. It was however happiness that was brought to a sudden and tragic ending on a winter evening in a severe snowstorm on Interstate 44.

The couple had earlier driven to the Holdenville Regional Airport at Forney Field to pick up Carrie's parents who planned to be with them over the holidays. The plane was detoured to Chicago because of weather conditions and Bull and Carrie were heading back to their residence at Fort Leonard Wood when a school bus hit a patch of black ice, lost control, and slid into the side of Bull's car pushing it off the highway straight into a ditch, causing it to flip and roll over.

Bull was thrown from the car and landed in a snowbank made when the plows came through earlier. Carrie, who always did everything according to the "letter of the law" was strapped tightly inside, secured by her seatbelts, and suffered fatal injuries when the car landed on the side where she was seated and crushed her.

At the hospital where Carrie was pronounced dead the attending physician proclaimed that she had also lost the baby. It was the surprise that Bull and Carrie had hoped to announce when her parents arrived.

The physical injuries Bull sustained all healed within a few months. But the love and enthusiasm that Bull Lambert felt so strongly toward the Army before Carrie came into his life never returned to that same level. He had experienced death in so many ways during his time in Vietnam and yet had no guidance for understanding the depth of this loss… the permanence of this pain. He would never be able to hold her… hug her… have her… ever. And their baby girl? He would never even get to know. He was lost and adrift and knew that could never change so long as he remained where he once was with her… with them.

He soon retired and upon returning home taught Criminal Investigation courses to police recruits at Missouri Southern State University in Joplin. After he was elected to be the Stone County Sheriff in 2016, he had the pleasure of recruiting two students from MSSU that graduated with degrees in Criminal Justice Administration. The first of these was Travis Holden followed four years later by Honey Holcomb.

Alison's mind was on these thoughts and sitting at her desk when she heard her name being called.

"Were you calling me for something?" she asked, peeking around the open door to his office.

"For something?" he repeated in a louder voice than she expected. "Of course it is for something," the sheriff continued. "And, I had to call you three times for. Some-THING. Where were you, ladies room again?"

Alison knew he was not as angry as he was putting on. Must be something hot is happening, she thought, while moving inside to where she usually stood by his desk. She looked down at the Springfield News-Leader that he was reading before calling her in. The headline read: Sheriff Stymied. The lead on column one read: Cops Cannot Catch Kylie Cooper's Killer.

"I want you to assemble everyone from C.I.D. that is in the building into the Conference Room. Come to think of it, bring along anyone from Ernie Mize's COMET boys too," he said still showing anger when he spoke.

When she turned to leave the sheriff coughed and cleared his throat before calling her back.

"I'm going to need a tall Starbucks for this meeting Alison," he said. "I'm going to be chewing ass and lighting fires… and whatever is needed to get them doing something to solve this damn thing that is causing the feeding frenzy with our friends in the Press."

*　*　*

Wednesday, August 28th, 10:00 A.M.

"Hey, the boss seems like he was coming apart this morning," Ernie Mize said after pulling up his chair at the opposite end of the conference table from where Travis sat.

Sitting to his left was Detective Platt who turned and asked, "You talking to me?"

"I'm just saying that all that shouting about nothing's getting done seemed like a worried man talking."

Arnie Platt did not like Ernie Mize and never tried to hide it. Still, he was outranked and had to always be on the alert that he did not rile him too much.

"Yeah, I was surprised when just before he ended our morning ass-chew he said something about heads will roll…"

At the far end of the table Travis and Honey overheard Detective Platt's remark.

"You know, I was also surprised by that," Honey said turning so only Travis could hear. Travis was anxious to get the meeting started but saw those three detectives from his C.I.D. unit had not yet arrived.

"I think our sheriff knows that we are working hard on this case… these cases… and just needs something he can use to quiet down the press."

Honey still looked concerned. "But… Heads will roll??"

At that point, the missing detectives arrived and found a place at the table. Seeing that this meant the meeting could begin, Honey Holcomb stood up and went to the Whiteboard where she would write on it the known facts and evidence in the Cooper murder case.

"Okay… Let's get started," Travis began while walking to the center of the room a few feet from where Lieutenant Honey Holcomb stood with a black marker in her hand.

"You all were included in this morning's brief by Sheriff Lambert and…"

A ripple of laughter was heard at the reminder of what went down at the morning meeting.

"Hey! Let us get back to being the serious, capable, well trained, and highly skilled detectives we have always been," Travis said trying to combine words of encouragement with those showing his authority. "Being fact finders, we want to be methodical in this investigation to discover all evidence… and just what findings that evidence will support. On these Whiteboards we want to record every step of our investigation including witness statements, forensic reports, crime scene photos, and the like. We will look at the victim's final days and weeks to allow us to really get to know her, her habits, who her friends were, and all that. We will go over the crime scene, treating everything as evidence and look for anything that does and does not belong there."

Travis paused at that point as he silently ran through the various steps that had to be followed in any successful police investigation.

"Let's be sure we make good use of the forensic equipment we have at our disposal… and communicate with each other throughout this." Travis looked around the room, checking to be sure his message was heard. "Finally, work together… as a team… the team of professional detectives you have always been."

Turning back to Lt. Holcomb he mentioned that she will be keeping the Whiteboard current showing each piece of evidence gathered to date, along with any witnesses' statements. "Lieutenant Holcomb will lead this investigation. I intend to reassign some of you to this case full time, meaning other cases we have under investigation will have to slide for a while."

Lieutenant Honey Holcomb then took over the meeting.

"For where we are right now, I have prepared the board in a summary format which I will review with you today," she began. "But we will be adding… or subtracting items as the investigation continues, so keep posted with it. The deceased is Kylie Cooper, white female, 31 years of age. Her father was Carl Cooper who owned a large tract of property known as Plyman's Point just off route 86 down by Table Rock Lake in Lampe. She died from poisons in her body after ingesting a combination of various drugs including Oxycodone with enough alcohol that resulted in her death. Suicide has been completely ruled out after lividity analysis disclosed that the victim's body had been moved several times after death occurred."

Seeing that there were no questions at this point, Honey continued. "Kylie Cooper was living with Michael Anthony Paladino, AKA Mickey Paladino, since May of this year at Indian Point. On Friday, August 19th he was found dead inside her home in the Branson subdivision. For now, at least, that murder is being investigated by detectives in the Branson Police Department since the body was discovered inside their district. The cause of death is from a gunshot, but we will know more upon receiving the Medical Examiner's report."

Lt. Holcomb moved next to the second Whiteboard in the room. "So, we have questions" she resumed. "Some of them have been posted here:

Where did Kylie Cooper's death occur?

What was the motive?

Why was her body moved… and by whom?

Is there a connection to the death of her boyfriend, Mickey Paladino?"

The presentation concluded when Captain Holden returned to the front of the room.

"Before Ms. Cooper's body was found our initial investigative effort focused on Mickey Paladino, her boyfriend. He was the closest person in her life as she was not married. But of course, his death now having been made known to us reduces—but does not eliminate suspicion of him.

Lieutenant Ernie Mize then indicated he had something to ask. "What if anything can be made of the sudden disappearance of Paladino's wife while these two murders happened?"

Travis looked over at Honey as if he were not sure either had an answer they wanted to provide at this point. Finally, after a few seconds he responded himself.

"Emily Paladino, age 33 years old, married Mickey Paladino ten years ago in April of 2014. She filed for a divorce in late 2023—which is still pending. They owned the restaurant in Branson known as Mickey Flynn's and have additional establishments in Saint Louis and one in a Chicago suburb, Wheaton. They contracted with a business named Central States Bar Management to run those restaurants. Meanwhile, she works at My Missouri Home in real estate sales."

Travis then motioned for Lt. Holcomb to continue with the Emily Paladino connection to this case.

"Emily went missing from her job on August 13th after showing one of her listings in Cassville. She remained a missing person case until Monday, August 19th. We were debriefing her regarding the reasons for being out of contact with anyone for so long when the death of her husband in Branson was made known to us."

Detective Ben Hodge, sitting the farthest away from the Whiteboards had to almost shout out his question.

"Sounds to me like there could be a connection… even a possible motive there, wouldn't you say Captain Holden?"

Travis walked closer to where the detective who had to shout his question was seated.

"What we know so far about Emily Paladino is that she was in divorce proceedings with the now deceased Mickey Paladino, and we are in the process of learning if there was anything to be gained by her with his death such as insurance money, or whatever. She is a Person of Interest but not yet a suspect."

The meeting ended with the reassignments of four detectives from the COMET unit and one from Internet Crimes being added to the special task force that Sheriff Bull Lambert wanted formed under Lieutenant Honey Holcomb to solve the Kylie Cooper murder.

"This task force will work under the direction of Lieutenant Holcomb, and I am expecting not only that there will be open communication but also full, willing cooperation by each member of this task force."

Captain Holden was looking directly at Lt. Ernie Mize when he dismissed everyone.

17

A motive—maybe!

Thursday, August 29th

THE DAY AFTER THE MEETING WITH the task force investigating the death of Kylie Cooper, Lieutenant Honey Holcomb met with Travis in his office. She told him that she wondered if putting Lt. Mize on this investigation team was a clever idea. "Travis, you know how sensitive Mize is about missing out on the promotion that got you those captain's bars."

Travis smiled. "Of course I know that. I suppose you want to remind me now of the contempt he feels for me, and you are wondering why I picked him… where he will now be reporting to me during the run of this investigation."

"You?" Honey Holcomb asked sounding like the captain had used the wrong pronoun. "Lieutenant Mize must go through me in this chain of command… I go to you. The rest of the task force… Ernie Mize included… goes to me, right?"

Travis reached his desk but stood facing his lieutenant while she was trying to make a point about her concern with the assignments he just announced. He paused briefly after hearing her question and then sat down at his desk while motioning for her to also be seated.

"And you must be thinking that our mutual friend Ernie Mize will have the same distaste in his mouth each time he has to face up to being lower on the command's Totem Pole than you… as he has concerning me."

Honey Holcomb nodded affirmatively indicating that was indeed what prompted her question.

Captain Holden opened the large desk drawer on his left and removed the Stone County Sheriff Police Detective Roster. He placed it where Honey could view it also.

"I have only six detectives plus you under my command in the C.I.D. unit. Honey, the sheriff is counting on me to solve this thing quick… he is taking a beating from some of those in the press looking to make a name for themselves in this case."

Honey Holcomb allowed the expression on her face to indicate that she was aware of the pressure they were under to find out who killed Kylie Cooper.

"I would put every one of us into C.I.D. on this one," Travis resumed. "But we still have other "hot" cases going. We are presently investigating two gas station armed robberies; one child molestation; several underage liquor violations, and one bank fraud… Six detectives are all I have available to cover the four hundred sixty-three square miles on land and the forty-eight square miles on Table Rock Lake that fall under the responsibility of the Stone County Sheriff's Department."

"You're right… you are right…" Honey said wishing now that she would have refrained from second guessing Lt. Ernie Mize's assignment to her task force.

Travis leaned across his desk and pulled her hand into his.

"Honey, if Mize pulls anything during this period do not wait to let me know…"

The intercom buzzed and when Travis clicked it to "ON" they heard the loud and friendly voice of Miss Helen calling from her desk in the Public Lobby.

"Travis?" she asked just to be certain she had pushed the correct office button on her intercom. "There's an insurance man here from Metropolitan for you."

Travis looked at Honey with an obvious question.

"Miss Helen, did you say there is an insurance man here... for me?"

"Yes dear," the elderly woman responded. "I'm with someone else here that is buying a fishing license so..."

"That's okay... Lieutenant Holcomb is nearby so I will ask her to escort the insurance man back to my office."

"Have you missed your monthly payment?" Honey laughed.

"I have no idea... nothing..." Travis sighed as he watched the lieutenant head out towards the Public Lobby.

When she returned, Travis recognized Verne Bauer immediately and they shook hands.

"Haven't seen you, Verne, since your daughter Vicki threw that beer bash at your house while you and Edna were at the Life Insurance Convention in Chicago."

Verne Bauer smiled. "I haven't forgotten how you came through for me then," he said. "That could have been a bad mark... not only for my daughter... but for me too... I mean my reputation... and all. Thanks for keeping that out of the press... and away from Judge Junior. That man would have loved to hang me out to dry."

"Hey!" Travis stopped him. "That's all in the past now... I was glad to help... Just one thing," he added. "What's Judge Junior got against you anyway?"

Verne sighed and took a seat next to Lt. Holcomb. "Before we got Al Duncan on our bowling team, we had no hopes of ever doing anything in the Thursday Night Men's League... But once we got him, we have been Champs ever since. Judge Junior tried every trick in the book to get Al on his team, Hangman's Bluff, and he tells folks now that we stole the championship from where it rightly belonged."

Travis's intention was to just engage their visitor in some friendly small talk but could see that Verne was getting himself all worked up to run the whole league history into the conversation.

"Verne, what is it that brings you in today? No more beer bashes, I hope?"

Verne paused now, seeming adrift in thought searching for what it was that he wanted to tell the Police Captain.

"Oh?… Oh yes… Hey Travis, you are working on that poor little Kylie Cooper case, right?"

Both Honey Holcomb and Travis answered at the same time.

"Right"……

"Right."

"Well, by now I'm sure that you and your detectives have found out that Kylie was living with that fellow Mickey Paladino while he was going through his divorce."

Travis was becoming impatient, hoping that Verne was not just making small talk about something that had been in the newspapers and on television.

"You have something you want to tell me, Verne? Something that I might not know?"

"Just this, Travis. Four months ago, I sold a one-million-dollar life insurance policy to that Paladino guy and at the same time sold another million-dollar policy on Kylie Cooper… all in the same afternoon while I was at her place over at Indian Point. Seems that she was using a good part of her inheritance and was in the process of buying in as his partner in that Ozark Lake Leisure Boats business and they wanted to finance a huge order for more luxury houseboats. I think that whatever bank they were talking to suggested they needed the life insurance to proceed with the loan application."

"Wait a minute, Verne… Are those policies in effect yet?"

"Damn sure!" They each had to take a physical… and passed it. Both passed it… right before they purchased more houseboats for their business."

Honey Holcomb was quiet up to this point but could wait no longer to inquire about who the beneficiary was in Kylie's policy.

"That's just it," Verne said. Mickey wanted to make Kylie his beneficiary and his lawyer told him to hold on until the divorce case was finished. The lawyer feared it would help Paladino's wife's case because of what it might show about the infidelity allegation she was using as her main reason for getting a divorce."

"So, Paladino took out the policy with no beneficiary?" Honey asked.

"Right… I told him that as soon as his divorce got settled, I would be back and help him complete the beneficiary form… You know, making Kylie his… Just like he wanted."

"But Kylie did name Mickey as her beneficiary?"

"Right."

Honey came over and stood next to Travis so that Verne Bauer was facing them both at the same time.

"You do know, Verne, that they are both deceased now, don't you?"

"That is just it. With them both dead… Kylie's million will go as she intended to Mickey Paladino… and his… and now hers too… goes to his estate… two million dollars… all in less than four months' time."

Travis' eyes went first to Honey Holcomb then quickly back to Verne Bauer.

"You don't know if Mickey had any other family… first cousin… anything…?"

"I do know," Bauer hurriedly interrupted. "That was something we did talk about when we knew he was supposed to wait on naming a beneficiary… He actually laughed because… well, he said he had to make sure that he kept living until we got the beneficiary thing straightened out or else…"

"Or else what?" Honey asked.

"It will all go to Emily… His wife… until she's not his wife… No other family… Nuthin!"

18

The Worldwide Lake Boat Sales connection

Tuesday, September 3rd, 10:00 A.M.

THE FIRST THING THAT CAME TO his mind after being escorted into Horace Haywood's office was that Homeland Security in Springfield, Missouri must be spending the government's money on something other than an adequate office space for their chief. His own office in Galena was at least one and a half times larger than the one he was now sitting in waiting for Haywood to finish with the telephone call he was on when he arrived. In fact, the desk in his own office would barely fit inside this one.

"Hey Bull, thanks for coming in this morning," Haywood said while standing up to greet the sheriff. "Hope you were able to enjoy your Labor Day doing something you wanted to be doing."

"Well Horace, I'll tell you this much," the sheriff said continuing their small talk. "Before all this happened, you know… the murders, things were going so slow I had made plans to take a week vacation and go to New Orleans and spend a leisurely week there with my sister."

Haywood sat quietly looking at Bull Lambert hoping he might cut this a bit shorter than it seemed was his intention.

"So… by my keen detection abilities I can see that plan never happened?"

"No… fuck no!" Bull Lambert said. "I've been as busy as I have been ever since they called off suicide and made it a murder."

"So… you worked the holiday?" Haywood said drawing things to a conclusion.

"Naw. I did not say I worked… just that it screwed my plans to leave this area for a week. I did enjoy a nice picnic… my deputy… you met her, Alison Monroe?"

"Huh? Oh, yes, that cute little gal that brings you the Starbucks every morning…"

Lambert looked a bit nonplussed. "So, you remember her… okay. As I was just telling you, she invited me and a few of the detectives working on the Kylie Cooper murder to her place for a nice Labor Day picnic. Big juicy hamburgers and brats, lots of her special potato salad, and just as important, enough Pabst Blue Ribbons to wash it all down. She had the big screen TV out on the back deck, so we also had the Cardinals game on. Yes, they won, and then she showed us the novel she is writing… all about this case we are working now."

"She's writing a novel… about the Cooper murder?" Haywood was disturbed by that last bit of news.

"Oh, the novel," the sheriff said, noticing how it could be something a law enforcement person should avoid doing at least while the investigation was ongoing. "There's no problem, Horace," he said trying to explain why he allowed her to be writing the facts of the murder investigation into a fictional novel. "Alison's job at police headquarters is not involved in any way in the investigation so…"

"But she does have access… You just told me that she…"

Sheriff Lambert leaned forward now, resting a forearm on the desk across from Haywood. "Turns out that Alison knew Kylie Cooper back in their high school days. When she is away from the job as my deputy, she likes to write and hopes someday to become a published author. She watches those TV shows like Dateline and 48 Hours… and those English mysteries on PBS and then she sees what we are doing here in Stone County Missouri and wants to write about it. I do not see any problem… but I promise you that first time there is one I will put a stop to it. Now then… Fill me in on that reason you wanted to see me this morning."

Although he still thought that situation could cause trouble down the line, Horace was more interested in doing just what the sheriff suggested, getting the conversation on the topic that was on today's agenda.

"Bull, as I mentioned a few days back when I was in your office, there are some very mysterious things going on at that Cooper farm over at Plyman's Point."

"Sure, you told me that your investigation discovered Carl refused to sell to Jari Abdou after finding out he was a Muslim who was working on his daughter Kylie to become one too… and then as soon as the old man was killed in that boating accident and the farm went to his daughter, she sold it to Abdou, right?"

"Exactly," Haywood confirmed. "After Abdou purchased it, he turned it into something like a Midwest corporate headquarters for his company, Worldwide Lake Boat Sales, which we know is merely a front for what is his real purpose. There are many reasons that we have our eyes on him but for now, let us review the connections he has in your domain."

The sheriff nodded that he was already in the circle on that part.

"Well, start with what we now know was the way Abdou finally arranged to buy the place after being turned down by Kylie's father,"

Bull Lambert said. "This is what we have learned after talking with various people during our search for Emily Paladino while she was a missing person. Kylie had been working as a singer in Branson… specifically, at Mickey Flynn's. When Mickey and his wife, Emily, opened two more restaurants, they soon discovered that they were in over their heads as far as daily management of them. So, they listened to their accountant… man by the name of Sherman Sutcliffe, his office is right here in Springfield, and turned the management part over to…" the sheriff paused and turned over several pages in the steno pad that Alison prepared for him to bring to the meeting with Haywood, looking for the company name.

"Let me help you there, Bull," Haywood said after losing some patience waiting for the sheriff to locate the information. "They turned it over to Central States Restaurant and Bar Management Associates… from Chicago."

"Yes… Yes… That's who it was… I mean… is." Lambert answered. "We've been busy trying to learn just who that group is involved with…"

"Okay… Let me fill in that data for you," Haywood said before the sheriff could open the steno pad's notes. "That group, Central States Bar Management, is silently owned by the mob… La Cosa Nostra, and their corporation papers filed with the State of Illinois list a fellow by the name of Guy Chevron as one of the company officers… along with someone by the name of Lucas Juliano who it is known has run other mob businesses."

"Who the fuck…??"

"Lucas Juliano used to run a Numbers game in the Chicago suburbs a few years ago," Haywood resumed. "Somehow he made the connection with the Big Boys and struck it rich… so to speak."

"But… other than have his Management Company run things at Mickey Flynn's, what is his connection to… Kylie Cooper? Or Jari Abdou?"

Haywood smiled. "Just how much time did you put aside for our meeting today, Bull?"

"Sounds like you got more to add," the sheriff responded. "Why don't you just keep filling in the blanks and if I got a time problem, I would stop you then, okay?"

"Okay Bull," Haywood said. before standing up and walking out to where his secretary could be seen. "Mrs. Maxwell," he called over to where she was running some copies. "Hold all my calls until the sheriff and I complete our discussions." He seemed more serious now than Sheriff Lambert remembered seeing him.

19

The danger at Plyman's Point

Tuesday, September 3rd, 10:30 A.M.

Before continuing the discussion, Sheriff Lambert called Alison Monroe to caution her about the book she has been writing. He wanted to do this in the presence of Horace Haywood to assure him that he understood that what they were about to discuss deserved the confidence in him that was being shown.

Horace Haywood seemed to relax upon being invited to listen to the sheriff's instructions to his deputy.

"Bull, not longer than a few months ago we received a heads-up from Washington that this fellow Jari Abdou, the same guy who bought the Cooper farm, has connections with one of those extremist Islamic terrorist radical groups.

"Is that the bunch that's called ISIS?" Lambert asked.

"More exactly," Haywood said, "they are who U.S. intelligence agencies said that they were concerned about. They are derived of inspirational supporters of al-Qaeda, such as Anwar al-'Awlaki, and who are increasingly motivating individuals toward violent extremism [in the United States."

Sheriff Lambert looked puzzled. "How does Jari Abdou fit into any of this?"

"Abdou worked as a cell organizer putting together resumes of potential supporters from within the Iranian mosques. He was a low-level threat but when he left Tehran to come to America it drew enough curiosity from TRAC that prompted us to open our own investigation."

"TRAC?"

"Right... that is an acronym for Terrorism Research and Analysis Consortium. They have resources all over the world that assemble information and profiles of terrorist organizations such as Al Queda, ISIS, and Boko Haram... even of various lone wolves. They also monitor and report on government counterterrorism campaigns. Thus far, the only verifiable information concerns Abdou's history in Iran. He was never arrested or charged with anything so, without any criminal record, he was able to keep his passport and enter the United States. His intentions here in America are only speculation."

"But you guys here in Homeland Security think... uh, speculate... that he represents a serious threat of some kind?"

"Well, we are quite confident that he did not leave Tehran just to invest and make money for himself here in Missouri. The Worldwide Lake Boat Sales provides a potential cover for terrorism cells to be formed and open new operations. It did not exist anywhere in the world before Abdou arrived with his group. We suspect that he chose Cooper farm because of the relative obscurity of the location. It is also a short drive to Missouri State University in Springfield where Hanna Mustafo, the sister of his cohort, a Muslim by the name of Rais Azari, was enrolled. Being on Table Rock Lake lent the credibility to his disguised purpose."

Sheriff Lambert was listening for anything a bit more specific about what the Homeland Security chief saw for any role he or his Stone County police might be expected to contribute.

"Horace," he began. "What do you think is the purpose of this guy, Jari Abdou, and his radical bunch… I mean, what's his reason as far as doing bad stuff in my Stone County?"

Horace Haywood shifted in his seat and paused to take another swallow of coffee before answering,

"Homeland Security knows that there are already more than two dozen sleeper cells… Islamic extremists sleeper cells… that are training and growing and planning for various kinds of potential disruptions here, within America. They are used to staying under the radar… taking up residences in non-urban locations… conducting secret meetings of their local leadership… under the radar of where one might suspect would be the focus."

Sheriff Lambert's confusion was written all over his face. And things were not being made any easier to understand so far with the explanation offered by the Homeland Security Chief.

"Are you saying that the business Abdou has set up… being a Sales Agency for those luxury houseboats… is all for show while he engages in something more sinister?"

"Yes, that's exactly what I'm saying," Heywood answered. "How he uses that fake business plan is what we are studying right now. We know that part of the sales they generate do get funneled into the financing for their new cells… some as far away as Chicago, some as close as Saint Louis."

"So, do you think that Abdou has set up one of those radical cells anywhere in Stone County?"

Heywood finished drinking the last of his coffee and then opened a file that had been sitting on his desk.

"That fellow that just got shot over at Indian Point… Paladino… He paid a down payment of $350,000 to Abdou for one of those houseboats and exclusive territory for sales of leisure boats on

Table Rock Lake. We know now that he met with Abdou on his houseboat trying to sell back that business shortly before he was later found murdered."

Lambert leaned forward in his chair hoping to be offered a look at the file the Chief was referring to but was surprised when he was rebuffed.

"So… Mickey Paladino who owns a very successful chain of restaurants decides he wants to go in the business of leasing houseboats along Table Rock Lake?" Lambert scoffed. "That don't make much sense… but even less sense that he decides he wants to sell perhaps most of it all back to Abdou… who instead shoots his brains out just for asking…?"

Horace Haywood laughed at the jump-to-conclusion frustration he heard in Sheriff Lambert's summary of what they had been discussing.

"Look Bull, I know that you must understand that is not what has gone down so far. Yes, Paladino bought the houseboat and the rights and yes for reasons we are still investigating and trying to learn, wanted to get all his money back out of it in less than three years after he bought it, even though it looks like it was by then making a nice profit. These are the facts… and the parts that do not yet make sense to you, or us, does not change those facts at all."

Lambert could see that he had succeeded in nudging the Homeland Security Chief a bit closer to having what might be called controlled anger than he intended. It was just that the more he listened the more he learned that the Feds seemed to know more about the recent murders in Stone County than he or his detectives knew.

"Horace, all I am asking is that you let me, and my crew handle the murder cases that happen in my… our Stone County, okay?"

Haywood stood up and walked across the room to retrieve another file. He looked like he was either irritated by the tone or in the way Sheriff Lambert was expressing himself or was using the opportunity to check back his own reaction so to avoid mushrooming their disagreement into something that would prove difficult to get past. When he returned to his desk, he brought the new file with him and opened it alongside the previous one that contained the information on Mickey Paladino.

"Bull there is more that I now feel must be shared with you… and before I begin let me acknowledge that I realize that you will be upset to learn that our investigation preceded the murders and gave us a head start in learning things that you now must feel belongs in your purview."

"Murders?" Bull Lambert asked. "You just told me about the Paladino investigation you had going before he met his due. Are you now adding the Kylie Cooper murder to what you folks were investigating… BEFORE she was found dead in the boat?"

"Okay, let's try to remember that we were friends before today's meeting and we will be friends when we finish," Horace said hoping to calm the sheriff before things got out of control. "The answer to your question about Kylie Cooper is… Yes! Just try to remember that our purpose for running that investigation was to learn as much as we could about the Worldwide Lake Boat Sales."

Horace was pleased to see that Bull Lambert seemed to be coming more relaxed and receptive to at least listening to the explanation of why his Homeland Security team became involved in what turned out to be two murders inside the sheriff's area of responsibility.

"We learned about Kylie after Jari Abdou started spending time with her. She was a singer in Mickey Flynn's club in Branson and we soon observed that she and Abdou often paired up with the two Paladino's going to some of the restaurants over near Silver Dollar City and along the Strip. Later, something happened that broke up Abdou and Kylie's relationship… we think he was hoping to convert her to his Islamic religion…

and then in less than a year later Emily and Mickey split up. The Paladino's separated at a time when their restaurant business was booming. They had already opened two additional Mickey Flynn Restaurants and were doing so well that they hired a management company to run everything for them. This freed Emily to return to her real estate sales position with My Missouri Home… and freed her husband to… well, be free. Soon he and Kylie were seen together out on Table Rock Lake in one of his catamarans… the one he named Mist Acken 1. We also learned that through Kylie's connections with Abdou, Mickey soon purchased the franchise he named Ozark Lake Leisure Boats that came with a luxury houseboat and a few expensive catamarans and included exclusive sales territory for the Table Rock Lake area from Worldwide Lake Boat Sales."

"Yes… yes, all of that I already know… you and I have run this through earlier… but… the murder… Kylie… where does that fit?"

"I thought you were going to ask where Mickey Paladino got his hands on the $350,000, he used for the down payment to buy his Ozark Lake Leisure Boats business from Abdou."

Lambert shifted uneasy in his chair. "Okay… I suppose that plays a role in all of this."

Horace smiled. "Mickey got the money from a loan made by the same Lucas Juliano… an officer in the Management Company running his three restaurants."

Once again, Haywood interrupted his conversation to fetch a third file and bring it back to his desk. Lambert noticed this file had a name too long to fit neatly in the tab and instead it was marked Central States Restaurant and Bar Management Associates in larger bold type on a label in the center, much easier for him to read from where he sat opposite Haywood.

"So, Paladino borrows $350,000 from Juliano to buy his Ozark Lake Leisure Boats business from Worldwide… which seems a bit stupid."

Haywood's eyebrows raised hearing the sheriff's comment. "I agree… but what was it that drew that analysis by you?"

"Well, it just seems that you don't want to borrow money from any company you have hired to account for the money your three Mickey Flynn's are bringing in."

"Bingo Bull… You and I are together on that observation," Haywood said offering a high five to the sheriff. "And, just as you would have guessed, things suddenly took a strange turn regarding that loan… just a week or so before the two murders happened."

Sheriff Lambert liked hearing the acknowledgement from the Homeland Security Chief that they shared the same conclusions. But the comment that followed about things going bad just before the murders caused him to edge forward in his seat. He wondered what it was that the fed's investigation learned that tied the loan to the murders that his detectives were hoping to solve. Instead of saying anything he merely nodded, which served to urge Haywood to explain more regarding that comment.

"As you already know, Bull, this fellow Lucas Juliano is just a mid-level front with the Cosa Nostra mob in Chicago. That sum of money, $350,000, is not much for them to get involved in as far as requiring their approval to loan out. But… if any part of the repayment plan goes south and looks like it could become a loss… Well, the man making the loan becomes the man responsible to the mob to pay back the loan."

"So, I guess you're saying that your boys learned that Mickey Paladino wasn't doing so well with that Ozark Lake Leisure Boats Company and couldn't make his payments, right?"

Haywood raised his hand in the 'Stop' position. "Not exactly that… but something happened between Lucas Juliano and Mickey Paladino that prompted rumors of a hit being issued at mob headquarters."

"Horace… are you telling me now that Paladino was murdered by the Chicago mob?"

This time Haywood raised both hands, palms out. "No… We don't know yet if the hit was approved… just that there was street talk that it was being ordered… most probably by Juliano."

"But… if they kill Mickey… how does that get Juliano off the hook regarding the bad loan?"

"Actually, it would not relieve him of that responsibility… and that is why we are pressing that part of our investigation to find that answer. We do know that the loan was backed by packaging the three Mickey Flynn restaurants as collateral. They all are doing gang busters… if you excuse the use of that term."

"So that is your answer… or one motive. If Mickey is dead the loan payments fall on Emily to make… and if she fails, then the loan gets recalled and Paladino and the mob become sole owners of three money making restaurants".

"True. But since, as you say, the restaurants are doing well enough to keep making the loan payments… which is what our investigations so indicate… it removes that… and the mob from having any reason to knock off Mickey."

Now it was the sheriff's turn to stand up. Something that Haywood just said turned on a light bulb of worrisome thoughts inside his mind.

"But just like if Mickey becomes too dead to make the loan payments… would not that become the same result if his wife, the co-owner, was killed off. No loan payments… collateral is seized. The restaurants… all three become Mob owned. Damn… that could be why they made that stupid loan in the first place…"

Haywood got up from his desk chair and walked over to where the sheriff stood.

"Bull, I am giving you these three files and turning everything concerning the murders over to you for your investigations into the deaths of Kylie Cooper and Mickey Paladino. We in Homeland Security have but one purpose here, and that involves Jari Abdou and that Sunni Muslim bunch that is up to no good with their Worldwide Lake Boat Sales. If we learn anything that can help you in finding out who and why Mickey Paladino and his girlfriend, Kylie Cooper, were killed we will share that with you. But there is one thing that I must ask… no, make that… demand from you."

Lambert stood eye to eye with the Homeland Security Chief with a look that challenged the use of the word "demand". Once again, he said nothing, allowing that the expression on his face be enough to urge the Chief to continue saying what it was that he would demand.

"We are amid what has become very delicate information gathering over there with Jari's group. We are aware they have plans… some of which we now know about. But there is much we still need to learn before making our move. What I am afraid of is that if your investigations lead towards them then it could well interfere with what we are doing here at Homeland Security. Later I will messenger over to you a package of background material we have assembled on Jari Abdou's bunch at Plyman's Point. That should help you know who in that bunch is and who we at Homeland Security need to call our own for any investigations or other police action."

"Sure Horace," the sheriff said. "You have the Muslim bunch in your sights, and I have some murders to solve. You are going to stay out of my business, and you want me and my detectives to avoid doing anything regarding the Worldwide Lake Boat Sales."

Hearing that, Horace Haywood extended a handshake to the sheriff. And then while he walked with him out to the elevator, he asked once again for the sheriff to closely monitor the book writing efforts of his deputy Alison Monroe.

20

Emily's role

Wednesday, September 4th

AFTER LEARNING THAT EMILY PALADINO was in line to receive the full life insurance benefits on the million-dollar policies for each of the two murdered victims, Travis called another meeting with the task force. Once they were all seated and Lieutenant Honey Holcomb was back at the Whiteboard, Travis began the meeting.

"I have asked Lieutenant Holcomb to summarize the evidence and interviews statements to begin and..."

Travis paused as, to his surprise, Sheriff Bull Lambert entered and took a seat by the door just inside the room.

Noticing that his entrance interrupted Captain Holden's meeting, the sheriff waved for Travis to continue. The other detectives, who were also surprised to see the boss at one of their Investigation Review meetings, took their cue and turned their attention back to where Travis and Honey stood.

"We do have an important piece of information that we were tipped on last Friday and that has just been confirmed," Travis said resuming control of everyone's attention. "I will let Lieutenant Holcomb inform you on that as she updates the Investigation history from what we discussed last week with the most recent information we have gained since."

Honey had just completed posting an updated listing of assignments for each task force member and at the mention of her name turned around and faced the assembled detectives.

"Reviewing what has been learned so far, on Sunday, August 18th, the body of Kylie Cooper, a longtime resident of Lampe, was discovered late at night by a young couple returning to their vehicle after attending a concert at Black Oak Mountain Theater on highway H. Their dog alerted them to a deserted rowboat that was along the shoreline just beyond Baxter Boat Dock and inside the boat was the body of Ms. Cooper."

Honey then pointed to a series of photographs showing the boat location and the body inside stretched along under the middle seat, facing up… with both eyes open. The photos of the young couple who found and reported the incident to the Stone County Sheriff's Police, along with their dog Archie, were also posted.

"On Monday, August 19th, the body of Mickey Paladino was discovered in a townhome owned by Kylie Cooper at Indian Point. We have learned that Mr. Paladino was living with her at that residence while going through a divorce from his wife, Emily Paladino."

Again, Lt. Holcomb referred to the photos taken at the scene and two of Mickey Paladino taken when he was alive.

"The cause of the death of Kylie Cooper was from her consuming excessive amounts of valium and other drugs including oxycodone along with sufficient alcohol and that combination prove to be fatal. The immediate indication was that Ms. Cooper committed suicide. However, once the Medical Examiner conducted a lividity analysis that revealed her body had been moved at least twice after becoming deceased the current cause of her death is listed as murder after earlier being labeled as undetermined. All this now raises the question did someone give or sneak the poison combination of drugs and alcohol for the victim to drink and what was his or her reason for doing so. Mr. Paladino's demise was much easier to determine as he was killed by a shot into the back of his head from a.33 mm (about 0.01 in). GLOCK. As of now we know the 'how' but not the 'why'."

Honey then walked to where a photograph taken when Emily Paladino was interviewed by detectives after being discovered walking along highway 65 near Silver Dollar City.

"Emily Paladino was suing her husband Mickey Paladino for divorce at the time of his death. She also knew Kylie Cooper who worked as an entertainer in the supper club Emily and Mickey owned in Branson known as Mickey Flynn's. In her lawsuit Emily stated that her husband and Kylie Cooper had become lovers, and the infidelity was a basis for the divorce."

"Have we learned if there were any threats made, like in anger, jealousy… whatever… by Mrs. Paladino to cause harm for either… or both, of the deceased victims?" Ernie Mize broke in.

"To date," Honey responded, "we have been unsuccessful during this investigation to learn of anything like that as a possible motive. When we brought Emily in after she was discovered near Silver Dollar City it was not then known of her connection to Kylie Cooper or even that her husband had been murdered. She was a Missing Person and her sister whom we planned earlier to assist us in our investigation was waiting to take her home following our interview with her. Emily was disoriented and seemed unable at that time to provide us with any useful information, so we arranged for her sister to take her from us, and we suggested then that appropriate medical examination of her condition take place."

"So… she just walked out of here without any further…" Lieutenant Mize grumbled aloud.

Travis motioned to Honey that he wanted to take over the meeting again.

"Ernie, you know that what we are presenting right now is a chronological summary… and when Emily walked out of here, we knew nothing at that time of her connection or connections to these murders."

"But we did know that there was one… soon to become two deaths that she had some connection with, right?" Ernie persisted.

Travis merely sighed showing that any further dialog with Lt. Mize at this point would prove fruitless.

"Moving on," Travis resumed as a few chuckles were heard coming from the other detectives reacting to their common knowledge of the long-standing enmity between these two men. "We did learn very recently that Emily can expect to receive a total of two million dollars from life insurance policies taken out on each of the deceased less than three months before they were murdered."

Once again, Ernie Mize broke in with a comment disguised as a question.

"Have we learned if Emily Paladino followed through on getting medical care… after she walked away from us… and if so, where is she now?

"On the same night she departed with her sister, Elizabeth Lane, she went to Ozark Community Hospital where she was examined in their emergency area and received oxygen and other antidotes for an overdose of a Valium-like narcotic. As to where she is at present, we believe that she either returned to her home or has gone somewhere else, to her sister's home in Tulsa."

Honey then returned to the Whiteboard and pointed to the list of persons that are known to be connected to Emily Paladino and the two murder victims.

"Emily is employed at My Missouri Home Realty, and we need to interview the managing owner, a Mr. Armand Locke, and the Office Manager, a Miss Twyla Turner to learn as much they may know about Mrs. Paladino's six days as a Missing Person. I have assigned Detective Arnie Platt to this."

Honey looked over her shoulder and saw that Platt heard and indicated he would follow through with that part.

"Kylie Cooper was the daughter of Carl Cooper who is deceased and with whom she was living before she started working as an entertainer at the supper club known as Mickey Flynn's in Branson. It was there that she met and subsequently became close with Mickey and Emily. We want to learn as much as possible about the affair she was having with Mickey Paladino as well as everything involving any other boyfriend she had during that time. Lieutenant Ernie Mize will gather that information for our investigation."

Captain Travis then took over the meeting.

"The last known person to be with Emily Paladino before she went missing, coincidentally during the times of the murders, is an ex-con by the name of Frankie Valenti. He is employed by Ozark Lake Leisure Boats, a business that mostly leases luxury houseboats on various lakes in the Ozarks. Lieutenant Honey Holcomb will bring him in and try to find out what his involvement is."

At this point, Sheriff Lambert stood up and came to the front of the room.

"As long as I have been involved in conducting or studying or teaching the process of investigating criminal activity," he began, "there were always those three magic words that needed to have answers before any crime would find a solution."

The sheriff turned and went to the Whiteboard, picking up the black grease marker on his way. He began writing... in large letters... while speaking.

"WHO did it? How was it done... and... WHY. was it done?"

When he finished, he turned back and faced where Travis and Honey were standing.

"I could have stayed at the Whiteboard and wrote three more words," he said. "But you all know them, right, mom?"

The sheriff pointed toward Lt. Ernie Mize who was completely flummoxed.

"I am sorry… my mind must have wandered. Did you say… mom?

The sheriff burst out laughing.

"Ernie, you are one dumb fuck sometimes."

Once again, the sheriff returned to the Whiteboard and wrote… M O M and turned back and pointed again at Mize who this time was paying closer attention.

"M O M is… uh stands for… method, opportunity, and… uh, means. That is, it, right?"

The sheriff smiled. "That is right, Ernie. I know you knew that all along and were just funning us."

The smile was gone when he aimed his next comments toward the man he promoted to run his Criminal Investigation Department, Captain Travis Holden.

"From where I sit, we have the answers to our M-O-M equation. Mrs. Emily Paladino is known now to have consumed the type of drugs used to kill Kylie Cooper. The opportunity is surely those missing six days in her life that need a whole lot more of an explanation. And the motive…? Come on people. Two million dollars!"

Facing Travis, the sheriff shrugged, indicating that he wanted to see that everyone understood where he was going with what he just said.

"Let us put our complete efforts into this case, Do the interviews and investigations that Lieutenant Holcomb assigned. But begin by bringing in the wife, Emily Paladino… even if that means… in handcuffs."

21

Emily selects her lawyer

Wednesday, September 4th, 1:00 P.M.

THE BRIGHTNESS OF THE EARLY AFTERNOON sunlight provided stark contrast to the first time that Elizabeth drove along Interstate route 44 toward Galena for a meeting (she thought…) with the sheriff's detectives. A significant difference this time was that Emily, who was still a Missing Person then, was now riding in the back seat of the car with her. She felt much more confident also because Frances was also with them now. It was Frances's advice that before they show up at the sheriff's office, as they had been instructed to do by Lieutenant Holcomb, that they meet first with Emily's lawyer at Emily's house in Kimberling City.

"The last time I drove on this highway it was storming like something I hadn't seen in years," Elizabeth laughed after catching sight in her rear-view mirror of Emily sitting quietly in the back seat looking far away in her thoughts. "And to think, that was just a couple of weeks ago when we thought that all which was needed was to find you."

Frances turned towards Elizabeth. "Yes, I remember how frightened you were by all that bad lightning and loud thunder when you called me wondering if you should just turn around and go back home," Frances said using her usual sarcastic tone.

"Why, that's not the reason I called you that day," Elizabeth said sounding offended. "I had just pulled off the highway at the height of the storm but heard a news report that a body of a young woman had just been found and I worried that…"

"I know," Frances consoled her sister while turning around to include Emily in their conversation. "Elizabeth really was afraid that she was only being asked to come to the Stone County Sherriff's office so she could identify the body they had just discovered in that boat over near Baxter Boat Dock."

Emily nodded, remembering the conversation she and Elizabeth had had the day after she was released from the hospital. Elizabeth described how everything seemed to just come apart all at once for her that day.

"It's seems so strange to think of the events in our lives that are going along in an almost boring fashion and then change a full one hundred eighty degrees in what seems a blink of an eye," Emily said referring to the more than three weeks that passed since she was home, or at least even close to her home in Kimberling City. "Of course, I was so out of it during most of that time that I was hardly aware of what day of the week it was."

Emily shuddered as some of the memories of those events began flooding her mind. "I had been swallowing valiums like they were candy just to keep myself from falling completely apart with fear"

"While I was waiting for you that night at Ozark Community Hospital the nurse mentioned they suspected that there was more than valium to blame for your condition that night," Elizabeth said turning just enough to make eye contact with Emily. "I know that she did promise to contact either you or me if the lab analysis disclosed anything other than valium that was causing those symptoms."

"Just where did you get that many valium tablets anyway?" Frances wanted to know. "You always were more into drugs than either me or Elizabeth. Did you have a prescription or were you back to your old ways… finding a dealer who could supply your needs?"

Emily shrugged showing her displeasure with those questions from her older sister. Why did Frances always find it necessary, Emily silently wondered, to bring up the trouble she had with using various recreational drugs.

"You do know that I quit using any drugs after my first marriage ended," Emily responded. "It was not until I opened our first restaurant in Branson that I got high on anything stronger than weed. Only after we got a cabaret license that allowed us to have live music did either of us even have any access to any drugs."

"So, it all started back up again when you and Mickey began hanging with members of the bands?" Frances asked.

"Not the bands so much," Emily said. "It was more when Mickey and I got close with Kylie Cooper who was singing with a local band called the Crazy Coyotes. It was around the time her father was killed in that boating accident. She was his only child, and he was her only living parent, so his death left her really hurting. She was using more drugs to cope with the death of her dad and eventually, the more time we spent with her the easier it became for Mickey and I to find an excuse to slip back into the cocaine, OxyContin, Percodan, or Vicodin lifestyle. Kylie always had those to hand out every time we spent time with her. Eventually she started bringing around a new boyfriend, Jari, and outside of work, all the four of us ever seemed to be doing was partying."

Frances and Elizabeth exchanged worried looks as Emily described the part of her life she managed to keep hidden from them. Living in three separate states, the sisters relied on

Facebook or emails or weekly telephone calls to stay in contact. About the only times that they were present in each other's life were at relatives' weddings or funerals or an occasional unplanned visit if one of them was ill or injured, like when Elizabeth broke her leg while skiing in Colorado six years ago. Keeping anything private from one another was not a tricky thing to accomplish.

A few moments of silence followed Emily's revelation of falling back into using drugs to get high or intoxicated. The two women in the front seat were silently recalling the troubles their younger sister had in her life in high school that kept becoming wilder through her first marriage to Randy Cone, troubles that all were related to drugs. Emily, sitting alone in the back seat, wondered if most or all her current troubles might have been avoided if she somehow found the strength to keep as far away from any drugs as she knew she should have.

The silence was broken when Frances turned around anxiously and faced Emily.

"You just said that Kylie was your source of supply, right?"

Emily nodded affirmatively.

"So… those valiums you relied upon and took so many of since that day Mickey showed up and surprised you in Cassville… Those were valiums you got from Kylie?"

"I guess," Emily responded. "I mean, I did have a prescription from my therapist, but I am sure that I must have run out of mine within the first couple of days after all this new trouble began. Come to think of it, when Kylie and I drove over to Plyman's Point to talk… or try to talk Jari into buying back some of the Ozark Lake Leisure Boats he sold to Mickey so he could pay off that loan to that gangster Lucas Juliano, I'm sure she offered me a good supply of something… I think it must have been valiums anyway".

"Baby sister," Frances's voice reflected the surge of anxiety that accompanied the worried thoughts she was having about those drugs. "Kylie's death was a direct result of drug and alcohol overdose… and they think the drug was OxyContin. Do you know if Kylie gave you anything like that? Were you also drinking anything?"

Emily sat mute and stared outside the car window as she tried to remember that drive from her home in Kimberling City to Plyman's Point to meet with Jari Abdou. She wondered if Frances's concern was valid… and, if so… was that an explanation for her loss of memory of the events that followed that meeting with Jari? After another five minutes or so of silence Frances decided it was time for more catching up with Emily on how she was dragged into this mess of troubles.

"Emily," she asked. "Are you sure that your divorce lawyer is who you need today to get legal advice before your meeting with the detectives? I mean, this is a murder investigation that they want to talk with you about."

Emily seemed distracted in her thoughts, and it was not until she heard the words, murder investigation, that her sister's question got her attention.

"Tomas is the lawyer I hired to divorce Mickey," she said. "But he does other things too, you understand. When Mickey and I opened the first Mickey Flynn's we had Tomas draw up the Partnership Agreement that Sherman Sutcliff, our accountant, told us we would need to report income to the IRS. Our real estate firm uses him often at closings and I know he prepares wills and those things too. Anyway, I have known him and his family since I sold them their house on Bonanza Drive, four houses down the street from the one Mickey and I bought when we got married."

"So… Tomas Cullerton is your… neighbor?" Elizabeth asked.

Frances shot a look over at Elizabeth indicating how less than convinced she was with Emily's choice of lawyers.

"Look, it's too late now to find another lawyer for Emily," Elizabeth pointed out. "We are due in Kimberling City in less than two hours for our meeting with him and that leaves us less than an hour later before we are expected to meet with the detectives."

"I agree," Frances mumbled. "But let's keep our options open. If it looks like they are trying to make Emily a suspect in either of the murder cases, I think we will need someone to represent her that handles those types of situations. Just those types."

22

A My Missouri Home connection

Wednesday, September 4ᵗʰ, 2:00 P.M.

Sᴇʀɢᴇᴀɴᴛ Aʀɴɪᴇ Pʟᴀᴛᴛ ᴡᴏɴᴅᴇʀᴇᴅ ʜᴏᴡ Lieutenant Holcomb made those decisions on which detectives would interview which person about which item of interest the Task Force had regarding the murders. In retrospect his assignment was just information gathering… the type that maybe when it would be combined with something important that a different detective got from a real suspect could lead towards solving these crimes. Would his efforts receive any recognition then? Yes, sure…

"Oh well," he said aloud to himself as he drove alone to the Springfield office of My Missouri Home, "I just have 4-2-GO and any assignment where I don't have to worry about taking a bullet before that great day arrives when I retire is fine-real fine with me." The last part of his private conversation prompted him to start singing… "Fine… I say Fine… I repeat… All is Fine with me babe… I have just 4-2-go… yes… that is 4-2-Go… and… and…" He abruptly stopped singing his little ditty noticing, a bit late, that he had stopped for a traffic light and with his window down he was drawing some embarrassing snickers from a good-looking brunette in the lane next to him.

The light changed and the woman pulled ahead and turned on to the next cross street. Arnie watched her turn before he slowly pressed on the gas pedal and proceeded on his way. "Four… To… Go…" the song was sure to become a number one hit when the big day finally arrived.

Upon arriving at his destination on Bradford Parkway he was surprised how the My Missouri Home building appeared so out of place with the remaining business section that surrounded it. Situated on a corner lot, the real estate office looked more like a large home in a residential neighborhood. Painted a bright yellow with white trim it made one think that it used to belong to a large family that raised nine or more children. Other than the large monument sign on which the words MY MISSOURI HOME appeared, was there any reason to doubt that a real estate office was still the main purpose for it.

Once inside Sergeant Platt became more certain that this was indeed a real estate sales office. Any walls that previously existed to form rooms in the house he earlier imagined had been removed and what remained was a well-furnished and profession-ally decorated open floor plan. A woman, in her middle forties, saw him enter and waved hello as she interrupted a conversation that she was having with someone in the only enclosed office at the far end of the floor. He met her halfway and said he was with the Stone County Sheriff's Police and had called ahead.

"Are you here about those parking tickets again," she asked with a smile. "Or are you Deputy Platt who has an appointment with our boss, Mr. Locke?"

"Well, let me see," he answered. "You're right and you're wrong… and you never want to be wrong with the law," he said faking a growl.

"Oh? And to what might I be wrong about?" she asked rising her eyes to meet his.

"I do in fact have an appointment with Mr. Locke," Platt said. "But I made Sergeant almost ten years ago, so the deputy thing was what you had wrong." His smile assured her there was nothing to become alarmed about.

"Well, I am sorry about getting your rank wrong. Perhaps if you will follow me now, I can take you to Mr. Locke's office as I know he is waiting for you there."

Once inside Armand Locke's office Platt turned and stopped the woman from leaving while reaching for his identification wallet to show them.

"You didn't say who you are," he smiled.

"I am the Office Manager, Twyla Turner," she responded with a proud upraised chin.

"Ah, good," he said. "And you are on my list to see today when I finish talking with Mr. Locke. So, hopefully you will be available then, so I will not have to make another trip from Galena."

Twyla felt a confidence boost to hear that she was someone who might have valuable information but as fate would have it, she was scheduled to be this month's honorable chairperson at the Downtown Springfield's Chamber of Commerce Fall planning meeting.

"I am very willing to answer any questions you may have, sergeant," she said after telling him of her important meeting.

Sergeant Platt looked first at Armand Locke then back to Twyla.

"You know, it isn't necessarily protocol but, what the f— uh… heck. Why don't you take the seat on that side of Mr. Locke, and I will sit here and ask my questions of each of you together?"

Armand Locke looked puzzled by all the back and forth between the detective and his office manager but refrained from doing anything that could leave an impression of being unwilling to fully cooperate.

"If that is the way it needs to be then I am certainly willing," Locke said looking at Sergeant Platt.

"Fine, then. You say fine… and Miss Turner looks like she says fine… and all is fine with me so let us get started. Emily Paladino works here and has since she returned after her restaurant chain grew so fast that she hired somebody to run those businesses. That is the way you remember it, right?"

"That is how I remember it too," Twyla answered before her boss could.

"But not long afterwards, Emily moved out and sued for divorce from her husband, Mickey…" Platt continued.

Once again Twyla responded first, interrupting the detective before he finished with his question.

"Emily did not move out of her house when she filed the divorce papers… he did."

Platt looked surprised. "You say that it was Mickey that was kicked out? Where did he go when that happened?"

Armand Locke cleared his throat indicating that it was his turn to say something.

"I think he stayed on one of his houseboats for the first few months."

Twyla's eyes lit up. "Yes, he did but I know that he was still fooling around with her… that Kylie Cooper… poor dear."

Platt knew all of this and was only getting their discussion going by asking questions he knew the answers to and were ones he understood they also knew the answers. He learned that technique early in his career as a detective. Sometimes a person being questioned by a police officer thinks that the questions are being aimed at something the officers think he or she did, and the best thing is to stay mum. But get them talking and make them feel that they know something about somebody else and then they relax and often give up surprising but valuable information.

"Do either of you remember ever hearing Emily discuss her feelings about either Kylie or her husband?"

Armand Locke looked sternly at Twyla who quickly understood the silent signal that told her to say nothing. Neither answered anything which told Arnie Platt that there was something being left unsaid that was of importance.

"Let's move on," he said hoping that going to his next question would divert their attention away from whatever the reason they had for clamming up on what they knew about something Emily must have told them.

"When I leave, I will need something showing how her sales were going before and after her split from her husband which you can email a PDF to me back at Police headquarters if it is not readily available today. But first… let me ask you this," he said locking eye contact with Twyla. "Did Emily have a drinking problem that you know about?"

"Oh no… it wasn't liquor… For her it was…" she paused hearing her boss once again clearing his throat.

This time Sergeant Platt decided to press for a complete answer. "It was what, Miss Turner? And try to remember that this is an official police interview, and you must under penalty of law provide full and complete information in your responses to my questions."

"I'm not saying she had a drug habit or was an addict or…," and again she paused… looking away from where Armand Locke was sitting… just searching for how to give a full and complete response… without it being too complete. "She was seeing a therapist, what with the sadness of finding out her husband was cheating on her with a woman she had made friends with back at her restaurant in Branson…… and I know that the therapist gave her prescriptions for valium. And something stronger. There were some days she had to call in and have a sales appointment rescheduled and Mr. Locke and I just suspected it was the valium…"

Arnie Platt was surprised by all this information which surpassed his highest hopes when given this assignment. So far, no one at the station or in the briefings mentioned that Emily Paladino was seeing a therapist… and was losing workdays because of a drug problem. This will turn heads at our next Task Force Update meeting, he thought.

"One last question. During the seven days… between August 13th after she showed a house she had listed in Cassville… to August 19th when we discovered her over by Silver Dollar City… Did she at any time contact either of you?"

"Oh? No, I knew that she was missing… I am the one who called the police and reported that," Twyla blurted out sounding both defensive and offended.

Platt looked next at Armand Locke. "How about you? Did you see her… talk with her… meet her somewhere during any of those six days?"

Armand Locke looked like the deer in the headlights. He stuttered… then cleared his throat. Then he reached for the telephone.

"I'm afraid that is all the time I can give you today," he said. "I have an important call that must be made right now…"

Platt stood up and prepared to leave. "I suppose that telephone call could be to your lawyer. But in the end, I know you will find out that I am entitled to the answer to my last question."

Sergeant Platt turned and walked past the rows of desks occupied with secretaries typing contract offers to buy or sell real estate. As he reached the outside door he looked back and saw Locke talking demonstrably to Twyla who was sitting with both of her hands locked together in prayer-like-form under her face which seemed frozen with worry.

23

An interview at police headquarters

Thursday, September 5ᵗʰ, 10:00 A.M.

TRAVIS WAS RELIEVED TO LEARN that Emily and her lawyer were waiting for him in the room used by the Criminal Investigations Department for questioning suspects. Earlier, when he instructed Alison Monroe to escort them there after they arrived at the station, he was concerned that the lawyer, Tomas Cullerton, might insist that the interview be conducted where there was no sound or video equipment. That was a point that Travis earlier conceded when Cullerton agreed to allow his client to be questioned.

Those arrangements were for a meeting scheduled for the previous afternoon that was changed only to accommodate the lawyer's request. During his meeting to prepare Emily for the meeting with the Stone County detectives, Tomas Cullerton said that certain facts were discovered causing him to seek a brief delay before bringing her in. In any case, Travis knew that the ball was back in his court this morning and he would get his wish to have the questions and answers recorded.

Before entering the room Travis walked behind the one-way glass that is used to monitor questioning of suspects from the hallway and saw that Cullerton had taken a seat on the side of where he positioned Emily so that when he looked her way the camera would not be able to show his face. Thus, when questions were asked, he could signal to her it was okay to respond or to avoid answering. This tactic could have some advantage if the questioning were later something played in front of a trial jury as it gives evidence for her claim of fully cooperating with the police.

When Travis entered, Cullerton rose and extended his hand in greeting him.

"I notice that you are alone?" Cullerton said making the statement into a question.

"Oh? You must be referring to the fact that I do not have a uniformed officer with me," Travis responded. "I do that when questioning a suspect, but this is just for information gathering purposes." The C.I.D. Captain hoped that this might establish a more informal setting for his questions thus diminishing any need to feel defensive in Emily's responses.

"And yet, I have noticed that the camera, the microphone, and the recording equipment remains in the "on" position," Cullerton quipped.

Travis decided that no response he might make would better suit his purpose and moved on to his questions to Emily.

"First let me say how much more alert you appear this morning than that afternoon you were found over near Silver Dollar City and brought in to help us learn why you had become a Missing Person."

Emily snuck a look towards her lawyer before responding.

"Yes," she finally said. "I am feeling better. Thank you."

"That was two full weeks ago," Travis continued. "Do you remember why you were in Branson, where you were found?"

Once again, she checked with her eyes for Cullerton's approval to answer this question.

"Captain Holden," the lawyer said while taking Emily's hand into his. "I have listened to what my client now remembers about all of that. It is a long story in that it began on August 13th and ended when she was found on August 19th. With your permission might I suggest that you allow her to start and say all that she now remembers between those dates without interrupting to ask questions? She has done nothing illegal and is anxious to tell you everything."

Travis Holden never expected that level of cooperation from Emily, yet alone on the advice of her lawyer. He did not know what else to say except… "Why?' Then he quickly explained his reaction. "I mean… I am happy to comply with your suggestion… as long as when Emily has finished that she understands that if I have questions that remain then I must go ahead and ask them."

Cullerton smiled. "Yes of course that is our understanding too. But when she tells you what she intends to say, I think you will come to understand how much she now feels that she is in some danger and…" he paused briefly and looked over at his client. "She needs police involvement in what is happening in her life."

Emily looked again over at her lawyer for assurance that she should tell everything, at least all the details that she now recalls. Yesterday, when she and her sisters met with the lawyer, he originally said that his advice was that she should decline to answer any police questions.

However, during his questions and her answers to about everything that happened after Mickey surprised her by being with Frankie Valenti when she went to Cassville to show a house she listed for sale, Mr. Cullerton expressed a concern that she may still be in as much danger as she was during the seven days she was a Missing Person. He suggested that she had done nothing that he was previously concerned about that could link her to any crime, let alone the murders. Instead, he thought now it was necessary to inform the police of it all.

After the lawyer patted her cupped hands and encouraged her to "begin at the beginning", Emily looked away from him and focused on Captain Holden.

"I was in Cassville," she said softly. "It was Tuesday, August 13th and Frankie Valenti…", she paused momentarily wondering if the detective knew who that was. "Frankie had made an appointment to look at the house I listed there, and I wondered myself why he might be interested in it. Frankie works at my ex-husband's business, we are in divorce proceedings, in Kimberling City and there are many similarly priced homes there closer to his job."

Tomas Cullerton saw that his clients was nervous and was rambling in her response with information that was straying from what he knew would be of interest to the detective.

"And when you arrived and learned that your husband had come along with Valenti that frightened you. Tell Captain Holden why that was the case," he said hoping to lead Emily back to more relevant issues.

Emily seemed surprised by her lawyer's question. "I was probably more startled than frightened," she said turning back to face the detective. "There is a court order of protection that I requested… and was granted… when Mickey kept coming to where I work at My Missouri Homes real estate… hounding me to give in on issues that we couldn't agree upon to settle the divorce. So, when I saw him, I knew that he used his employee to set me up… away from any police protection."

"And yet, you went somewhere with him and Valenti?" Travis wondered.

"No, I drove and let Mickey ride with me. Valenti drove behind us."

"Why did you decide to allow Mickey to ride with you? You did have an Order of Protection, right?"

Emily stole a quick peek at her lawyer before continuing. "Yes, I knew I did not have to spend any time at all with him. But then he mentioned that our restaurants could be foreclosed on… unless I acted that same day. Well, I was curious how that could be since I knew we were not in arrears on any payments."

"So… What did you find out?"

"Mickey told me that he needed to borrow a lot of money when he started that new business… the Ozark Lakes Leisure Boats. When Valenti told him about how the company we hired to run the business for the restaurants, Central States Bar Management, could also loan him the money he needed, Mickey went and took out the loan."

"And they are the ones who are foreclosing on your restaurants," Travis asked.

"Yes, that is what Mickey told me. He said that it all happened because Mr. Cullerton called and told them that Mickey forged my name on the loan application."

"I'm surprised you didn't just stop the car and push him out of it when you heard that," Travis said hoping that by showing he was on her side it would lessen her reluctance to be open and tell everything.

"Well, we did exchange some nasty words. I told him that I planned to call Mr. Cullerton to verify what he just told me and that is when he said he hoped I would because it could just save both of our lives."

Captain Holden was surprised by that disclosure and looked over at her lawyer Tomas Cullerton.

"Yes," the lawyer said. "I can verify that… or most of what Emily has just told you. While I was busy assembling the financial information regarding who owns what for the divorce process, I came across the loan application that Mr. Paladino submitted to Central States Bar Management when I checked everything through the County Recorder's Office.

When I saw that Emily's signature was on that application, I knew immediately that it was a forgery. I knew that Emily had an appointment to see me within the next few days and thought that would be the best time to inform her of the forgery. In the meantime, I sent a letter to the lawyer, Bronson Cummings, and later spoke with him on the phone. He is the attorney for the one named as the executive with Central States Bar Management on the loan… a man by the name of Lucas Juliano. I told Bronson Cummings that I knew Emily did not sign that document and that the Partnership agreement that she has in force with Mickey does not allow for any encumbrances that are not directly benefitting the business they had mutual ownership in… the three Mickey Flynn's Restaurants.

"What happened after your call to Bronson Cummings?"

Tomas Cullerton laughed. "I found out that they recalled the loan… gave Mickey Paladino a mere two days to come up with the money… and then they planned to go ahead and try to foreclose on the collateral… the three restaurants."

Travis found all this quite interesting and suspected that there was more yet to learn about that loan and the threatened foreclosure. But he really needed more from Emily regarding that threat Mickey mentioned.

"Emily, you said that when you told Mickey you planned to call your lawyer, he told you that he hoped you would because it just might save both of your lives. Did he explain that threat any further to you?"

Emily lifted her gaze from the table where she had been aimlessly focused during the conversation between the police detective and her lawyer. Remembering that conversation in her car when Mickey told her something had to be done right away to stop the disclosures because it could save both of their very lives, her eyes widened with the anxiety that began at that moment and rose exponentially each passing day until nearly two weeks later when she found herself finally safe at Elizabeth's home in Tulsa along with their older sister Frances.

"He told me that it all began when he heard from Kylie that Jari Abdou was about to sell exclusive rights to his company's boat sales at Table Rock Lake. Mickey already had bought one boat from Jari... the catamaran that he named Mist Akin 1. He was growing bored ever since we signed with Central States to manage the restaurants, and this looked exactly what he wanted to do..."

"So, he took Valenti's suggestion and borrowed the money from Lucas Juliano's people to buy the boat business, right?"

"Yes," Emily said. "But to get the full amount that he needed he told me they insisted that the full ownership of the three restaurants be put up as collateral..."

"And he never went to you and asked if you would agree?" Travis sounded astonished.

"No... You see we were separated and getting set to divorce and... well, he just knew that I didn't trust him any more... not after finding out how he cheated on our marriage... with a personal friend of mine."

Travis saw that this last response edged Emily close to breaking into some serious crying. To give her a chance to recover he directed his next questions and comments to her lawyer, Tomas Cullerton.

"What did you find out about the "save our lives" comment Mickey made?"

"When Emily mentioned that to me yesterday it shook me up. This fellow, Lucas Juliano, it turns out is a hood. When I was advised by Bronson Cummings that they intended to proceed with an attempt to grab the restaurants through foreclosure I checked out the Central States Bar Management Business that he is associated with. I saw his name on some items that I recognized were related to the Cosa Nostra in Chicago. Any threat coming from him… at either Mickey or Emily… or possibly both of them has to be taken seriously."

"Taken seriously? What did that mean?"

"So, yesterday when Emily told me what she just told you about being threatened I knew it was time to bring this all to you. Her two sisters were with us yesterday and hearing that Emily was in danger they also urged us to go to the police."

"I know now that you asked your attorney to stop the foreclosure which didn't work out so well," Travis said turning back to Emily. "But you must have been concerned about the threat on your lives that Mickey mentioned."

"Yes, we were very worried. That is why Mickey persuaded me to drive to Indian Point where Kylie Cooper lived. He said she had a plan to ask Jari Abdou to buy some of the boats and if they got enough money, they would simply pay off the loan to Juliano. Our thinking was that if the loan was paid off… completely, even though the deadline was supposed to have come and gone by then, that there would be no legal reason to justify the foreclosure, and no reason to carry out any threats."

"Mickey seemed to ignore that the reason there were threats to him, and probably Emily's also, was because he tried to put one over on the mob when he forged Emily's signature on the collateral papers in the loan," Cullerton pointed out.

"Did Kylie contact Jari Abdou, as you suggested?"

"Yes, and she wanted me to ride with her over to Plyman's Point, where Jari's company is, since he and I always got along so comfortably when he was dating Kylie and we hung around together."

"What happened when you met with him there?"

Emily frowned with the memory of the disappointment she and Kylie felt when Jari said no to their offer. "He said he was a boat seller, not a buyer of used boats."

"So, we left and then told Mickey how that plan came up empty," Emily said. "We were then back at square one, soon to face foreclosure of our restaurants, and still concerned about Mickey pissing off the wrong people enough that he, and maybe both of us, were in some deep trouble."

While saying that both were in deep trouble Emily appeared emotionally spent. Travis hesitated to ask any further questions for the moment and along with her lawyer, Tomas Cullerton, just sat mute. A full three minutes of silence followed until Emily decided to continue.

"Mickey suddenly produced a new plan. He said that we all remembered how much Jari loved being with us at our Mickey Flynn's restaurant in Branson, He knew that Jari understood that the restaurants were all doing quite well financially and perhaps if we shifted the collateral away from Juliano's Central States Bar Management and used it to get the loan from Jari Abdou it would resolve all our problems."

"So is that what happened," Travis asked.

"Not exactly," Emily said. "I was getting divorced from Mickey and wanted no part in being tied in any business dealings with him. So, I told Mickey that the only thing I would agree with was that he could sell his fifty percent ownership in the restaurants to Jari. It was quite possible that by now his half of the ownership of the three restaurants had more equity value than the amount he owed to Juliano. I could see that Mickey considered how that would put things to a happy conclusion. He would not have any ownership in the restaurants, but he would have the loan paid off to the mobster Lucas Juliano, and still own all of Ozark Lakes Leisure Boats"

"So, Mickey went to Jari with that proposal," Travis asked.

"He did. And when he returned, he told us that Jari was interested but had to run some of it past his superiors in Sydney and that he would let us know by mid-week."

Emily's information was now leading up to the questions Travis wanted most to ask and get answers to regarding where each of them were after Tuesday, August 13th up to Monday, August 19th.

"Emily, while you and Kylie and Mickey waited for Jari Abdou's decision, did you stay together… perhaps at her place or over at your house?"

Emily checked again with her eyes to see if this was something her lawyer did not want her to answer. Cullerton sat motionless which Emily interpreted to mean that she should feel free to respond.

"No, we did not all go to my house. Because of the situation concerning how Mickey suspected that he was in some danger with Juliano's boys, they decided to hide out on the little houseboat he kept over at Baxter Boat Dock. I went with them that first night just because it was late and if I was in some danger I did not want to be alone at my home in Kimberling City. My plan was afterwards I would call my sisters and go stay with one of them for a while."

"But you were missing until August 19th," Travis said. "Your sisters, the people you work with at the real estate office, all called us and wanted to investigate what happened to explain your disappearance."

Emily's eyes dropped down, almost closed, revealing her shame in what she was about to admit to the police captain.

"After we arrived on the houseboat and figured we were finally safe, you know, away from where anybody would be expecting us to be, we relaxed. It was the first time I can remember even taking a breath since being surprised by Mickey earlier in Cassville. Before long we had a few drinks, just to regain some calm in ourselves. Then, while Mickey went down to the galley to see what he might later cook up for our dinner, Kylie and I had a few more drinks and…" her voiced drifted into silence.

Cullerton reached over to Emily seated next to him and once again took her hand into his trying to both comfort her while at the same time urging her to resume where she had left off.

After another moment or two had passed Emily pulled her hand away from the lawyer's, sat up and suddenly showed a more determined look in her expression than any time earlier.

"I suppose I should not tell you this but after a while of just being on the same boat with my soon to be ex-husband and the woman he snuck off and slept with behind my back, causing the end of our marriage, I just decided that I needed to get as wasted as possible. I hoped I would just fall dead asleep and upon waking up find out this was all just a bad dream."

Travis indicated that he understood where she was going with this and suggested that she should just continue.

Once more Emily looked over at Cullerton who merely nodded it was all right to tell the C.I.D. captain what happened next.

"Well, I didn't want to drink enough wine to get as high as I knew I had to get so I asked Kylie if she still had any more of the OxyContin I saw her take while we were back in her home at Indian Point while Mickey was busy trying to make deals with Jari. She did… and I did… and soon Mickey did too. Mickey had some coke, and I contributed the few valiums I still had with me. We got so out of it that we never made it back down from the deck into the cramped galley long enough to fix anything to eat… which was our plan before the OxyContin was handed out.

We all passed out sitting in those awful deck chairs that first night. The sun woke me up the next morning and I saw we had spent the night up on the deck of his 57-foot houseboat right out where anybody on a passing boat that wanted to look would see us."

"So, you made it through that Tuesday night safely," Travis said. "But wasn't your original plan to then contact one of your sisters?

Emily nodded her head up and down indicating a positive response to his question. "But there was still a waiting time. Jari mentioned to Mickey that he expected to hear back from his people in Sydney no later than mid-week. If he got the approval to buy out Mickey's share in our restaurants and Mickey would then use that money to clear them from being used as collateral in the loan from Juliano, I would have to stick around long enough to know those things. I mean, I had to know if Jari was going to be my new partner… and if there was still any reason that I had to worry about anything bad happening to me from Mickey's enemies."

"Were you feeling any better about staying with the others on the houseboat while waiting to learn Abdou's decision?"

"Oh no, not at all," Emily replied with more emotion than the detective expected. "The only thing that got me through that period was staying as numb as the drugs would keep me."

Captain Holden was surprised by that response. "I thought that you indicated that you, and the others, used up the drugs you had with you on that first night you were aboard the houseboat."

Emily let slip a smile that indicated she had only told a minimum of the drug-use so far.

"Mickey was able to get a lot more of them when he arranged for some food and other supplies to be brought out to us. He decided to abstain from any more oxeyes or valiums or the like for himself. He wanted to stay as clear thinking as possible knowing that he still had that deal pending with Jari. But he did give Kylie and me enough of what was included in the supplies that he arranged to be brought to us. Between the Ambiens and quaaludes and Seconal's and Nembutal's I think we must have emptied his entire horde. In any case, it was enough to keep Kylie and I either numb or asleep that whole week… which was the only way my emotions could survive being there with them."

"So, tell me," Travis asked with some impatience. "What happened when Jari finally gave all of you his decision?"

Emily sighed and continued staring at the wall behind Travis, seemingly engaged in a war with her memory. Both the police detective and her lawyer said nothing during the next few moments allowing the extended silence to provide the pressure necessary to push her back into talking.

"I'm not very certain that I remember the days very clearly while we waited on the houseboat. You have to try and understand the horrible pressure that Mickey was experiencing which both Kylie and I felt too, perhaps, to a lesser degree.

It may have been Wednesday that we heard from Jari… Tuesday or Wednesday… But he contacted Mickey and told him that his people in Sydney turned down the proposals Mickey suggested. But he gave us a glimmer of hope when he said that the Sydney people authorized him to have ready by the end of the week a new proposal that would completely bail us out of the spot we were in and get Lucas Juliano off his back. Jari did not want to explain this any further but he said that he would meet us on the houseboat on Friday."

"Was that information enough for Mickey to just sit and wait until Friday?" Travis asked.

"Mickey pressed him for more information but when Jari resisted Mickey finally agreed to lay low until Friday. He told Jari that his employee, Frankie Valenti, was bringing food and other necessities out to the houseboat.. In order to avoid being followed by Juliano or his thugs he did this using one of the boats Mickey had for sale at Ozark Lake Leisure Boats, a 24-foot Glastron Runabout which he used disguised as a person fishing out on the lake. He drove to the side of the houseboat facing away from the shoreline so to avoid being observed making his deliveries.

He told Jari that he would prefer that Jari use that same technique when he was ready to come aboard the houseboat on Friday."

The attorney, Tomas Cullerton, stood up and stretched.

"We've covered almost everything that Emily discussed with me yesterday and hopefully you have enough to determine how to provide her with the protection that I, and her sisters, think that she now requires.".

Captain Holden more than agreed with that statement but hesitated disclosing that sentiment just yet. He still had to find out if Emily knew how convoluted the designations of beneficiaries in the two life insurance policies ended up making her the one who would receive the two-million-dollar windfall.

The information that Emily mentioned about the drugs the two women took during that week on the houseboat, especially hearing that they had access to OxyContin and valiums, the two drugs mentioned in the report from the Medical Examiner, was a real revelation.

Travis thought he noticed something in the way that Emily paused when she mentioned how she and Kylie consumed enough drugs to pass out or at a minimum stay high. When she said Kylie's name she hesitated and seemed to be checking with her lawyer about something. After she apparently was signaled to continue talking it was in a very deliberate manner. Travis could tell she was withholding telling anything more than her attorney had practiced with her to say before agreeing to this police interview.

Using Frankie Valenti to bring supplies out to the houseboat was the first tie-in with him and the others during the general time frames of the death of Kylie Cooper and a day later, Mickey Paladino. That was perhaps the biggest news.

However, before Travis could get to asking Emily about these items, her lawyer had pulled back Emily's chair and was in the process of escorting her out of the room. Travis understood that he had no legal means to hold Emily. Instead, he thanked her and her lawyer for spending so much time answering his questions.

He wanted to make sure that she would be safe, as that was the main concern that persuaded her lawyer to allow her to answer his questions.

"If you are staying at your home on Bonanza Drive in Kimberling City, I will be better able to provide you with round the clock police protection," Travis offered.

Emily looked first back to where Cullerton was standing already out in the hallway.

"Why yes," she replied. "I was going to return to Tulsa where I intended to stay with my sister. But I think that I can arrange for at least one of my sisters to stay here in Kimberling City with me to take advantage of your offer of police protection.

Travis smiled and said that he would meet immediately with the sheriff who would arrange for the protection they discussed.

24

Pieces in the puzzle

Friday, September 6th, 8:00 A.M.

SHERIFF LAMBERT WAS SURPRISED that Emily opened so much in her responses, especially with her attorney seated next to her. And when told that Travis requested around the clock protection for Emily the sheriff agreed, at least for a minimum of one week.

"With all this new information that needs to be investigated, the drugs the women took, the connection with Valenti bringing supplies to them in that Runabout, along with the stuff Sergeant Platt discovered, our Task Force is in danger of being short on manpower," Travis suggested. "You have any objection if we just assign one of the uniforms to stay with Emily?

"Can we afford the loss in parking ticket revenues," the sheriff responded with a sly grin.

The morning meeting the sheriff called for was to discuss the media leaks of their investigation's progress. The evening edition of the Springfield News Leader ran a front-page story reporting that the Branson Police had turned over the Mickey

Paladino murder investigation to Sheriff Cole Lambert's Criminal Investigation Department. The reporter quoted Lieutenant Ernie Mize as the source. The way the article was written it made it look like Bull Lambert was making a "power play" trying to consolidate everything under his personal authority.

Sheriff Lambert remembered how his opposition during the recent election cycle used a similar theme trying to label The Bull as The Bully.

"Do you want me to come down heavy on Lieutenant Mize," Travis asked.

"No, I don't think it would do a damn bit of good right now," Lambert said after pausing to consider that option. "Ernie was just being Ernie… just trying to find another way of looking more important than he suspects he is. No, just at the next Task Force meeting make mention of it and that's when you might threaten to bounce a few heads together if it continues."

Immediately after their meeting with the sheriff Travis and Honey had plans to drive over to the sales office of Ozark Lakes Leisure Boats. Honey stopped first to see if Sergeant Ben Hodges, who she assigned to trail Frankie Valenti around for a few days, had dropped by and posted any update on the Task Force Whiteboard. Seeing none she hustled out to meet Travis in the parking lot.

"The sheriff seemed calmer than I expected to find him," Honey said after getting into the waiting car.

Travis turned briefly and smiled. "Who could stay angry with someone as sexy as you are sitting with your legs crossed in his direct line of vision?"

Honey turned away and looked straight forward. "Why Captain Holden… I do declare," she said sounding as close as she could imagine that a proper Southern Belle might sound. "I thought you got all your "needs" like that settled and taken care of last night… I do declare!"

They both cheated a glance back at each other and then broke out laughing.

"You know, Honey, I wasn't out in the hallway watching or listening when you questioned that small time hood, Valenti," Travis said. "If your session with him would have come after mine with Emily you would have known about his use of a small powerboat boat to make deliveries to Mickey's houseboat and could have made him explain what was in those deliveries. Of course, he would have clammed up."

"But I was surprised," Travis continued, "when I heard about how you intimidated him enough that he spilled out what he knew about being with Emily Paladino when Mickey violated the Order of Protection and snuck out to Cassville to talk to her. You weren't showing him your legs or talking Southern Belle stuff just to make him forget he was talking to a cop, were you?"

Honey decided to ignore the teasing from Travis. "So, you missed my interrogation of Frankie Valenti, huh?" Honey asked sounding disappointed. "I learned earlier from our friend, Lieutenant Ernie Mize that Valenti was seen over at Plyman's Point which was under surveillance by the COMET Task Force. Mize was following through on a tip he got making a drug bust at a party in Lampe that was organized by some MSU students five, maybe six months ago."

Honey opened her purse and withdrew an opened package of Wrigley's Spearmint and offered to remove the wrapper before handing a stick of it to Travis. 'I may have suggested that we knew that there were ex-cons there at the same time that Valenti was and that the terms of his parole required him to avoid any contact with known criminals... You do know that Frankie Valenti was on parole from Statesville when he got the job working as a bouncer at Mickey Flynn's... right?"

Travis smiled. "Of course, I knew that" he said. "Just not the part about there being known criminals staying on Plyman's Point."

"Well, perhaps I left out the word… maybe… when I said they were there. But in any case, it put him on the fast track back to the Big House if we ended our session less than on friendly terms. Once I suspected that he figured it would be better for him to at least answer my questions, I began with wanting to know why he was shopping for a home to buy in Cassville since there was such a wide selection closer to where he worked at Ozark Lake Leisure Boats."

"Yes," Travis agreed. "I remember feeling surprised that he was so quick to say that his boss, Mickey Paladino, told him to make an appointment to see a house that Emily listed and that was the first one he came across online from the My Missouri Home Internet web page. Right away he dragged in Mickey."

"He volunteered that it was all set up by Mickey who rode over to the Cassville house secreted in the back seat so he could surprise Emily when they arrived there," Honey added.

"So, you managed to put Mickey, and his thug employee Frankie, with Emily on the day she disappeared. That's all good, but did you learn what it was that Mickey found so important that caused him to violate the Order of Protection Emily got from the judge in her divorce case?"

"Well, that took a bit more effort. I suggested that his story about just leaving the two of them in Cassville and driving alone back to his apartment in Kimberling City, where he first said he stayed for the next week because of some illness that suddenly struck him, was going to be so easy to check out… or not, he suddenly remembered more… a lot more."

"That's when he mentioned that he followed as Mickey rode with Emily over to Kylie's home at Indian Point, right?"

"Right. His story now was that whatever Mickey had to say that persuaded Emily to go with him to Kylie's was not something he could know since he was not in the same car with them when they came to that decision."

"Makes sense… I doubt that Mickey would have any reason to share that information with Valenti," Travis reasoned. "Still, we know now after Arnie Platt made a second trip to question Twyla Turner alone when Armand Locke was not around. She named Frankie Valenti as the one who connected Mickey with Juliano about a huge loan so he could buy the catamarans from Jari Abdou to start his new Ozark Lake Leisure Boats business. And we know what Emily told us about his connection with bringing out supplies to them during their hideout on the houseboat. And that was during that last week before the murders."

Honey paused a moment while considering how these latest bits of information were adding up.

"Well, Frankie was not able to alibi for his time on either August 17th or the 18th…"

Travis glanced momentarily towards Honey. "The dates that Kylie and then Mickey were murdered…"

"Yes, I know that puts him square into the picture… at least a Person of Interest. But there's something about him that keeps telling me he was small time before he was convicted of two felonies and was sent to prison for having cocaine in his possession when they caught him driving the getaway car in a robbery. And he has been a small timer since he got out and worked as a bouncer at Mickey Flynn's and then just a mechanic at the boat business," Honey added slowly as if she was weighing her thoughts before speaking to them out loud.

Travis slowed the car as they entered the parking area just north of the Ozark Lake Leisure Boats office. A man stood waiting outside the only other car in the lot.

"That must be Sherman Sutcliffe," Travis told Honey. "I wonder what it is that he felt is urgent enough to want to be meeting with us today."

25

Plyman's Point

Friday, September 6th, 9:00 A.M.

DEPUTY ALISON MONROE NOTICED a considerable change in her boss's disposition following the meeting with his C.I.D. Task Force leaders. When he arrived earlier that morning, she noticed he carried under one arm a folded Springfield News Leader which led her to believe that he was still quite angry about the Ernie Mize news leak.

That all seemed quite settled after Captain Travis Holden and Lieutenant Holcomb came out of the closed-door meeting with the sheriff. The voice she heard when he called her to come into his office was more like the relaxed, confident one that was his normal way of speaking.

"Alison, I wonder if you would allow me to buy both of us a large cup of Starbucks finest this morning," he said when she entered the office.

Before she could respond he pushed back his chair and while

walking around his desk he pulled his wallet out and withdrew a Twenty.

"If you would be kind enough to run over there and get our order it will be my treat," he said handing the money to her.

Alison liked the way Sheriff Lambert never treated her like a gopher, the way some bosses just expected the secretary to drop whatever she was doing and go-for or fetch a coffee or something similar. Sheriff Lambert always insisted on making it seem like a reward for something she had recently done for him. The result may have been the same… just not as demeaning. As she turned to leave his office she heard the intercom on his desk phone buzzing.

"Good morning, Miss Helen," the sheriff answered. "What is that? A uniform what? Oh yes, that must be the package I was expecting… What? No, you can stay right where you are. I will send Alison out to bring it to me."

He looked over at the entrance to his office and was relieved to see Alison still there. It was as if she anticipated that the call from the front lobby desk where Miss Helen was calling from would result in her being needed for something.

"Would you be kind enough to help me avoid our lovely Miss Helen this morning by going out there and signing for the package that Homeland Security arranged to be delivered by Springfield Messenger Service?"

After Alison said she would be happy to do that the sheriff added one last request.

"If you will, bring the package to me right away… and then hurry back with the order from Starbucks!"

Alison expected to find either a parcel or, at a minimum, something wrapped or bundled. Instead, the item she signed for was merely a legal-size envelope that contained only a file weighing barely more than what four or five first class letters would be the rate on her trusty postal scale. In any case the sheriff opened it as soon as she brought it to him.

The cover letter was signed by Horace Haywood, Chief Southwest Missouri Homeland Security and listed the items in the file.

- Known occupants of suspected terrorist cell at Plyman's Point, AKA Worldwide Lake Boats Sales
- Photos of occupants
- Copy of TRAC Report
- Vehicles observed
- Surveillance reports for dates in August and September 2024

Also included was the Homeland Security summary of the most recent TRAC Star Report.

Sheriff Lambert sat down and began reading from the top item.

Plyman's Point:

We have learned that Jari Abdou's mission from the Sunni Muslim Mosque that he is affiliated with in Sydney is to establish an income producing business that would serve as a front for their desired purpose of recruiting and training Muslims already living in the United States who believe in the ISIS cause.

The training to become a domestic terrorist, a lone wolf type, is headed up by Rais Azari (identified later in this report). In less than four years Jari Abdou and his ISIS followers managed to find and then purchase a former campground known as Plyman's Point on Table Rock Lake just off route 86 in Lampe. At that location he brought in a small sales force to operate the Worldwide Lake Boat Sales business which provided cover for the training of lone wolf recruits.

Jari's initial cadre consisted of one fellow loyalist from the mosque who came with him from Sydney and two Americans who belonged to Muslim Mosques in Springfield, Missouri. The oldest and most skilled in terrorist planning is Rais Azari, age 42, who was the one that accompanied Abdou from Australia. Azari was someone who the Sydney police suspected but who avoided being charged in a plot to behead an Australian citizen in a main commercial area of that city, hoping that the shock would gain the attention of other Sunnis who might then join their cause.

As of 2013 there were an estimated two and a half million Muslims in the United States. In the whole state of Missouri there are less than twelve thousand and only approximately three hundred in the Springfield area. Such a small local population of Muslims in Springfield is perhaps one reason Jari Abdou settled there. It is under the radar as far as getting any attention from our government's efforts to search out any terrorist threats.

Hanna Mustafo, age 28, is a naturalized American citizen. She was born in Sydney, Australia and later sent to live with relatives in Joplin, Missouri when her parents were murdered during an anti-Muslim riot in Sydney. Her older stepbrother is Rais Azari. She was a student at Missouri State University and active in the Muslim Student Association when she was recruited by Jari Abdou who was at that time scouting for potential additions to his team.

Mustafo majored in accounting and other business courses at the university. Abdou discovered that Hanna was enrolled in a course called Managerial Finance. We know he monitored lectures she attended on the Comprehensive study of the Finance Function in the Business Enterprise, Capital Budgeting, Leasing, Working Capital Management and Multinational Finance.

Her participation in the study groups where she was recognized for making significant contributions make her an invaluable addition to his Plyman's Point plans. His confidence in her financial brilliance has increased substantially since she moved in there. It's at the level now where it is believed that Jari relies completely on her for the financial planning and decisions the group makes.

Callum Rasheed, age 29, is American and from Joplin. He belonged to the same Muslim Mosque that Hanna Mustafo joined in Joplin and then later the one they both attended in Springfield. He was a student at Missouri State University during the same time that Hanna attended there, and he graduated with a degree in accounting and is a Certified Public Accountant.

Much of his time is spent freelancing with various accounting firms in Springfield, Branson, and Eureka Springs. We believe that he was brought along with Hanna Mustafo to live at Plyman's Point when she was recruited and that his presence is tolerated by Abdou and Rais Azari so as not to lose her.

Three additional residents with names and photos were included in the package but had no additional narrative attachments like those that accompanied the other four.

The TRAC report mentioned the same references that Homeland Security identified regarding Abdou and Azari. It also mentioned a possible connection that Azari may have made in St. Louis citing his monthly attendance at a Sunni Mosque in that city.

Sheriff Lambert read more swiftly through the Homeland Security Surveillance report covering dates in 2024 from January through early August as it contained so many redactions that the information proved to be unreadable.

However, beginning Friday, August 9th through Labor Day, the report had fewer redactions and the information contained in it was more closely related to the incidents being investigated by his Stone County detectives.

On Monday, August 12th, using the authority under the NSA Electronic Surveillance Program portion of the Patriot Act we have been tapping the phone calls at Plyman's Point and on this date heard a call come in for Abdou from a person later identified as Kylie Cooper. She informed Abdou that a loan that Mickey Paladino got to purchase the original houseboat and catamarans from Abdou came from a source closely related to the Chicago mob. The loan was being recalled for undisclosed reasons and Paladino needed to raise a half million dollars fast or face the usual mob consequences.

The purpose of her call was to arrange to meet with Abdou and determine if he could get them out of the jam they were in with the mob by buying back some of the boats that Paladino owned in his Ozark Lake Leisure Boats business. Abdou and the caller discussed which boats were to be returned at various potential prices but did not come to any agreement.

Sometime later Mickey Paladino called Abdou. He inquired if Abdou could make a new loan in the amount of a half million dollars to Paladino if the three Mickey Flynn's restaurants were used as collateral. Abdou said he would consider that offer and call back.

Abdou then called Sydney, Australia, and spoke with (name redacted), an underling to Abu Bakr al Baghdadi. The discussion focused on the advantages that ownership in the three restaurants and their locations near target urban areas would give them.

Jari Abdou said that each restaurant enjoyed substantial cash flow which could be siphoned off to fund new lone wolf assignments. He said the restaurants provided a channel to become insiders within the cities they were located, disguising their terrorist plots while at the same time gaining information, they would not otherwise find easy to get.

But the main reason Jari said he thought that it was not only important but imperative for them to get Paladino off the mob's hit list was because if they took him out while he was in the Branson-Kimberling City area it would mean heavy police activity trying to catch or solve whatever crimes were involved.

Abdou explained during the call that he had very quietly established their headquarters at Plyman's Point, and everything was going according to the plans that they were sent to follow in America. As far as he knew their company, Worldwide Lakes Boat Sales, was not suspected as being anything other than that. This ruse would be in jeopardy if something happened that made it necessary for an increased police involvement in the surrounding area.

They shifted the focus of the conversation to several ways that they could be certain that if they chose to make the loan it would fail, and they could foreclose on the three restaurants they would insist on being put up as collateral. However, after much analysis they determined that even if the restaurants were assigned as collateral for the loan, they would still be providing more than sufficient income for Mickey and his wife, Emily, to pay the loan made by Abdou.

It was decided that planning for foreclosure would be unlikely to be successful and, even if it went that way, it would be too time-consuming. Sydney suggested that the best plan was to purchase the restaurants outright by offering the Paladino's enough money to pay off the mob loan, roughly a half million dollars.

If that proposal needed to be sweetened, an offer to forgive the balance owed for the boats sold to Ozark Lake Leisure Boats by Worldwide Lakes Boat Sales could be added to their proposal. Thus, for roughly one million dollars Abdou's group would take full ownership of not only the three Restaurants but also the name Mickey Flynn's, which could extend their profits by opening new restaurants in additional sites. Paladino would have the money he needed to pay off the loan from Lucas Juliano and things in the Table Rock Lake area would be expected to return to normal.

When the person on the phone in Sydney asked Abdou what the plans were if their proposal to buy the restaurants was turned down, the reply was he would remind both Mickey and his wife Emily that the deadline to pay off the mob loan was already past. The restaurants were going to be owned by

Jari through his proposal to purchase them or by the mob who would get them through foreclosure when the payments were delinquent and in default… something they would accomplish by murdering them both, leaving them, of course, unable to make any more payments.

A chill went through the sheriff's whole body after reading the final paragraph in the report from Homeland Security. The murder investigations that were still ongoing were moving with swift speed towards discovering who ended the lives of two of the people on the houseboat, Mickey Paladino, and Kylie Cooper, but were yet unresolved. Only Emily Paladino remained alive from that group. The person or persons responsible for the murders were still out there, somewhere, and whatever the purpose was that drove them to commit the murders meant they still needed to finish the job by murdering Emily Paladino.

After reading the report containing the taped conversations that preceded Abdou's visit to the houseboat on the Friday before the murders, Sheriff Bull Lambert was more convinced than ever that Emily Paladino was in grave danger.

26

An accountant's story

September 6th, 10:00 A.M.

Travis parked a few spaces away from the only other car in the otherwise empty customer parking lot for Ozark Lake Leisure Boats. A man standing next to that car waved" hello" and then walked over and introduced himself as Travis and Honey exited their unmarked Stone County Police Criminal Investigation Department Chevrolet Impala.

He tipped his hat brim towards Honey and after reaching where Travis stood, extended a handshake.

"Thank you for meeting me away from the police station," he said. "I am Sherman Sutcliffe. We talked yesterday."

Travis acknowledged their phone conversation and then asked why Sutcliffe felt it was important that they talk away from police headquarters.

"I am a Certified Public Accountant, and I am afraid that being seen talking with police could cause some to suspect that there might be a problem with my business… or one of my clients.

Let's just say that for whatever reasons I have, good ones or not, I am happy that we can do this my way."

At that point he turned towards Honey and very politely asked if she was an employee at Stone County Sheriff's Police.

Travis quickly apologized for not introducing her right away." This is Lieutenant Honey Holcomb," he said as she pulled open her Stone County Police Identification wallet to show to him.

Then, showing some impatience, Travis turned back to him. "You said on the phone there was something you needed to talk to us about concerning the murder investigation, right?"

"Yes, by all means. But if you would prefer, I might suggest that we go inside the office. They have been closed for business since the death of their owner, Mickey Paladino. But I do have the keys to get us inside if you so desire."

"Are you telling us that you are employed at Ozark Lakes Leisure Boats," Honey asked.

"Not exactly," he said. "As I mentioned when we introduced each other, I am a Certified Public Accountant and have an office in Springfield. I did the accounting for Mickey and Emily when they opened their first Mickey Flynn's restaurant and Bar in Branson. When their business became so successful they decided to expand, and they opened new Mickey Flynn's in Saint Louis and then Chicago. It was me that lined them up with Central States Bar Management to run the business for them."

"How did that work out for you," Travis asked. "Your helpful suggestion kind of meant they no longer needed your service."

"No, it didn't mean that at all," he laughed. "Central States has been in the business for more than forty years running restaurants. They have valuable expertise in food and liquor purchasing, hiring, buildings and equipment, workman's comprehensive rules, insurance and all that sort of stuff. They leave the accountants to do our thing. We have no problem getting along."

"So, you stayed as the accountant for the three restaurants, right," Travis asked and noticed that Sutcliffe's smile indicated he was correct. "But now you are also the accountant for Ozark Lakes?"

"Sure, Mickey needed an accountant for his new business and naturally he chose me… I mean my accounting firm. I have three full-time accountants and one or two others who fill in when business is going well enough to warrant contracting with them on a part-time basis. It was one of them that I assigned to work at Ozark Lake Boats Sales that tipped me off that there was a connection with someone I introduced to Mickey that now has an involvement… or may be involved somehow in his murder."

At that point they reached the door to Mickey's office where Sutcliffe ushered them inside.

"Sorry, but with everyone gone right now there is nothing available for me to offer as refreshments," he apologized. "But we do enjoy the privacy I desired."

"You were saying that you recently found out that you introduced someone to Mickey who now is involved in his murder," Honey asked.

"Yes, but I used the words "may be involved"," Sutcliffe corrected her. "The company that Mickey chose to run the business end of his restaurants, Central States Bar Management, has been doing that service for more than forty years in Illinois, Indiana, Wisconsin, Michigan, and Missouri.

I've done the accounting for perhaps twenty of their clients and always found them to be honest and professional. So, I harbored no reluctance, at that time, recommending them when I suggested that it was the best alternative for the three restaurants that Mickey and Emily Paladino owned."

"You said you were fine with them—when you recommended them," Honey said. "That implies that you have since changed your mind?"

"Yes. I learned after I made that recommendation that a consortium that is suspected to be a front for Cosa Nostra purchased that business along with their name. I would not have recommended them to Paladino if that were made known to me."

Travis wondered if this soul cleansing was the only reason Sutcliffe wanted to meet.

"Did you know about the change in ownership at Central States when you suggested that Mickey see them about the loan to make the down payment to purchase the Ozark Lakes Boats franchise?"

Sherman Sutcliffe frowned at the implied suggestion in Travis's question.

"I did not. I most certainly did not suggest anything of the sort to Mickey," Sutcliffe said with as much self-righteousness that he could muster to attach to his response.

"In fact, that is exactly why I asked to meet with you. I knew that if the police discovered Mickey was doing business with gangsters, they would want to learn how that came to be and wonder who else was involved."

Neither Travis nor Honey were impressed with his outburst, feigning indignity, even insult. However, hoping to keep him talking Travis decided to shift the focus to his next questions.

"If it was not you, then who was it that brought Mickey to them? Do you know who… and how did you find that out?"

"Yes, I know who it was. At least who I was told was the one who connected Mickey with them to get the loan. It was his employee, a man by the name of Frankie Valenti."

At the mention of Valenti's name the two detectives sitting across from each other exchanged looks of surprise.

"We do know that Frankie Valenti worked for Mikey Flynn's as a bouncer around the time that they first contracted to have Central States operate the restaurants," Honey said. "But to say that Mickey turned to his bouncer when he needed to find a source to make that loan seems quite a stretch."

Sutcliffe's expression revealed the disappointment he felt that his disclosure about the Valenti connection was received with such doubt.

"You may call it a stretch," Sutcliffe said looking directly at the female detective. "But I know it to be the case."

"And you know it because of what reason," Travis asked, taking back the lead in the discussion.

Sherman Sutcliffe leaned forward in his desk chair looking like the proverbial cat that swallowed a mouse.

"As I explained earlier," he began. "The accountant that I hired for the Ozark Lakes business told me that he learned that information during a discussion with the man who said he connected Mickey with someone who could make the money available quickly. That man was Frankie Valenti."

"Now, tell us the identity of your employee, the accountant you assigned to the Ozark Lakes business so that we can arrange to talk further with him," Travis said.

"Of course I will tell you who told me, who my accountant is at Ozark Lakes," Sutcliffe said, still showing his displeasure at the direction the police interview was going.

"His name is Callum Rasheed. You can talk with him at his address over in Lampe at a place known as Plyman's Point."

27

Progress

September 6th, 1:00 P.M.

THE C.I.D. TASK FORCE MEETING was briefly delayed waiting for Lieutenant Ernie Mize and Sergeant Ben Hodges to show up. Everyone else was in attendance or had been accounted for when Captain Travis Holden entered the room. Lieutenant Holcomb mentioned that they were waiting for the two absentees by name.

"Are our missing members still on their lunch hour," Travis asked. "I would say we begin without them, but we have some new information to disseminate, and everyone has to be up to speed on these items."

Travis had no sooner finished talking when the missing detectives entered the room and took their place on chairs close to where Honey stood near the Whiteboard.

"I know it looks like I am late… like we are late," Mize said turning around to face the others. "It's just that we seem to be having a Task Force Update session every other day now. What gives…?"

Travis was perturbed that Mize never even apologized for holding up the meeting but decided to express his anger in a softer response.

"You're right again, Lieutenant Mize," he said without even looking in the direction of where the latecomers were seated. "You are always right. As you just said, it does look like you are late!"

Lieutenant Holcomb then took over and opened the meeting by pointing to the Whiteboard where four columns headed by names of persons or places with photos of persons questioned were numbered as follows: 1. My Missouri Homes 2. Frankie Valenti 3. Emily Paladino and 4. Sherman Sutcliffe

"Each of these interviews occurred during the last forty-eight hours and uncovered new and valuable information that we want shared with all the detectives working on these murder cases. In the first interview conducted by Sergeant Arnie Platt we learned that Emily Paladino has a long history of drug use. We also found out that Frankie Valenti was the person that linked the now deceased Mickey Paladino with a mob loan shark by the name of Lucas Juliano. Sergeant Platt was particularly successful with his questioning of the Office Manager at My Missouri Home, where Emily Paladino works, by the name of Twyla Turner. The owner is Armand Locke, who opted to call for his attorney when Platt's questions were directed at him. Both of their photographs are on the adjacent bulletin board for your review.

By way of information, we received from Homeland Security Special Agent Horace Haywood we know that Mr. Juliano is associated with a business called Central States Bar Management which is located on Chicago's northwest side and is managed by another known Cosa Nostra member named Guy Chevron. That business is a suspected mob front now but has a long and up to recent times, good reputation. Central States was, and still is, running operations at all three restaurants owned by Mickey and Emily Paladino."

Honey then pointed to the Whiteboard entry, Item number 2 Frankie Valenti.

"I questioned Frankie Valenti and found him to be forthcoming and surprisingly responsive. That is, he became that way once he understood that we were looking into some friends and companions that he made over at Plyman's Point which could mean a parole violation charge if we pursued that during our investigation. Frankie served a short stint at Stateville for drug possession while he was driving the getaway car involved in an armed robbery.

Valenti admitted that he secretly brought Mickey Paladino with him when he arranged for a house to be shown to him by Emily Paladino. This was on August 13th, the same day that she became a missing person. He also placed Mickey and Emily together at Kylie Cooper's residence at Indian Point on that date. When asked, Frankie could not provide an alibi for August 16, 17, or 18."

Honey then walked closer to where Travis was standing.

"We learned during Captain Holden's interview with Emily that Valenti was called upon to bring supplies, at least twice, to the houseboat where Mickey, Emily, and Kylie hid from the mob during the period Tuesday, August 13th to Friday, August 16th. He did this using a runabout powered by a small power motor. This type of watercraft could move across Table Rock Lake and get much closer to the shore than any boat the size of a houseboat. It does raise at least a suspicion that it could have transported Kylie's body where she was found gently placed in an abandoned rowboat along that shoreline."

Honey stopped talking, wanting to be certain that each of her points were understood, before continuing when she was alongside Travis. "Again, from Captain Holden's interview with Emily we learned that both she and Kylie consumed drugs with sufficient frequency and quantity to remain barely conscious throughout that week. What else did Valenti bring to the house-boat along with food and liquor? From one of Sergeant Platt's interviews with Twyla Turner we now know that it was Valenti that linked Mickey Paladino to Lucas Juliano for that loan. This information was confirmed just earlier today when Captain Travis and I questioned their accountant, Sherman Sutcliffe.

"Captain Travis was able to question Emily Paladino but only with her lawyer present. Nonetheless, he was surprised by her openness. Some of what he learned that was new during that interview has already been discussed this afternoon, such as Emily's drug use and the time she was in hiding on Mickey's houseboat. Also, the relationship that Frankie Valenti had with the three of them on the houseboat was supported by things Emily told Captain Holden."

At this point, Travis stood up and addressed the detectives.

"Yes, I was surprised by how willing Emily was to be so open, especially with her lawyer being there with her. Tomas Cullerton told me that he is convinced that his client is in a lot of danger and that is why he agreed to the questioning session. He wants us to provide protection around the clock for her. I talked with Sheriff Lambert, and he is now on board with that and has assigned a uniform team, two of them, to stay with Emily and her sister outside her home in Kimberling City around the clock.

There was a lot of ground covered when I questioned Emily. But there was a lot that was not stuff she knew something about. She was spending that whole time in a drug induced stupor. She told me the reason was that on the one hand she could not tolerate being on the houseboat any longer than necessary because it meant being with Mickey and Kylie, the two who betrayed her.

The other reason she wanted to stay as high on whatever drugs she could find on board was because she had grown very frightened. She learned from Mickey that when he forged her name on the collateral papers for the loan from the mob, he not only provided their value to be of use in that manner, but he also did something even worse than that. He double crossed the mob. The only thing the mob considers worse than squealing on them is cheating them. Both usually come with the death sentence when found out.

So, we are planning to bring Emily back in for more questions and hopefully get answers to those items we just discussed. But also, we are eager to find out what more she can remember about those last few days on the houseboat. We do not know if Kylie died by accident or was murdered by someone slipping excessive OxyContin mixed with valiums and other combinations of barbiturates that, when consumed with the alcohol that we suspect she drank, eventually stopped her heart, and killed her.

Whatever the case, we do believe she died while on the houseboat and her body was later transported to the shore, under cover of night, and placed in the abandoned rowboat. Right now, we do not have any evidence to suspect that Emily participated in any of that wrongdoing. But as time continues to pass, it is possible that she will remember more than she has up to now told us."

Honey noticed that there were indications from some of the detectives that they had some questions of their own now.

"We have one last interview to mention, the one that Captain Holden and myself had earlier today with the accountant for Mickey's restaurants, Sherman Sutcliffe. Then we will open it up for questions and discussions from you."

"I won't take much more time this afternoon as we all have a lot of work ahead," Travis began. "Just one thing that came from the Sutcliffe interview was substantiation that it was Frankie Valenti who set Mickey up with Lucas Juliano for the loan that he used to get Ozark Lake Boats business started. Sutcliffe did say that Central States Bar Management was a well thought of business until it was bought by Chevron as a front for the Cosa Nostra.

What this tells us is that when Mickey told Emily that they had a lot to be frightened about it was right on the mark. It also means that since Mickey is no longer in the picture, and that loan is still outstanding, Emily becomes their target. The mob cannot afford to allow anyone to get away from paying for what Mickey pulled off."

Ernie Mize was the first to stand up with his questions.

"Did you confront Emily with what we learned about the two million dollars she's going to receive from those two life insurance policies? What I mean is did she, make that does she, even know about them?"

"I did not ask her about those policies then because her lawyer ended our session before I could," Travis said. "It's going to be high on my list when we bring her back for more questions."

"One last question, if I could," Mize persisted. "Has the coroner or medical examiner made a final finding on Kylie Cooper's death? Is it still undetermined, or suicide? Or accidental. Murder?" Ernie Mize's tone left little doubt that he was sending a large dose of ridicule in the direction of Travis.

"No, Ernie. Neither of them feels they have enough information yet to make that call. That is our job, to gather as much evidence that is to be found and hand it over to them."

Lieutenant Holcomb began wrapping up the Update session for the Task Force when Travis suddenly interrupted her.

"We are reminded after reading the Springfield News Leader's scoop regarding Branson police turning over the investigation of Mickey Paladino's murder to Sheriff Lambert's C.I.D. unit about the rules and procedures for criminal investigations that we are required to follow. The sheriff was happy to see that one of us, he said it was Lieutenant Mize, might be singled out for once again bringing to our attention the need for strict adherence to that standard."

28

Alison and Owen go On Guard

September 6th, Friday 4:00 P.M.

Deputy Alison Monroe loved being where all the command decisions were made. Her assignment as the Office Manager at the Stone County Sheriff's Office did just that for her. During the current investigation into the recent murders in Kimberling City and Branson, Alison was busy writing her first mystery novel. While she watched the comings and goings of the detectives during the daylight hours, she spent her nights writing about them in her fictional mystery story.

Alison had access to the notes taken at the Task Force Update meetings which kept her current but still, there was something missing. She wanted now to find a way to help solve the mystery of who-done-it. It required that she find a way to ask the sheriff to assign her to the C.I.D. unit during their investigations of the Cooper and Paladino murders.

Sheriff Cole Lambert, more commonly referred to as Bull Lambert, was more of a military battlefield General than someone with a similar rank who stayed behind the lines or back at a desk in the Pentagon during wartimes. Both types of Generals made decisions regarding strategies for fighting battles. The Generals behind the lines were more of what is called theoretical types. Generals who led their troops into battle were more reality types.

In Stone County, the sheriff was more likely to be "at the scene" than directing the action from somewhere safer. In criminal investigations "The Bull" was not only the Director, the person in charge of investigative strategies, he insisted on being an active participant when the plans were put into action.

Alison planned to refer to the need to be more involved that were so much a part of the sheriff's personality, when she found the opportunity to approach him about how she now felt. She was a uniformed patrol deputy when the opportunity to become his Office Manager came her way. Throughout the whole time she worked, mostly as his secretary, she continued to meet the requirements that all the police had regarding semi-annual pistol and rifle qualifications at the firing range.

She was hopeful that the sheriff would take that into consideration regarding her request which she planned to submit at the appropriate opportunity.

*　*　*

Saturday, September 7th, 1:50 A.M., Tempo di Bolero

Deputy Owen Horner woke with a start hearing the barking of a small dog. Turning first to his right, then towards the passenger door with the window lowered to allow a draft of cool nighttime air to enter his squad car, he wondered where the noise was coming from. It stopped now as he considered if he should get out and walk around looking for whatever woke up the pooch.

Owen sat straight up, searching ahead through the windshield, then through the rear-view mirror, then forward again. He laughed at how startled he had become. There was nothing to be frightened about, he thought to himself. It was just that the dog heard or smelled a rabbit or raccoon and did what dogs do... bark.

A thought came that prompted a smile. Soon Owen was singing the lyrics to "Who let the dogs out?" Before he was more than through the first verse it happened again... bark... BARK-BARK!

"Wilma," someone was heard yelling inside of the house two doors down farther on Bonanza Drive. "Wilma... WILMA." The barking stopped when the second Wilma carried a louder, angrier tone.

"I guess the doggie's name is Wilma," Owen thought to himself. "Or else, Wilma is maybe his wife's name?" Then after reflecting on it he decided it had to be what he first thought.

"It was definitely a dog that was barking," he reasoned.

Deputy Horner looked at his watch and saw it was almost 2:00 A.M. He yawned and nestled snugger in his car seat. Owen was not one of those police officers that loved action. Sometimes a high-speed car chase was exciting, but when his fellow cops used the word action they referred usually to a stick-up, or burglary or a good old bar fight, or something of that ilk. Owen's objection to those activities was that was a good way to get injured... killed maybe.

No, except for the boredom of sitting through the dark hours of the nights and the mornings before sunrise, this assignment to the twenty-four-hour protection detail was not so bad. He figured the reason he was selected for this nighttime slot was because he was not married. Married cops had more reason to be sleeping during the night hours. They needed to be home in bed with their wives. Single police officers, or anyone still not married, could sleep anytime since they had no wife or children to keep them awake if they had to try to get their eight hours in during daylight.

"Life can be fairly… unfair sometimes," he whispered hoping not to disturb Wilma again.

Just then Owen thought he saw something, a light beam that bounced off the curtains in the Paladino house he was guarding. His heartbeat reacted the same way it did when something frightened him. He stared at the window where he first thought he saw the light flicker then disappear. Was someone inside using a flashlight rather than turning on a lamp? But why? A minute passed, then another, without any repetition of the light. Was it his imagination? No, something caught his eye, a moving light caught his eye. It flashed while he was staring at the house with the dog.

Owen quickly considered the steps he should be taking to investigate the possibility of someone with a flashlight inside the Paladino house. He should just get out of the squad car and go to the house, look inside, and at least knock on the door. No, that would just serve to wake up the two women inside and maybe cause them to be surprised by whoever the intruder was when they came to open the door.

Then suddenly there was a loud noise as if someone had knocked over something inside. At the same time, the beam of light he first noticed shot wildly up and down and then steadied and moved away from the front windows as if the person holding the flashlight had fallen and then stood up and was fleeing.

Now convinced he was not imagining these events, Owen grabbed for the radio and called in that he needed help on Bonanza Drive in Kimberling City. He wasted a precious few seconds trying to recall the three-digit numbered code that alerted the desk sergeant about the type of situation at the scene. Was this a 501? No… That is not it… a 501 is… He was blank! Because of the urgency of the situation Owen's mind was in near panic mode. He just simply could not recall the exact code that police officers learn to use when requiring help. But by saying where he was and that he needed help sent… fast, Owen was sure the message would be received, and he bolted out of his squad car and ran toward the house.

Hoping that his ears might be able to tell him what the darkness inside the house hid from his eyes, Owen leaned the side of his face against the window closest to the front door just as a frightened, loud scream came from inside… a woman's scream! Owen jerked his ringing ear away from the window and turned just in time to see someone running around the side of the neighboring house towards the corner.

His first impulse was to give chase. But that scream he heard stopped him. Was that person injured? Was he needed to be inside now and tend to whatever her emergency needs might be?

Owen went back to the front door and while pushing the doorbell yelled that he was a police officer followed by the command to OPEN THE DOOR!

A woman, tall enough to look through the narrow glass window higher up on the front door, peeked out and seeing Deputy Horner outside, pulled it open.

Before Owen could get even one foot inside the house, he heard the squeal of tires and out of the darkness a black sedan without the headlights turned on rushed past him and was quickly out of sight.

Owen turned to face the woman who was dressed only in a nightshirt and asked if anyone inside needed medical help. She seemed confused and stumbled out an answer that sounded like she did not know… she needed to check… Then more squealing tires, this time it was a black Lexus, Owen thought, but could not be positive as it sped past them in the same direction as the first car.

Deputy Horner glanced back at the woman in the doorway who was as startled as he was by the two cars that just raced by.

"We're okay, I think," she said in a voice still trembling from the frightening series of events. "Just go… Go after them!"

The deputy turned and ran back to his squad car. He hurried to get behind the steering wheel and realized the voice he was hearing was the sergeant's back at the sheriff's office yelling for him to please identify the situation.

Owen turned on the Mars blinking red lights and had to then turn the vehicle into the nearby driveway to back around and begin the chase. He had only travelled two or three blocks when it became obvious that neither vehicle was anywhere in sight.

Deputy Horner strongly suspected that wherever they were now they would want to get as far away as they could from the subdivision that bordered Kimberling Airways. They would get over to route 13 and from there, depending which direction they proceeded in, would head towards Branson, or Cassville, or out of state to nearby Arkansas.

By now, the adrenaline rush that began charging through him with the high activity on Bonanza Drive, was sufficiently harnessed as he searched for the two cars that sped away. The police radio codes that he could not recall minutes ago now flowed easily through his memory as he reached again for the radio.

After getting through to the Night Commander Owen called for an 1199 which he hoped meant Officer needs help followed by Code 3 which he knew for sure meant ASAP, after which he provided a verbal report of the situation. Within minutes Owen heard on his radio a **BOLO** call for all cars to Be On the Lookout for a black sedan with one driver being either chased or followed by a dark colored Lexus, also one driver.

"These vehicles fled from after breaking into a home that was under the protection of a Stone County surveillance unit near the Kimberling Airways area and believed to be on highway 13."

Hearing that the pursuit of the fleeing cars was now being taken over by highway patrols in the area, Owen turned around again and sped back to the Paladino house on Bonanza Drive. As he pulled in front of the house, he saw that it was still completely dark inside. A front porch light shined across the yard and spilled on to the sidewalk where Owen saw two women huddled together. They were frightened and confused and eyed him with suspicion as he walked toward them. Their names he was about to learn were Emily Paladino and her sister, Elizabeth Lane.

29

A chase and a crash

Saturday, September 7ᵗʰ, 2:20 A.M.

PILES BECK DROVE WITH ONE EYE on the road ahead and the other on his rearview mirror checking on the car behind him. He was surprised by its sudden appearance and wondered if it could be a cop or a private dick hired to watch over the person he was sent to kill. Being that he was unfamiliar with the frequent curves in the road that seemed to suddenly appear from nowhere, he had to lower his speed to just over seventy miles per hour. Unfortunately, that allowed the other car to stay too close for Beck to lose it.

Even at that lowered speed Beck almost lost control of his 2024 Dodge Challenger. The 305-horse powered muscle car would have easily escaped from pursuit if Beck could only find a straight stretch on state route 13 that was longer than the length of a football field.

Beck saw an intersection ahead and made the turn onto state highway 86. The road straightened enough to allow him to kick up his speed to 90 MPH but a quick check in his mirror showed that the Lexus was still less than ten car lengths behind. He zoomed past a large lighted billboard advertising Ozark Valley Nature Park before noticing a smaller road sign indicating Trace Hollow Road was coming up soon. Beck maintained his speed until he saw where this road cut into route 86 and then made the 90 degrees turn onto it at almost 50 miles per hour. The rear end of the Dodge Charger fishtailed on the loose gravel surface causing him to lose control. Suddenly he crashed into a large sign giving directions to Plyman's Point. The Dodge Charger flipped over once and rested on its roof.

Though slightly dizzy, Beck was able to escape from the crashed car, with the wheels still spinning, by climbing through the opening where the windshield popped loose when the car roof tented upon impact. Once away from the wrecked Dodge, Piles looked back to where he last saw the Lexus just before he made that poorly thought out turn onto Trace Hollow Road.

He had to wait until the cloud of dust that was kicked up during his turn and subsequent crash settled but saw nothing beyond his upturned Dodge. Either that driver left the scene already or never even attempted the turn and kept going on state route 86.

Knowing that the Highway Patrol were most probably alerted and looking for him, and whoever, that driver of the Lexus was, after they exited the Kimberling City area on route 13, Piles decided to walk the opposite direction farther down Trace Hollow Road. He expected that he might find a car or pick-up truck sitting in a driveway. Then, with his experience in securing unattended automobiles which led to him serving a short sentence at Cook County for car thefts when he was just out of high school, it would be no time before he would be back on the road, hopefully avoiding any police notice.

Beck stumbled down Trace Hollow Road without coming across any houses or cars until he arrived at the intersection at Trellis Drive. One sign pointed in the direction of Hurley Estates while the opposite arrowed sign read Heroy Circle. From a high point along the road, he could see about two hundred yards down where Table Rock Lake was partially lit by the Moon.

He could make out a boat slip almost hidden from his view by trees set back from the shoreline. Piles began walking in that direction but not before checking to be sure that the Ruger .380 caliber pistol that he carried in his waistband holster had not dislodged and got lost during the crash. Unfortunately, the cell phone that he carried attached to his belt must have slipped away during the crash and was missing. Feeling that he was recovering from the dizziness he felt climbing away from the wrecked Dodge Charger, he set out looking for that place identified on the sign his car struck, Plyman's Point.

* * *

3:00 A.M.

Honey Holcomb was awakened suddenly by the unexpected noise coming from her cell phone on the nearby nightstand. Her mind, still in a fog from the wine and exciting sex she enjoyed with Travis only a few hours earlier, hesitated momentarily before deciding to answer after clicking it on.

"Honey, wake up." She recognized it was Travis but, only half asleep, wondered why he needed to be calling her.

"Hey mister," she said with her eyes half closed. "Didn't you just get up to go potty?"

"Honey. WAKE UP." This time he sounded more demanding.

"Okay… Okay baby, I'm awake… I think. What got you up… so early?"

"Honey, I am at home. I just got a call from Mack at the station that there has been some big trouble over at Emily Paladino's house."

Just the mention of trouble and Emily Paladino's house in the same sentence provided all the push that Honey required to regain full awareness.

"Travis... Is she okay?"

"Yes, she is only shaken up from the terror of someone breaking into her house. Get dressed and meet me down at the station. We must move her... and her sister out of there... within the next few hours."

30

Plymans' Point

September 7ᵗʰ, 3:15 A.M.

A s had been their practice for all previous training cycles, the departure from Plyman's Point was planned for dawn. It was done this way to lessen the likelihood that the personnel who were leaving would draw notice from neighbors or, for that matter, highway patrols.

In some of the previous groups there were as many as seven men who received the lone wolf training that was provided at this unsuspecting, out-of-the-way site along sleepy Table Rock Lake. If everyone departed simultaneously it prompted the possibility that questions might arise concerning the purpose of their stay at Plyman's Point. In this group there were only three who were picked to be trained but their departure in just a few hours from now, at dawn, would be conducted just like the others.

Jari Abdou, who last addressed these men three weeks ago when they first arrived, spoke again to them in his office after each had finished gathering up the few personal items they would take with them when they would depart from this camp. He echoed what Rais Azari, their instructor, told them regarding the importance of maintaining absolute secrecy regarding their role in the War against Islam's enemies.

"This is so important in the eventual outcome of our holy purpose," Jari explained. "We have neither the numbers nor the military power to win this fight other than in the lone wolf terrorist style in which you have been trained here."

Jari knew that the importance of guarding the secrecy of their identity and their lone wolf mission had been spoken about as often in their training as the bomb making and guns procurement subjects that were taught to them. Still, to make that point one more time before trainees left the training camp Jari always brought it up during his final good-by to them.

"From this moment forward as you embark on your holiest of missions to serve almighty Allah, you can place your trust in no other. If there is any chance that you can or will be identified, you must be prepared to stop that from happening. No one here can make that decision for you as it has now become your lone responsibility."

As the hour drew nearer for their departure, Hanna Mustafo came in and gave each of them a Visa prepaid credit card that was loaded with a five thousand dollars balance. Behind her Rais Azari followed into the office. He had just spent his downtime while they waited for the scheduled departure by cleaning the weapons that were kept in the rifle rack inside Jari's office. Carrying a Bushmaster Predator AR-15 rifle he placed it in the rack next to the Smith and Wesson M & P-OR15 Semi-Automatic rifle already there.

A noise from outside caused everyone to turn towards the path leading up to the Quonset hut office front door where they saw someone running. Callum Rasheed arrived breathing fast and then abruptly stopped. He looked first at Hanna and then to Jari.

"There is someone sneaking around outside," he said. "It is a police officer... I am sure I heard a siren earlier out on route 86... but it stopped and then... I saw someone... more than..."

Rais Azari did not wait any longer for the winded Rasheed to finish. He attempted to pull the Bushmaster AR-15 from the rack but was stopped by Jari who told him to wait.

"I'll go out there and see what's going on," he said. In fact, you and Hanna should come along with me."

Jari then turned and looked over at the three newest trained soldiers of Allah.

"Two of you can grab a rifle and cover us, one from that window and the other from this door. No one must be allowed to see you or know of your presence here."

As Rais and Hanna caught up with Jari he cautioned that the last thing they needed at Plyman's Point was a confrontation with the police.

"If it is the police we have nothing to start a struggle over," Jari said. "We haven't broken any law and I damn sure don't want for any of us to be seen carrying any guns."

Then, pointing back to where they left Callum Rasheed and the three trainees, Jari pulled Rais closer.

"If it's not a cop then it must be someone looking for something to steal... and our boys back in the office can put a stop to that."

Rais stopped and grabbed Abdou causing him to also halt.

"Why would anyone think there is something we have they may want to steal from us," he asked.

Jari brushed himself free of Rais' grip and looked quickly back to where Hanna stood behind them a few paces.

"When I was negotiating that deal to buy the three Mickey Flynn's Restaurants with Mickey, I had to convince him that I had a half million dollars in cash back in my office but that I had to first show the contract to our people in Sydney. Turned out that bastard had forged Kylie's name… again. So, I gave up on making the deal."

"But… Mickey Paladino is dead??" Hanna seemed surprised.

Jari shrugged and began walking again towards where Callum said he saw the person on their property.

"I know that Mickey is dead. But he died owing a bundle to the Chicago Mob and… my guess is that he told them all about that money that we had ready to buy the restaurants."

Hanna did not continue walking together with Jari and Rais after what she just heard. Instead, fearing that Callum could be in danger back at the Quonset hut, she turned and began running in that direction.

Jari decided against trying to catch her and motioned for Rais to stay and help him find out who and how many people were out there where Callum pointed to when he saw someone.

As Hanna hurried along in the darkness and neared the open office door, in her haste she tripped on a tree root and fell.

Callum Rasheed, seeing her and then not seeing her, panicked, fearing that her sudden disappearance was caused by the intruder. He took off in the direction she was approaching from after first telling the men with the rifles to cover him from their positions inside the office.

The spot where Hanna tripped and fell was along an S curve the trail made around two large trees. Cullum, running at full speed, never saw her until it was too late. Hanna, who was dazed by the fall she took had just made it back up on her knees when she was struck full force by Callum.

The collision resulted in each of them briefly losing consciousness. Hanna recovered sooner and was relieved to recognize that it was her lover, Callum Rasheed, who was sprawled on the sandy ground nearby. She crawled to be closer and to help him regain a sense of awareness whereupon she appraised him of the potential dangers that she learned of moments earlier.

Suddenly, Hanna froze in mid-sentence.

"What is it, Hanna," Callum asked. "Do you see someone?"

Hanna began crawling again, this time back towards where she was when Callum ran into her, all the time sweeping the ground with her hands.

"Come and help me find it, Callum," she pleaded. "I lost it… the flash drive… the encrypted files…"

* * *

Being handed a rifle and told to cover the Camp Commander and their Instructor while they chased an unknown intruder caused a surprising rush of adrenaline to the trainees inside the Quonset hut's office. Was this just a test, their final test before departing the camp, to determine if they had what it would take to succeed in their lone wolf war?

If this whole thing is a charade, then each has thus far passed with excellence. No one balked when two of them were handed a loaded rifle. Each positioned themselves where Commander Abdou told them to be. They watched, not only for supposed enemy intruders, but just as importantly, where the Commander and the other two people headed into the darkness away from them.

When Callum Rasheed reacted to seeing and then not seeing Hanna Mustafo and then told each of them to cover him as he ran into the darkness, what were each of them to think? It had to be a way of testing them. Their instructors needed to be certain that they could and would react when orders were given to them.

Their nerves heightened to surprising levels of intensity watching Callum Rasheed suddenly disappear only a hundred yards down the path. They heard a frightening loud noise… more a thud of some kind. And then… nothing.

The trainee who was assigned at the window looked quizzically over at his fellow trainee at the open door. Surely doing nothing at this critical moment was tantamount to failure. He walked away from the window to be alongside the other trainee and pushed him aside. Taking his rifle and aiming it into the night sky he fired a clip of ammunition.

The sounds that were made echoed through the surrounding forest making it impossible to tell from which direction they originated.

When his fellow trainee recovered from the shock of watching what just occurred, he could hardly speak above a whisper.

"Are you sure? Are you sure you should have done that?"

The sounds from the gunshots threw a fright into Hanna and Callum causing them to stop searching for the lost encrypted files. They took off running in the direction they last saw Jari Abdou and Rais Azari.

Both Abdou and Azari were similarly shaken by the gunfire that came from somewhere in the wooded land surrounding Plyman's Point. Hearing footsteps behind them that sounded like five, six people were in their pursuit, they likewise started running toward Trellis Drive… away from Table Rock Lake and away from where they were certain they heard the gun shots. Whoever was after them had guns, rifles… they were sure the noise indicated more than pistol fire. Rais Azari cursed his commander for earlier stopping him from having his rifle with him now.

31

Quiet, just not for long

September 7th, 3:30 A.M.

NIGHT WATCH COMMANDER JOHNNY MACK had been working the graveyard shift at the Stone County Sheriff's Office ever since his promotion to that rank ten years ago. He had opportunities to get back to days but when push came to shove, he passed on them preferring the constant activity that came with any police duties during nighttime hours.

Some nights were less active than others, but weekends and holidays made up for any that were quiet, thus boring, by comparison. Still, Mack could not recall anything in his memory like what was happening at this time.

It began when something went wrong over on Bonanza Drive in Kimberling City where the sheriff's police had a 24-hour guard detail assigned. The deputy on duty made a strange call into the station that violated procedures by failing to use appropriate code numbers. However, his verbalized message was clear and indicated that there was a break-in at the home being guarded and that additional help was requested.

Just as Mack was notifying patrols in that general area to respond, the deputy called again, this time using the procedural codes, albeit not necessarily the correct ones, that requested a BOLO, Be On the Lookout, be sent over the radio to all police squads in the area for two black sedans travelling at high speeds on state route 13 away from the Kimberling Airways private airport.

Mack knew that the C.I.D. unit had concerns for the safety of the persons being guarded at that location and called Captain Travis Holden's cell phone to appraise him of the event. He had time for only two or three more swallows of coffee when he answered a call from the sheriff who wanted to be informed of everything going on at that time.

Mack told him what was known so far about the break-in and was not surprised when the sheriff said he was leaving his home in Reed Springs and would be at the station as soon as he could make it there. Mack told the sheriff that he had already contacted Travis who was also on his way in.

Then, an afterthought, Sheriff Lambert told Mack to call Alison Monroe and tell her to report to his office at her earliest time.

Compared with the activity that followed less than five minutes after the phone calls to Sheriff Lambert and Deputy Alison Monroe, all the preceding events were made to seem, by comparison, nothing more than business as usual.

A 9-1-1 call reported an accident near state route 86 and Trace Hollow Road. Mack put that on the police radio immediately and within seconds a patrol car involved in the earlier BOLO call responded that he just arrived at the scene and requested medical help be sent even though he could find no one in the vehicle but it appeared unlikely that the driver would be found alive and unhurt.

Another 9-1-1 call from a resident on Trellis Drive reported a prowler who set off the car alarm on his Ford Taurus parked in his driveway alongside his house. Within minutes two more emergency calls came in with similar complaints.

Sergeant Mack was familiar with the entire area where the accident was first reported to occur and where the subsequent calls about the attempts to steal a car were coming from. He reasoned that the inhabitant of the damaged car was the same person prompting the 9-1-1 calls and radioed his suspicion to the deputy who was investigating the car crash. Mack told him to proceed down Trace Hollow and then Trellis to see what he could find out.

The deputy called back within minutes reporting gunshots being heard. He thought they came from the area around Plyman's Point and requested immediate assistance. Mack put that call on the police radio adding a code 3 and within minutes two sheriff's deputies responded they were near and were on their way.

* * *

4:00 A.M.

Travis was the first to arrive at the station and looked around for Mack to get the most current update on the break-in at Emily Paladino's house and their whereabouts.

"The deputy who was guarding them placed them into his patrol car and is on his way here," Mack told him. "Meanwhile, we have a shoot-out going over at Plyman's Point… two of our units are there and three more are closing in…"

Travis knew that Sheriff Lambert had earlier issued direct orders to stay away from Plyman's Point to all the deputies and detectives until further notice. Something big and mysteriously secret was happening there. The sheriff had an agreement with

Homeland Security to let them have their first call on any police situations there.

He walked closer to where Mack was receiving another call from a unit that just arrived at the staging area being set-up along the Plyman's Point property line marked by signs reading "No Trespassing. Private Property."

"You said… a shoot-out…?" he asked Mack when he got his attention.

"That's correct," Mack responded. "Someone, a D.U.I., spun out and crashed over at route 86 and Trace Hollow Road. When he could not right his car, he must have taken off on foot down Trace Hollow. We got several 9-1-1 calls that said he was trying to steal a car and next thing I know is that the patrol unit we had checking the accident heard gun shots… coming from the area around Plyman's Point."

"Where do things stand at this time," Travis asked.

"The sheriff heard it all going down on his radio while he was on his way here and ordered a "Stand Down", Mack told him.

Travis noticed that Honey arrived at the same time Deputy Owen Horner was leading Emily and her sister into the police station. He told Honey to bring them all into the C.I.D. Unit's Meeting area until he could arrange for a safe place for them to be moved to temporarily.

Then, just as Travis was asking Deputy Horner to brief him on the break-in and the two cars that fled the scene, in walked Sheriff Lambert with Alison Monroe two steps back.

"Morning Travis," the sheriff greeted him while motioning for him to follow along with Deputy Monroe into his office.

"I see that we have the Paladino woman and her sister safe for now," he said. "I thought about that problem we have as to where we can hide them from whoever it is that wants to harm Emily."

The sheriff was at his desk but had not sat down yet. He turned to Alison.

"You have been asking for a detail that can get you more directly into the kind of police work that Captain Holden does," he said to her. "As I drove in from Reed Springs just now, I asked myself, where would be the last place that anyone would expect Emily to be hiding? Where would she be the safest soon… until we can figure this case out?"

Alison knew Sheriff Lambert as well as anyone ever did and was quickly able to decipher the reasons for the questions, he was teasing her with.

"Sheriff," she said without another second of hesitation. "I am positive that if you let me hide Emily at my house, we can do all of that in secret… and Yes, I accept this detail," she hurriedly added.

The sheriff smiled and turned next to Travis.

"I am expecting any moment that a very angry Chief of Homeland Security is going to rush in here demanding some serious answers about what we have going on right now over at Plyman's Point," he said. "I will leave it up to you or Lieutenant Holcomb to figure out how to secretly transport Emily over to Alison's house and work out the details for whatever they will need there.

All three in the sheriff's office turned together to see the disturbance outside as Mack was trying to block the efforts of Horace Haywood to get past him.

"Sheriff…" Mack called out.

"Get out of my way," Haywood was heard saying as he struggled to get past him.

Travis led the sheriff out of the office to where the two men were arguing.

"Mack," Travis said as he approached. "He is okay. The sheriff is expecting him."

"Horace," Sheriff Lambert said in a timid manner. "Come on into my office and I'll fill you in on how this all began over at Plyman's Point, and we see what needs to be done about it."

Travis signaled to Alison to come out of the office and follow him and then turned back to Mack.

"We are going to be in the C.I.D. Unit's Meeting area with Lieutenant Holcomb in case the sheriff is trying to reach me."

* * *

4:15 A.M.

Before meeting with Lieutenant Holcomb regarding the plans to move Emily over to Alison's home until the threat on her life was addressed, Travis told Mack to call in two of the members of the Task Force, Lieutenant Mize, and Sergeant Platt. He knew that the situation going on over at Plyman's Point required urgent investigative work to identify the driver of the wrecked Dodge Charger who was now likely the cause of the gunfire and to coordinate with the deputies at the scene the eventual capture of him.

Upon returning to be with Lieutenant Holcomb he was briefed on the plan that she made to keep the move secret.

"Alison will leave the station alone and drive to her house and prepare for Emily and her sister," she explained. "I will drive them over there and be certain to avoid anyone who might be interested in following us."

Travis said that this met with his approval but wondered what was being arranged to maintain constant protection for them other than leaving that to Alison.

Honey paused before responding to his question long enough to allow Alison to speak.

"Captain Holden," she said with a bit of a smile. "I have been dating another deputy for the last few months and I hope that if you think I need more help that you pick him."

Travis shot a glance over at Honey who nodded her silent agreement with Alison's request.

"Fine then," Travis said. "I do have one question remaining though." He walked closer to where Emily and Elizabeth were sitting. "Are you both in agreement with these plans? I cannot say yet how long this will be required, but whatever the inconvenience is it is necessary."

"We aren't concerned about any inconvenience," Elizabeth said. "Emily's attorney has convinced us that she is in danger and needs constant police protection. Our sister Frances had to return to Tampa but will stay in touch with us in case there is something we need."

32

In the darkness there is comfort

September 7th ...

GUY CHEVRON ONCE SHARED a conversation with Piles Beck that never seemed more appropriate than the way his night had gone so far. It was something that had a life lesson, a moral as Guy described it, and it was about how there is always a calm before a storm, which everyone already knows. But Monsieur Chevron pointed out that it is always just as true that there is calm after every storm. Knowing that little axiom (a word that only the dandy Frenchman would think to use.) made it easier to stay steady and do things as best you can do when the going gets tough.

Piles was going to have to spend the next few hours sitting right where he was, safe in a thicket, hidden from anyone that would do him harm. Things were quiet again and allowed his mind to replay the events that led to where he found himself.

He remembered it beginning after the Dodge Charge spun out and flipped. He escaped but he was lost! Hoping to sneak down closer to Table Rock Lake and the homestead known as Plyman's Point where he might drive away with one of their vehicles, he was surprised by the sudden problems he ran into.

First, he blew it trying to hotwire a pick-up he spotted while walking along Trellis Drive. Blaming the mistake of setting off the truck's alarm on the fact that he had not tried stealing cars since he passed age thirty, he remembered stumbling into a trench on the adjacent property that woke up the residents inside when he could not resist yelling out…" Oh FUCK!"

By the time he managed to limp down to where there were five vehicles to pick from in the corral at Plyman's Point, he discovered that he had lost the element of surprise feature that was so valuable to have when doing this kind of business.

For some crazy reason, he thought the people inside the Quonset hut were still awake. He crept closer to see if he could determine how many were in there and what to expect if he were discovered. Suddenly, someone was running from another building set back farther from the lake. Once the man was inside Piles heard him tell the others that there was a prowler on their property,

He thought about running back towards the entrance trail but that was where he came from and highly likely was being sought by the people whose alarm went off. There were boats in the slip down by the lake, but the two Quonset huts stood between him and that hiding place.

Before he could decide where to go, he saw two men and a woman leave the office in the Quonset hut and start walking directly towards him. He turned and began limping as quietly as he could into the wooded areas just off the path. It was much darker once he was under the dense tree branches that hid most of the available light from the moon.

With the pain in the leg that he injured when he slipped in the trench earlier causing him to put most of his weight on the opposite side, he stumbled behind a thicket patch only a few feet away from the path. He settled there just in time as they walked around a large tree that caused the path to be built in a half circle.

He was relieved when these people walked past within less than five feet without seeing him. But suddenly they had stopped. Had one of them seen him and was telling the others where he was? He thought about just taking off and running, but where? He could not see but only a few yards in front of him. Besides, his leg hurt so bad that all he could do was to limp and surely that would leave them no trouble in catching him.

Then, the woman who was walking a bit behind the two men turned and began running back along the trail. Surely, it had to have been her that saw him and was now in pursuit. With no plan other than staying as still as he could, he braced himself for the inevitable.

But luck must have just smiled on him. As soon as she reached the closest point to where he stayed hidden in the thicket, the woman tripped and fell with such force that she seemed to have lost consciousness. The two men that she had been with were by then too far away to be aware of her accident.

Now was his chance to get back on the path and head for the boat slips he had seen by the lake. He figured that everyone that had been inside that office earlier were the ones who came out looking for him and it should be clear sailing to get down to the lake.

But no, once again he was surprised. He had forgotten about the man who first alerted the others about the prowler. Piles saw that man as he left the office in the Quonset hut running towards him and calling out for someone named Hanna.

The collision that occurred between the two of his pursuers was almost comical. Peeking through the thicket he was hiding behind; he saw the woman rising on her knees just as the man ran around the tree and SMACK… both were face down in the grass alongside of the path.

The force from which she was struck caused a locket that was hung around her neck to break free and fly into the very ticket that hid him from detection. The woman regained consciousness first and cautiously approached the man who was slowly recovering his own sense of awareness. He saw them embrace and engage in whispered conversation. Suddenly, the woman surprised the man by turning and, instead of getting back to her feet, continued on her knees, crawling in an almost spread-eagle fashion.

The woman was near panic and when the man called out to her wondering if she had seen someone, she answered sounding very terrified that she needed his help to find something she lost when they collided. Piles remembered thinking he heard her call it something. Something like… Piles?

How could this woman have known his name? He recalled how he felt a shiver of severe confusion until he heard her repeat back to the man, who was by now also on his knees and by her side that her desperate search was for the encrypted files.

Now, laying low behind the thicket back from where the woman and man who crashed into each other were before they heard the guns being fired and took off running, Piles Beck sat rubbing his injured leg. The thicket that successfully hid him was on ground above the path just high enough that allowed him to see immediately that the shots came from the office door in the farthest Quonset hut. Unless the shooters inside came out and walked toward his location he was as safe there as he could think of being anywhere. He reached out and pulled a chain necklace with a golden locket attached to it from the edge of the bush in front of him.

"Well, it's certainly not one of those encrypted files she was looking so hard to find," he thought.

33

Find that other car

September 7ᵗʰ, 5:15 A.M.

ERNIE MIZE WAS NONE-TOO-HAPPY about receiving the urgent telephone call from Mack at the station to report ASAP. What was so damn urgent that Travis Holden needed him to be at work so early? What could it be that his arch enemy thought he needed help from him anyway?

Ernie pulled into the parking lot at the Quick Stop Convenient store before arriving at the police station. He needed a cup of coffee, and he hated the stuff that came out of the machine at work. He often wondered why the sheriff didn't just put in a new coffee machine that made his own favorite, Starbucks. Not that it would have made a difference to Ernie. He hated Starbucks too.

As he entered the Squad room where he had his personal locker he saw Arnie Platt talking with Travis just outside of Sheriff Lambert's office.

"Just like that brown nose to get to work before me," Ernie

grumbled loud enough to be heard by a deputy changing for work at a nearby locker.

"Are you talking to me, Lieutenant?" the deputy asked.

Ernie turned, surprised that he was overheard talking to himself.

"No… Just happy to be here and ready to start work," Ernie replied allowing his sarcasm to reveal his true feelings.

By the time he eventually got to where Captain Holden and Sergeant Platt were standing locked in a serious conversation, he sensed that indeed something big was happening and he had better appear ready to contribute.

Travis made no mention of the extra time it took for Lieutenant Mize to report. Instead, he quickly finished giving instructions to Sergeant Platt and told Ernie to follow him into his office.

"Ernie, we've had a wild morning… lots happening… most all of it quite serious," Travis told him. "There was a break-in at Emily's house by at least one person… maybe two around 2:00 A.M."

Mize looked surprised. "I thought we had a 24-hour watch on that place."

"Well, we did, and it did not stop whoever it was that wanted to get inside. But no one got hurt, Emily and her sister are not only safe but are in the process of being moved somewhere that we think will keep her out of harm's way."

Ernie bit his lip to stop from adding…" Safe? Like she was supposed to be until this morning?" He let his facial expression carry that thought for Travis to notice.

"Two cars were involved with the break-in and one of them crashed later over on route 86 near Ozark Valley Nature Park. The driver got out of the crashed car and walked around, we think, looking for another car to steal."

"So… Have we caught up with that guy yet?" Ernie asked.

"Not yet," Travis sighed. In any case we think the guy found his way over to Plyman's Point and either he or they began a shooting war."

A smug feeling jumped alive inside the perpetually jealous mind of Ernest Mize.

"You say there is a shooting event going on over at Plyman's Point?"

"Yes, that's exactly what I said." Travis caught a whiff of the joy that news seemed to provide for Ernie. "The sheriff… and Horace Haywood are right now inside Sheriff Lambert's office deciding how this plays into their concerns about what's been going on there."

"I bet the Homeland Security Chief is pissed," Ernie gloated. "In fact, I bet Sheriff Lambert is shook up some too."

Travis decided to ignore the implications that sneaked inside everything Ernie Mize had to say. Instead, he told the lieutenant what the reason was that he was awakened and called in to work.

"Get the license number of the car that crashed and see if we can identify who that guy is that has created all this trouble. I need to know who he is… what it was he wanted to be doing when he broke into Emily Paladino's house in Kimberling City, and anything and everything else you can find out about him by noon… Today."

34

Stand down ordered

September 7ᵗʰ, 5:15 A.M.

"I JUST WANT TO KNOW ONE THING," Bull Lambert said after bringing Horace Haywood into his office and closing the door.

"One thing?" the chief of Homeland Security asked lifting both eyebrows. "You must be one lucky sheriff. I have a litany of questions needing answers."

The sheriff smiled but insisted that his question get answered first.

"How in the world did you almost beat me here this morning? I mean, all the way from Springfield…"

"Actually Bull, I got the call probably around the same time this morning that your patrol deputy came upon the upended Dodge Charger at Trace Hollow Road and 86. If you recall, I did mention to you that we've had Plyman's Point under surveillance for quite some time."

The sheriff nodded that he recalled being told about the surveillance back when the Homeland Security Chief first informed him about their concerns of the activities at Plyman's Point.

"So, now what do we have going on there right now," Haywood asked.

"Well… just as soon as I knew that our patrol deputy made a call for more assistance because of some shootings there I rushed to tell our Night Commander, Mack, to broadcast my orders for all deputies to Stand Down. Those that are there already, and the squads that are on their way, will not enter Plyman's Point until I give them a GO."

Sheriff Lambert hoped that hearing that would appease the Homeland Chief a bit. He knew that Haywood had every right to be pissed off. They had made an agreement that all of Plyman's Point belonged to Homeland Security for the near future. But Sheriff Lambert also knew that what occurred early this morning that resulted in three or more of his Sheriff Police patrols to be at that location was not really a violation of their agreement.

Sheriff Lambert was in mid-sentence trying to emphasize this rationale when the intercom buzzed, and he heard Captain Holden's voice.

"What's up, Travis?"

"Sheriff, our deputy that was the earliest arrival just called in saying that some people who claim to be the owners at Plyman's Point have come out and made a demand that all police leave immediately."

Sheriff Lambert stole a look over at Horace Haywood to gage his reaction. Seeing that the Homeland Security Chief seemed hesitant to interfere, he clicked back the TALK button.

"Travis," he began using a tone that reflected both the anger and the insult that he felt at being told by that property owner what he must do. "The Stand Down order is immediately rescinded. Instead, inform all deputies who are engaged at this event that I want the people who say they are the property owners brought in for questioning."

There was a brief pause as Travis considered whether the sheriff was overreacting after hearing the demands to get the police away from Plyman's Point.

"Sheriff?" Travis asked. "Shall I allow the deputy to inform them why they are being brought in for questioning?"

Sheriff Lambert kept his eyes on Horace Haywood the entire time during his discussion with Travis.

"Sure, tell them that we have reports of gunshots on the property, and we have two responsibilities that must be met. One is the safety of all people on the site. The second concern is to investigate and determine who fired the guns and was anybody there injured or worse."

Travis hurriedly answered Roger to that and clicked off the intercom so that he could radio the sheriff's instructions to all personnel at the site.

While changing the Stand Down order to one that would require entering the property, Sheriff Lambert never took his eyes away from Horace Haywood. But after having done that, he was surprised by how small the effect of it was on him.

"Bull," Haywood said, appearing more resigned than upset. "Once there were reports of gunfire there was nothing else you could do. Do not worry about how that settles with our agreement. I guess, sometimes fate itself must rule what we all end up doing."

Sheriff Lambert was indeed happy with the response he just heard from the Homeland Security Chief. He had acted on impulse when Travis told him that his deputies were being "ordered" to leave. But impulse is often the truest teller of a correct decision that has to be made.

"So, where does all of this now leave Homeland Securities plans?" he asked.

Horace Haywood just shrugged his shoulders. But his eyes indicated that something like what just happened was already anticipated for and would not result in a plan failure.

"Bull," he said while positioning himself to sit in the chair opposite the sheriff. "I hope you will assign your most skilled detectives to handle the interrogation of whomever is being brought in right now for questioning. Hopefully, you can instruct that only questions concerning the shooting be asked at this time and that nothing be said, mentioned, nor asked that refer to our suspicions that Plyman's Point has other purposes."

"Of course," the sheriff responded. "I'll assign Travis Holden and Lieutenant Honey Holcomb. Both are intelligent and experienced in conducting interrogations and are persons that can accommodate our dual policing needs."

"Okay, that sounds like how we want to proceed," Haywood acknowledged. "Now, who is leading the investigation going on right now at the site concerning the gunfire questions?"

"I've already taken care of that," Sheriff Lambert said. "Even before the property owner mouthed off making those foolish demands, I assigned Sergeant Arnie Platt to take charge of things there once I found out more about the extent of the problem."

35

Dawn but not done

September 7th, 5:30 A.M.

THE THREE LONE WOLF TRAINEES were growing restless. Was all that activity that took place an hour ago real? They made a calculated guess that it was all a charade, something the instructor, Rais Azari, or perhaps his boss, Commander Abdou thought up and acted out to test them.

However, with the sky starting to brighten as dawn was arriving, many doubts were brewing inside each of them. All the camp's cadre eventually left, leaving them alone. Either they had faked much of what just happened or experienced real incidents and were now long gone. Even the spray of rifle fire that one of the trainees unloaded did not receive the expected response.

As organized as they discovered the training was throughout the three weeks they were in training camp there, this morning's actions caused more confusion than anything else. From everything that they had earlier been told it was now getting time to depart. Except for the fact that Hanna Mustafo had previously handed each a prepaid Visa credit card for their initial expenses, nothing further had been explained. How were they supposed to depart from the camp? Who would drive them to the airport in Springfield where they expected to be handed flight boarding passes and head to their specific destinations?

The last instruction that was given came from Commander Abdou who told them to stay inside the office and provide cover for those who left to respond to a mysterious prowler. But if it turned out that the guess they made earlier and acted upon was in error… and there really was a major problem, then just staying in the office was no longer an operative choice.

The trainees discussed these possibilities amongst themselves without being able to find agreement on a course of action. Finally, the man who fired the rifle earlier decided that he was leaving. He had his personal belongings and the prepaid credit card that he was given and even his choice of weapons that were close by in the unlocked rifle rack.

"But we have no transportation," one of the other trainees complained.

They knew that there were two cars and two pick-ups in the corral but knowing that even if they could get them started, they would then have to drive out on the same gravel road that was alongside of the path that the others took and who-knows-what would be waiting for them there.

Looking back at the boat slip they noticed the eighteen foot Bowrider that Callum Rasheed used often to go to work at the Ozark Lakes Leisure Boats sales office near Baxter Boat Dock. The trainee who earlier made the decision to fire the rifle shots bragged that he had already driven that boat once when Callum offered him an early morning cruise around the lake when he arrived at camp a few days earlier than the others.

The three waited close to another hour to see if Abdou or Azari or anyone else would return. But suspecting that there was indeed something bad and unplanned that happened to them, they set off for the boat slip down on the lake. Each carried their personal gear and one weapon which they took from the rifle rack inside the office.

From his location behind the thicket patch Piles was able to watch three men… all armed with a rifle, leave the office in the Quonset hut and head down to the boat slip in the lake. Wisely, he decided to wait longer before leaving the security of his hiding place.

The sound of the Bowrider starting up was noisy enough to be heard by Sergeant Arnie Platt who had just begun leading a squad of sheriff's deputies down the path toward the Quonset huts and the lake.

Piles Beck slid deeper inside the thicket after spotting the deputies coming towards his location. With their focus on first the Quonset huts and then to the lake where they observed the three men leaving in the Bowrider, they moved silently but quickly past the hiding place Piles had chosen and not moved from.

It took Sergeant Platt's troops almost fifteen additional moments to clear the Quonset huts and the surrounding wooded area and be certain there were no additional suspects before they could descend to the boat slip from which the three men had escaped. Hurrying back on the path to get to their vehicles, they ran right past Piles once again.

He waited another twenty minutes after hearing the sounds of the police cars leaving en masse and heading back out on Trellis Drive. Piles slowly moved from behind the thicket and began limping his own way down to the lake.

"Nice of them policemen to make sure there's nobody left to surprise me," Piles thought happily, but silently, to himself.

Unable to catch up with the three unknown men who snuck away from Plyman's Point in a Bowrider, Sergeant Platt and his squad of sheriff's deputies hurried back to the cars.

Sergeant Platt's was the only unmarked police car so he waved the ones with Mars lights and sirens to lead the way, telling them that the destination for the Bowrider was around the Baxter area.

Using his cell phone Platt called into the station and told Captain Travis Holden what just went down.

"Why do you think they were going to Baxter," Travis asked.

"Because Captain, it is likely they will want to get off the lake as soon as possible and then look for some other means of ground transportation," Platt replied. "Baxter Boat Dock is the closest public location to find an empty slip and park the boat."

"Give me a description of the Bowrider, Arnie," Travis said. "I'll have the Missouri State Police Water Patrol Division ready, and we can use them to help round them up.

36

In custody

September 7th, mid-morning

BULL LAMBERT AND HORACE HAYWOOD watched together as Sergeant Ben Hodges paraded the three people the deputies pulled in along with Jari Abdou who objected to any police presence at Plyman's Point. Each was put into separate holding cells until they could be identified and then questioned.

"Who do you want us to begin with?" the sheriff asked Haywood. "I have only Captain Holden ready to conduct the first interview. Lieutenant Holcomb is on her way back to the station from Kimberling City and should be here within a brief time."

Horace Haywood appreciated being consulted by the sheriff before conducting the interviews. He sensed that the accommodation was being made to help reconcile what both he and the sheriff viewed as an accidental violation of their earlier agreement to keep Plyman's Point under the sole police responsibility of Homeland Security.

"I think the first thing that we need to learn is who was responsible for the shootings," Haywood pointed out.

"I agree," Lambert said. "I have received a report from the deputy that entered the property that there were no others found other than three men seen leaving via a power boat. So, unless any of them were injured it looks like the gun shots all missed a target."

"Okay, then let's focus on finding out why the guns were fired and by whom. I already heard from our agent who was watching the incident happen from his offsite location that it was timed with someone who was seen sneaking down Trellis Drive and then turned into the driveway entrance to Plyman's camp".

"That was probably our suspect from the crashed Dodge Charger," the sheriff added.

"Right, but why did he choose Plyman's Point?" Haywood wondered. "Was he simply returning there? I mean, was he someone who was living or staying there who turned out to be one of the groups with the three men your deputies saw later leaving the area via Table Rock Lake?"

"Could be that way, I guess," Lambert thought aloud. "But the way he seemed to have started trouble all down Trellis Drive, setting off car alarms and the like, makes me think he was just looking for stealing his transportation out of that area."

Haywood agreed with that explanation and suggested that they jot down a list of questioning topics.

"I know that none of the people who were transported into the station were booked since there was no arrests," Haywood said. "But once your deputies have already taken down their identities, let's see if we can get any of them to explain their relationship with the others there."

Sheriff lambert added "relationships" to "Who fired rifle shots" to the list he was preparing for Captain Holden to inquire about. "Is it okay with what you are concerned about there if we try to discover the names of the three we saw leaving when we entered the camp?"

"Sure, that would be helpful," Haywood responded. "Just make sure that nothing is asked or mentioned regarding their purpose for being there. We are close to completing our investigation into that but there are still a few items we hope to uncover before putting a finish to their mission. When you end up releasing them, I want them to return and do what they think they still have time to do."

"Okay, that's all in line with what we have been talking about before this morning," the sheriff acknowledged. "Now then how long do you need us to keep them all retained?"

Haywood smiled, seeing that Sheriff Lambert already guessed that his crew of agents had already descended on the property and were in the process of planting listening devices and taking notes of any file information they might see.

"As long as they do not ask for help from any lawyer, I imagine we can hold them for the better part of the day," Lambert said waiting for a response to his earlier question.

"Five... maybe six hours will give us all the time we will need, Bull... and thanks."

* * *

When he heard that Arnie Platt was chosen to lead the squad of deputies into Plyman's Point, and that they succeeded in chasing three suspects and since were joined with the Missouri State Water Patrol Units, Ernie Mize looked at his current assignment as nothing more than "busy work" that was probably intended by the sheriff to keep him away from the big stuff.

It took less than ten minutes to get the license plate numbers on the crashed Dodge Charger, and almost less than that to run that information in the Missouri Department of Motor

Vehicle records to determine that the owner was one Charles Beck of Chicago.

Remembering that the sheriff added to his assignment that he wanted as much information about that car owner, Ernie used the Stone County password to log into the Missouri State Highway Patrol site and clicked on the link for CJIS, Criminal Justice Information Services.

He found a link to the criminal history of Charles Beck and clicked on it. Two photos appeared immediately and below them was a narrative of his criminal record that began at the Cook County Court's system showing he had been convicted of petty theft five times; auto theft eight times; and burglary twice. He spent time in Cook County jail; Lake County jail; and DuPage County jail. The auto theft convictions bought him a stint at Stateville.

It was while reading Beck's history at Stateville that Lieutenant Mize saw something that, as far as he was aware of, no one had yet discovered during the current investigations of the two murders the task force was working on.

Ernie Mize may have just uncovered the most important link in the murder investigations and could not wait to bring news of it to the sheriff.

No reason to involve "Boy Wonder and his girlfriend, Honey the Hustler," he gleefully thought. He waited only as long as it took to click on the small green square marked PRINT.

By the time that Piles limped his way down to the boat slips he discovered that just before the three men who barely escaped being captured by the Stone County deputies took off in the Bowrider, they managed to free the dock lines from the cleats for the two other small boats and pushed them away from the dock out into the middle of the lake intending for the police to require other means for their pursuit.

Fortunately for Piles, they disregarded the little fourteen-foot Crestliner tied to the dock at a point much farther away from the Bowrider they hurriedly boarded and then used to escape. Piles knew as soon as he stepped inside of it that even without ignition keys, the small 9.5 horse powered Evinrude outboard would be a snap for him.

With truly little effort and within mere minutes after he was on the boat, Piles was heading out on the lake away from the shoreline of Plyman's Point. Once he was out in the middle of Table Rock Lake, he realized that two potentially serious obstacles remained before he was free.

The first concerned fuel as the gage was showing below the empty line. The other was direction. All he knew for sure was that he watched as the Bowrider with the three men aboard took off in one direction, but he had no idea of their intended destination. Piles chose to go in the opposite direction and once again had no idea of an intended destination.

37

Questions for number one

September 7th, noon

"THE REASON WE BROUGHT YOU… and your associates into the station this morning is that we are investigating gun shots that were fired on your property before dawn this morning," Travis said in answer to Jari Abdou's question after he was brought from the Holding Area into the Interrogation room.

"I see," Abdou said. "But if I may, why was it necessary to take us all off of the property… OUR property…? Couldn't your questions have been asked there?"

Travis, who was sitting directly across from Abdou, shrugged his shoulders. "Maybe so," he replied. "Our problem with that was we had no way of knowing anything more than where the gun shots came from. We did not know if the shooter was perhaps one of you who met us at the property line. We didn't know if the shooter remained behind the four of you and was perhaps threatening you… or others."

Jari Abdou shook his head in a continuous back and forth during Travis's explanation indicating he was not finding it believable.

"How long do you intend to hold us here?" he asked.

Travis looked surprised. "You want an answer even before you have heard the questions," he laughed. "How long will it take you and your associates to cooperate with us and answer the questions we have regarding the gun shots this morning?"

Jari again shook his head in a no-no manner. "I don't believe that I have to answer your questions. Am I correct?"

Travis gave him one of his practiced 'disappointed expressions'. "Are you saying that you will not respond to my questions concerning the gun shots that were heard at Plyman's Point this early morning?"

"You are answering my question with a question, sir. Do I have to agree to be questioned by the police or not? I am demanding that you respond."

Travis was only playing for time during this cat and mouth game with Jari Abdou. He fully expected that Abdou would be uncooperative. He also knew that Homeland Security needed a few more hours to drop the listening devices in secret locations back at Jari Abdou's Quonset huts and office and residence.

"Actually Mr. Abdou," Travis began. "I do not understand why you thought earlier you could make demands on our deputies that responded to a potentially life-threatening situation at your place. And I damn sure don't understand why you think I should feel the least bit intimidated now, listening to you issuing new demands."

Travis signaled to the deputy standing guard by the door that he should return Jari Abdou to the Holding Area at least until the others were allowed to indicate their intentions to be more cooperative… or not, during their questioning session.

As the deputy approached him, Jari stood up and once again demanded his rights.

Travis, having already been informed by Sheriff Lambert of Abdou's citizenship status, knew that Jari was putting on an act, hoping that Travis could not detect that he was bluffing about his rights, suggesting he was holding the trump card while all the time it was just… the Joker.

*   *   *

Ernie Mize was as surprised as he hoped the sheriff would be when he first learned the connection that the driver of the crashed Dodge Charger had with someone who was already designated as a POI, Person of Interest.

"This piece of investigative success should elevate my standing with the boss," he softly said as he walked towards the front office.

He spotted the sheriff inside his office as he approached and ignoring the protocol that required being either invited or simply requesting to see the sheriff first, he barged into the office bursting with the important news he learned.

Sheriff Lambert was on the telephone and looked up, startled by the unannounced intrusion. He continued his conversation on the phone, but the frown that he produced left no doubt about the displeasure he felt.

After closing the discussion by commenting that he had to cut it short because someone had an emergency that he had to deal with, he turned towards Ernie.

"Well, what is it?" he demanded to know. "You've got something so important that office rules don't apply anymore?"

Ernie never felt so deflated. Here he was, about to announce a new lead in the murder investigations, and he was being treated with as much respect as a misbehaving pet puppy.

"Sheriff, I have the name of the perp with the Dodge Charger," he said in a cautious voice.

"The sheriff sat silently waiting for Ernie to supply the identity of the person he was earlier assigned to discover.

"The fella's name is Charles Beck, AKA Piles Beck… out of Chicago," Ernie felt momentum shifting his way as he spoke. "After I learned that information, I went through the Missouri Automated Criminal History to learn as much as there is known about this guy."

Lambert waited again without saying what was on his mind as he listened to the lieutenant giving his verbal report much more drama than it most likely deserved.

"Now comes the surprise," Ernie sounded like what he was about to say had to be fast or he might just wet his pants. "Beck has a history, small time stuff, some big. Like Grand Theft Auto. Did some time in Stateville…"

The sheriff did not look at all as interested as Ernie imagined he should at this point.

"Did you think to use this information and put out an APB so that we might actually capture this. Beck fellow?" the sheriff asked.

"Well. No, I have not done that just quite yet," Ernie said with just a twinge of disappointment reflected in his response.

"You see… There is more…"

Bull Lambert was rapidly becoming impatient. "More?" he asked. "Come on. Out with-it Ernie," he demanded. "We've got a lot on our plate today already."

This was it, Ernie thought. This is the time to drop the bomb. Lambert is going to be so surprised…

"Well???"

"Sheriff, the perp we are looking for, Beck, had a roommate in Stateville who plays a big part so far in our two murder investigations."

Again, Lambert said nothing but instead opened his hands and squeezed his outstretched fingers in a rapid give-me what you've got motion.

"Boss, what I'm trying to tell you is that Charles Beck, AKA Piles Beck, knows our POI Frankie Valenti well enough they could be like brothers to each other."

The silence coming from the sheriff seemed much different suddenly than it was just seconds earlier while he waited for his lieutenant to complete what he was so excited to report to him.

"This really is news," he said, showing how surprised he had become. When Sheriff Lambert rose to his feet, he produced a satisfied kind of smile that told Ernie Mize he had just done well.

38

Ready for the next step

September 7th, afternoon

Horace Haywood prepared to leave the Stone County Sheriff's Office shortly after watching Captain Holden's failed interrogation of Jari Abdou.

"I really didn't think that we would find Abdou wanting to open up and answer questions," he told Sheriff Lambert. "But it's really no matter, other than we still do not have an identity of the guy they were shooting at."

"Oh that," Bull Lambert said feeling guilty he hadn't mentioned Lieutenant Mize's success in identifying Piles Beck as the person who walked down to Plyman's Point after wrecking his Dodge Charger.

"So, he's not connected to what Abdou's bunch are involved in?" he asked.

"Doesn't seem to be," Lambert said. "But strange as this seems, he does appear to be close with someone we have on top of our suspect list in the murder cases we're working on."

The Homeland Security Chief smiled. "Lieutenant Mize, you say, is the detective that made that discovery?"

"Right you are," the sheriff laughed.

"Well, I'll be," Haywood said just as his cell phone caught his attention.

Sheriff Lambert only heard Haywood's end of the conversation before realizing that it was something that did not involve him or his county police. He began walking back to his office giving Haywood a polite goodbye, see you later, only to notice that he was being asked to wait up.

Haywood hurried through the remainder of his cell phone discussion and took the sheriff by the arm, walking with him into the office.

My agents have finished setting the listening devices where they can do us the best," he said. "But we will need your boys to keep Abdou and his associates here and incommunicado for maybe another hour."

"Sounds like your boys found something more than they expected over at Plyman's Point?" the sheriff asked.

"They did and I'll explain all that later on," Haywood said. "But I can tell you this," he added, not wanting to look like he was holding back something that the sheriff should know about. "Looks like we found evidence that clearly establishes what their purpose really is… and it's never been anything related to Worldwide Lake Boat Sales business."

Before leaving Sheriff Lambert's office, Haywood turned back and held up two fingers.

"Make sure, Bull, that Abdou enjoys his stay here for at least a couple more hours. I'll give you our all clear when we leave Plyman's Point."

"I'll do that Horace," the sheriff confirmed. "But you mentioned you want them kept away from anyone, including each other?"

"Oh yes, thank God I almost forgot that," Haywood said showing relief that it could now be explained. "We cannot let them use any means to call out to anyone who might then hustle over to Plyman's Point while my agents are still there working. We also want to keep them from talking with each other until they return to Plyman's Point where we should be able to hear their discussions ourselves."

*   *   *

The Missouri Highway Water Patrol Unit had three police boats in the vicinity of Baxter Boat Dock within fifteen minutes after receiving the call for help from Sheriff Lambert. However, they saw no signs of the Bowrider that was reported to have three suspects aboard that fled from an ongoing police investigation concerning gunshot activities.

Staying in radio contact with Sergeant Platt and his Stone County deputies, they patrolled Table Rock Lake parallel with the efforts of the police on land. Surprisingly, it took over two hours before the Bowrider was flushed from its hiding place. Sergeant Platt's deputies discovered the boat tucked between two similar boats secured to a private dock hidden in a cove that was accessed through a narrow channel. The men in the Bowrider fired shots at Sergeant Platt's men who had surrounded the dock thereby eliminating any exit on land as an alternative for escape.

Instead, they started up the Bowrider and took off at full speed through the narrow channel leading back to Table Rock Lake. Suddenly, unaware that the buoys in the channel warned of certain dangers, the bottom of their boat struck the top of a large tree that was left hidden below water level when the man-made lake was created years earlier. The boat was sent high off the water and landed portside sliding along the shoreline until it crashed into another private boat dock.

By the time that the first Water Patrol Unit arrived the boat had settled and two men with rifles strapped around their shoulders were observed crawling along the starboard side of the watercraft. The First Officer on deck on the Missouri Water Patrol boat used the boat's public address system to command the men to surrender and put away the rifles.

Instead, both men pulled their rifles around their shoulders and took aim at the police boat. The deputies who were on land and who chased the Bowrider from its hiding place arrived and yelled for the men to surrender.

The standoff lasted no more than another minute before the two men on the damaged Bowrider threw down their rifles and raised their arms in surrender. The Water Patrol Police Unit stood guard as Sergeant Platt and a deputy coaxed the two men to land where they were handcuffed and taken away.

"There were three of them," Sergeant Platt yelled over to the First Officer. "I'm going inside and find the other."

The waves that were stirred by the engines on the Police Boat crashed against the damaged Bowrider causing it to violently rock up and down.

Platt managed to lean over the top on the starboard side that remained above the water where he saw the man he was searching for wedged between the steering wheel and the windshield. The lake water that entered the boat was at his shoulder level… and rising.

Arnie yelled to the Officer on the police boat that he needed a rope that he hoped to secure around the steering wheel and as they pulled the wheel back, he could help the man get free.

All went exactly as if it had been practiced many times. Within less than ten minutes the deputies on land had their prisoner and were taking him back through the marshy shore to where other Stone County Police squads were located.

"That was one fine job you just did there, sergeant," the First Officer said patting Sergeant Platt on the back.

Arnie laughed and then briskly shook his head back and forth releasing a thorough spray of lake water from his thick gray hair to shower his fellow police officer.

"Just for that, wise guy," the Water Patrol Unit officer laughed while shaking some of the water off his shirt, "you'll have to buy the first round when awards are passed out celebrating our mutual success."

39

Closing in to closing the case

September 7th, late afternoon

TRAVIS REALIZED THAT ANOTHER Task Force Update session should be called as soon as possible. A lot had happened just since dawn and much needed to be reviewed and coordinated. However, the late afternoon capture of the three men who escaped by boat from Plyman's Point earlier required his full attention.

Travis had already been advised by Sheriff Lambert that the Homeland Security Chief wanted to meet with them before they booked the captured men. That meeting would have to be this evening and Travis wanted to use any time up to then talking with Sergeant Platt and perhaps the Missouri Highway Water Patrol Unit Commander to make certain that all applicable procedures were followed.

After Lieutenant Holcomb returned from Alison's house she went over everything with Travis that she did there to be as certain as she could be that Emily and her sister would remain safe until whoever was a threat to her was captured.

"I went with Alison through every room on every floor in her house and checked that the doors and windows were all locked. We made sleeping arrangements for Emily and her sister to be in a bedroom that is next to Alison's. We arranged for the deputy who has volunteered for this duty assignment, to perform twenty-four, seven-day guard duty, to sleep on the sofa bed in the living room."

Travis' mind struggled to give full attention to Honey's report but thoughts of everything else that depended on decisions he had to make… and make soon, were giving intense competition.

"You said you got a uniform to volunteer for the 24/7 duty assignment?" he asked as much to show Honey he was listening to her as for any other reason.

"OH? Um. Yes," Honey responded realizing that Travis might not find the same logic she did in making this selection. "Turned out that Alison has been dating a deputy for some time now… and he was quite happy to volunteer after she asked him."

Travis looked at Honey and could see that she wanted to tell him more but was hesitating for whatever reason he could not guess.

"Honey," he said softly. "Just tell me his name."

"Well, you see it's the same man that was guarding the house, Emily's house, this morning when……"

"Are you telling me that Alison has been dating Owen Horner, Deputy Owen Horner… and you knew that and… didn't tell me until now?"

"Well yes, I did know that, at least I knew that this morning when Alison got him to volunteer," Honey said. "I'm sure that he is capable… and just who else would be more certain to give it his all?"

Travis sighed and then pulled her closer into his arms.

"Baby, for the record I do not agree," he said. "But, with all that I must do… and be involved in right now, I know what makes the most sense is to just trust you. And that is all I need now to approve your choices."

Honey, still in his embrace, looked up just as he finished talking, and kissed him.

"For the record," she said mimicking him, "I trust you too. So, why don't you sit back for a minute, gather your thoughts, I will order the pizza, and while we eat supper you can fill me in on everything."

Travis gave Honey a good squeeze and then suggested he could summarize what had occurred for her even before she ordered their dinner.

"Well, to begin with," he began. Three of our Task Force members were central components of separate police actions that took place today."

Travis then recounted their involvements.

"Ernie Mize managed to discover a connection that was either unknown… or missed, that Frankie Valenti had more direct involvement with certain people and connections that eventually resulted in the two murders."

"Ernie did that?" Honey said looking quite impressed.

"Arnie Platt managed to chase the three gunmen out of their hiding place at Plyman's Point and then coordinated their subsequent capture while saving one of their lives," Travis continued.

"Arnie saved one of their lives?" Honey sounded equally impressed.

"And Sergeant Ben Hodges assisted Sergeant Platt in the roundup of the Abdou foursome and coordinated the steps that had to be taken during their retention to keep them from making any contact on the outside or with each other."

While Honey took a time-out to order the pizza, Travis's mind returned to the other pressing needs he had.

There were other links in the chain of proper police investigative work that needed his attention. The driver of the Dodge Charger, Piles Beck, had escaped from the area during the confusion that surrounded his involvement there. Travis needed to put someone from his Task Force in charge of finding him… soon!

The fact that Beck was driving the type of vehicle that was reported connected to the break-in at Emily's house concerned the C.I.D. captain. The presumption had to be that it's the same person who wanted to do harm to Emily, and is, at present, on the loose, capable of making another try at her.

Discussing these concerns while sharing the pizza that she ordered, Honey alerted Travis to another thread in their investigation of the break-in that was receiving no attention yet.

"Deputy Horner was guarding Emily's house and when he reported the break-in, he said that there were two cars involved," Honey remembered. "We believe that the lead car was driven by this fellow, Piles Beck. But who do you think was driving the second car… it was reported to be a black Lexus?"

Travis just shook his head. "I have no idea," he responded. "I suppose it had to be someone in cahoots with Piles Beck but, on the other hand, when Beck crashed the Dodge Challenger, whoever it was did not stick around to give him any help."

"No, instead he had some reason to not stick around. He had something in his car that if discovered by police would be serious trouble for him."

Travis took the last piece of the pizza and began wiping his hands with the paper towels that Honey brought back to his desk when their dinner arrived.

"Honey, could you stay on top of this angle… I think it's important that we find the driver of that second car," he asked.

The intercom buzzed and clicking it to on Travis heard the voice of Sheriff Lambert.

"Travis, Horace Haywood has arrived and is in my office… so light a firecracker and stick it somewhere that can speed your ass along through the hallways and into my office, okay?"

Travis laughed and looking over at Honey clicked back on to say he was on his way.

When he arrived at Lambert's office Travis was greeted by the Homeland Security Chief, Horace Haywood who was already seated across from the sheriff. They were engaged in a hushed conversation as their voices were both barely above a whisper.

"Come on in, Travis," the sheriff said regaining his normal way of speaking. "And close that door before finding a seat."

The sheriff suggested that Horace Haywood start over again with what he had been telling him before Travis arrived.

"Well, as it turned out, that little episode this morning over at Plyman's Point that I feared was going to either blow up our surveillance strategies or at the very least put a severe kink in them, was quite a good break for us."

Travis looked first at the sheriff and then back at Haywood.

"I'm thinking that your agents did more than plant some listening bugs while we were holding Mr. Abdou and friends?"

Horace Haywood smiled. "Your guess is right on the mark. We were able to find, and using Minox miniature cameras, photograph letters and documents that should prove invaluable to us."

"And you had enough time to put everything back where you found it so Abdou might think his mission, as he called it, is still a secret," the sheriff added looking over at Haywood.

"That's right," Haywood confirmed. "But the reason that I am sharing this information with you and the sheriff is because those three escapees who fled from the camp via boat, and whom you have secured now in their own little prison cells, had just completed training to become domestic terrorists. We think they were scheduled to depart from their training site at Plyman's Point this very morning."

Travis looked pleased but his face revealed the confusion that accompanied the news that his deputies had just captured three terrorists.

"Since we've had Abdou and the others here all day I suppose they do not know yet what happened to their students, right?"

Horace Haywood smiled again. "Maybe, that's all that I can say," he said. "When they get back to Plyman's Point and find the… uh, students as you have just referred to them, gone they will make contact… or try to contact them. Of course, that won't happen now but with the listening devices that we left there we hope that we can capture the contact information and techniques they use for that purpose.

The sheriff pushed back his chair from the desk and stood up and stretched. "It's been quite a long day, boys… a bit too long for this fifty-six-year-old stud."

Travis took the hint that his presence was no longer needed there and also rose to leave.

"I trust you understand that this is all Homeland Security hush-hush stuff, at least for now," Haywood said while extending a handshake to Travis. "It's just you, and the sheriff that are in on it… and until I say otherwise let's hold true to that promise."

Travis understood the importance of maintaining complete secrecy. As he left the two men by themselves, he walked out with one thought concerning what he had just heard. How was he going to manage to avoid the efforts of Honey Holcomb later that night when her curiosity was going to be at its peak?

40

A pickle, a peck.
So, where is Piles Beck!

Sunday, September 8th, 7:00 A.M.

S ANDRA STEVENS WAS ALWAYS the first employee on the shift to ring in at her job as a Security Guard at Ozark Valley Nature Park. This month her schedule called to report for work at 8:00 A.M. Since the drive from her home in Springfield often took up to three quarters of an hour, she always began the trip around six thirty allowing an extra thirty to forty minutes for unexpected delays that might otherwise cause her to be late.

Going to her locker Sandra passed the Video room where along the north wall eight monitors captured the view of all activities at the Fly-Fishing School and the trails used for walking, biking, Segways, and open-air trams. She was surprised that she did not see either Simon Pfarr or Norb Wilson staffing this post.

During her shift on days there were always two security personnel assigned to the Video Room, but she suspected that since the park was closed at night, they had less reasons to pay that kind of strict attention to the monitors. She entered the room expecting that the other bank of monitors along the west wall was where she would find at least one of them.

Once again, that section where eight more monitors provided viewing at the Ozark Valley Nature Park Entrance; Wilderness Chapel; the Valley Café; and the waterfalls was unattended. Sandra was concerned by this breach in procedures but was not yet worried that the night guards might have experienced any problems. Nothing along that line ever happened at Ozark Valley, especially at night when they were closed to the public.

She finished at her locker preparing herself for work and then sneaked another peek inside the guards Video Monitors Room before heading for the Valley Cafe where she always spent her early time before her assignment on the Day Shift started.

Marie Delmar was just finishing making coffee when Sandra walked inside.

"You want some coffee you are going to have to wait over there with the boys this morning," she told Sandra after greeting her. "With all the news and everything I am just running behind on my schedule."

"Oh, that's alright Marie," I'm a bit earlier myself this morning," she replied. "You mentioned seeing the boys?"

Marie kept getting the preparations for the breakfast menu out for the cook but took time to point over to where the customer tables were. Sandra looked where she pointed to and saw the two Night Security Guards who were sitting at a table engrossed in something happening on the television.

Sandra greeted the men when she approached nearer to where they were sitting but received only a quick look back at her from Simon.

"Yō, Sandra," he said while turning quickly back to the television set mounted on the wall above the double rack holding selections of Trail Maps and pamphlets for Fly Fishing School, Segway and Open-Air Tram schedules.

The television had on the news showing various officials discussing the police activities that took place on Table Rock Lake and along State Road 86 on Saturday. Just as Sandra sat down at the table with the two Security Guards, she saw a photo of someone that must have been taken when he was being arrested somewhere.

Underneath the photo she saw that his name was Charles Beck. The TV reporter said that Beck totaled his Dodge Charger sometime after midnight on 86 and Trace Hollow Road and then abandoned the wrecked vehicle and is suspected of attempting to steal at least two cars that belonged to residents on Trellis Drive.

A Stone County detective who asked that his name not be used said that police have determined that the wanted man, Beck, then stole a small Crestliner from the private boat dock at Plyman's Point and escaped from the police by heading towards an area where Table Rock Lakes narrows to just small creek size before crossing under State 86 at the entrance to Ozark Valley.

"We suspect that Beck may have then contacted an accomplice to pick him up near that location," the police detective said.

Sandra turned to the two Night Security guards sitting with her.

"Did you both hear what I think I just heard?" she asked. "That fugitive might have used the creeks that feed from Ozark Valley into Table Rock Lake and if that is true then he just as well could have used that creek that flows under 86 to find his way into our Park?" Her speech was faster than usual and was filled with excitement.

Simon looked first to see what Norb's reaction was, deferring to his higher seniority rank.

Norb's expression revealed his surprised reaction to Sandra's speculations.

"Look," he began, hoping to sound more convincing to them than he felt himself. "If he had come in here one of us would have known about it. We do have cameras everywhere. If someone were in here last night or early this morning, I am sure we would have been able to see them on one of our monitors."

"That's right," Simon added. "No way could he have got in here."

"Yes, I'm sure that you both should have been able to see them," Sandra sighed, unable to fully disguise her doubts. She left them at the table watching the news.

After clocking in to begin her shift Sandra asked her supervisor to be assigned to the video room. This was usually the least requested assignment unless there was threatening weather, and her request was swiftly approved. Once inside the room Sandra moved to the Review Monitor and set the time she wished to begin her search for Saturday, eight P.M., the time the Nature Park closed.

41

A mere dream or...?

September 8th, 9:00 A.M.

IT WAS JUST ALL THE EXCITEMENT of going into hiding, Elizabeth thought, or her sister's restless night reflected the intense anxiety she must have felt hearing from Deputy Horner that the person suspected of the break-in was on the loose. Neither of the sisters had been able to fall asleep when they initially went to bed.

Elizabeth awoke first on Sunday morning and was already finished using the guest bathroom when Emily finally stirred from her nightmare filled sleep.

Sitting in front of the large mirror opposite from where the bed they shared was located, Elizabeth continued brushing her hair.

"Time to get up, sleepy head," she laughed recalling how their mother roused them on school days when they were kids.

"It can't be," Emily complained. "I feel like I just fell asleep a few minutes ago."

"Well, you had quite a night tossing around dreaming about some strangeness with your Ex and a missing cashier's check."

Emily sat up being reminded of her dream and covered her face with both hands.

"You mean I was talking in my sleep?" she asked.

"You were not only talking," Elizabeth answered. "You also seemed like you wanted to run somewhere. Don't you remember waking up screaming?"

"I was screaming?"

"Loud enough that brought our host Alison in here and even Deputy Owen from downstairs."

Slowly the memory of her dream returned and her whole body began to tremble as it must have done when something happened that prompted the screaming that her sister mentioned.

Elizabeth put aside the hair brushing and rushed to comfort her sister.

"Will it help you to try to remember what was happening in your dream and just talk about it?" she asked while attempting to comfort Emily.

The details of her dream were still mostly hidden from her. She saw Mickey and she believed someone else and they were in a kitchen and then she had to run somewhere. But where? Why was she so terrified?

Emily told these remnants of her dream to Elizabeth and to Alison who came into their bedroom to see about breakfast plans.

"Yes, you were quite frightened," Alison confirmed. "It took some effort by your sister to calm you enough that you could go back to sleep."

"I remember thinking that the police would start looking for me and that I had to run... to hide from... No, wait!" Emily's dream was becoming more lucid, more real, and more threatening.

The two other women in the room could see that Emily's mind was now engaged only in the events of her dream and the reliving of it was both frightening and painful.

"Mickey and... someone were fighting and I... I saw something in Mickey's hand, and it was swinging up and down. And I heard a noise... then Mickey fell. or was pushed and hurt his head, I think, ... blood coming out. I needed to run... It was all my fault...???"

Emily began weeping uncontrollably and collapsed into Elizabeth's embrace.

* * *

Saturday was a long day for both Travis and Honey, and they were not able to leave work until close to 10:00 P.M. Because of that they decided that a full night's sleep took priority over spending the night together and each went to their separate homes.

When Honey arrived the next morning, she saw Travis inside the office with Sheriff Lambert.

"Did you catch the time when Captain Holden showed up today?" she asked Mack who was just ringing out.

"That's not in my job description," he laughed. "Good thing, too, or most of you detectives who aren't required to use time-cards to report your work hours might find your paychecks a bit on the smaller side."

"Come on, Mack" Honey laughed. "I am certain that you know we put in far more time than most people suspect we do. But did you catch what it was about that the sheriff wanted to see him this early?"

"Well let's see," Mack began. "It could have concerned that the news this morning is all about what they called 'the raid' by Stone County Police over at Plyman's Point yesterday."

"Oh?" Honey looked surprised. "I have not had either the TV or radio on yet this morning. "They called it a... raid?" Honey needed to take a deep breath knowing that what happened was anything but a raid. She knew immediately how that description would sit with the sheriff, and recalled how his political enemies were consistently trying to reference him in their speeches and campaign literature as "Cole Lambert, the Bully Sheriff of Stone County".

She hoped that Mack could stay around a bit longer and fill her in on what else the news reports may be saying when her cell phone indicated an incoming call from Alison Monroe.

Honey took the call immediately fearing some trouble had or was happening where they were guarding Emily Paladino and her sister. She was relieved to discover that the call was only about a dream, or a nightmare as Alison described it, that Emily had during the previous night and early morning.

With everything going on now, Honey grew impatient with Alison's insistence that she hear all about the strange dream. She suspected that Alison was doing what she could to fill this guarding Emily assignment with as much importance as she could give it.

But when Alison told her how Emily said the dream was as real as anything she ever dreamt before and that it was about her husband Mickey fighting over some weapon with another person that Honey decided to give this conversation her full attention.

While Alison continued to report Emily's dream Honey's mind flashed back to the Branson Police report of their investigation in Mickey Paladino's homicide. He died from a gunshot to his head. There were no witnesses. His death occurred the day following the discovery of Kylie Cooper, his girlfriend, who was found deceased in an abandoned rowboat near the Baxter Boat Dock.

As was the usual practice the Branson Police Department released only preliminary information to the press concerning the homicide of Mickey Paladino. Although their release mentioned he sustained a gun shot in his head as the cause of death, there was no mention of where his body was discovered.

When Honey heard Alison's report of the dream, she was startled hearing that Emily thought she saw Mickey with someone else in the kitchen. That was in fact where the body of Mickey Paladino was found.

Honey scribbled down some of what she heard from Alison and underlined the kitchen, the arms swings, the someone else, and the fear that Emily worried that she would be sought out by the police.

Perhaps the dream was one of those that defy conscious logic to understand where they originate from or what connection they might have with some part of a reality that was experienced. "A lot of people have weird dreams," Honey told Alison. But were these dreams… or memories returning after being driven deep inside some hidden part of Emily's mind?

"I need to discuss this with Emily," Lieutenant Holcomb told Alison before ending the phone conversation. "I'll call you when I know more about some other things going on today and let you know when to expect me. But until I can get there do not encourage her to tell you anything more about that dream."

Alison seemed a little put off by that instruction.

"But what if Emily feels like talking more about it to me… or to her sister like she did this morning?"

"If that happens, try to explain to her that you have told me about the dream and that since I will visit with her later today it would be better if she merely writes down some notes about anything more that she remembers…"

After they each hung up Honey pictured Alison running back to Emily hoping to engage her in further discussions of that dream. It would not be either helpful or damaging to the investigation. However, Honey felt it was imperative that she interview Emily before either she or her sister Elizabeth decided to discuss the dream first with her attorney, Tomas Cullerton.

"There could be parts of Emily's lost memories that reveal more than her attorney would advise being awakened," Honey thought to herself.

42

Spotted

Sunday, September 8th, 9:30 A.M.

ACTING ON HER SUSPICION THAT the fugitive being sought by the police could have ended up inside the Ozark Valley Nature Park, Sandra Stevens went immediately to work at the Video Review monitor to see if she might be able to if it were true.

She began the search timed for when the Park closed on Saturday night. Earlier she heard on the television news report of the incident that the man stole a boat from a private slip at Plyman's Point and was observed heading in a direction that may have offered an escape route along the narrow creeks that feed into Table Rock Lake from within Ozark Valley.

She focused on video searches that showed the entrance off State Highway 86 knowing that it was at that point that the water ran under the highway into the lake eventually. The two Night Security Guards, Simon Pfarr and Norb Wilson stopped by before signing to go off duty and wished her luck on what Norb referred to her 'fishing expedition.'

An hour had passed and the excitement that Sandra felt beginning her search was waning fast. The occasional spotting of a raccoon and later a skunk did nothing to impress upon Sandra any confidence that she would discover the object of her search sneaking inside the park.

Then suddenly, there was movement along the tree line between the entrance and the Gift Shop. Sandra was not at first sure that it was not another nocturnal animal. But what she was now watching moved in an upright manner and when it began walking faster out of the trees Sandra was certain it was indeed a human being.

"Oh my God," she exclaimed loud enough to draw the attention of another employee who was just outside of the Video Room.

"What is it?" he shouted as he ran inside to be of whatever assistance that was needed. "Sandra... What in the world..."

Sandra pulled her co-worker closer and pointed to the image now appearing like he was preparing to open a window at the rear of the Gift Shop. Her eyes moved quickly to the time reader at the upper corner of the video. It read... 2130 hours.

"The fugitive who the police are looking for was here... right there at the Gift Shop... at 9:30 P.M. last night," Sandra exclaimed. The joy that rewarded her for first suspecting this result was swiftly overtaken by a mounting fear as she realized the possibility that the person was still in the park... perhaps, remarkably close to where she sat watching the monitors.

*   *   *

The Patrol Unit at the Stone County Sheriff's Office was headed up by Captain Holland Wolf, a thirty-year veteran on the force. As he came up through the ranks during various stages of his career, he willingly worked the most difficult assignments and the least desired schedules, all so that he would stand out and be in an advantageous position for each opportunity that came along for a promotion. After finally reaching the highest rank in the Patrol Unit as Captain, the only reward that he allowed himself, insisted upon for himself, was having every Sunday off.

"Today is Sunday," he said to Lieutenant Ernie Mize while they visited over some coffee. "So, why am I here?"

"I'll bite," Ernie responded as he looked up from the morning newspaper.

"I'm here because every other department borrows from mine each and every time they are short compliment."

Ernie returned to the newspaper but to show he was still listening grunted "uh huh."

"So now my Patrol Unit, which should have four sergeants and nineteen healthy, willing, patrol police officers have so many on loan to either your COMET Section or detailed to Administration or serving court papers to persons being evicted and stuff like that. I lost one of my Patrol deputies to a Special Assignment for Witness Protection for a woman connected to those recent murders. Then there are those three others who are unavailable for duty because of calling in sick or just plain not available because of injuries sustained while on duty. Hey! Are you even listening to me, Ernie?

Ernie was only half listening to Captain Wolf's complaints about how being shorthanded meant that he had to give up his usual Sunday off. Years ago, when they both worked in Patrol, Holland Wolf found so many things to fuel his anger and bitch about that people stopped calling him by his first name, Holland, and changed that to Howling... Howling Wolf.

"The Wolf is howling today" was the old joke.

Their conversation was abruptly interrupted by the Dispatcher who was heard paging Captain Wolf to advise appropriate action in response to a 9-1-1 call.

"Well, what is it now?" Captain Wolf asked.

The Dispatcher told him they just received a call from a supervisor at Ozark Valley that the fugitive that escaped from Plyman's Point yesterday has been identified on their video surveillance reviews and they believe he is presently hiding somewhere on site there.

Captain Wolf looked over at Lieutenant Mize and smiled.

"Well, now there is a good reason that fate arranged for me to come to work today… Sunday!"

Captain Wolf instructed the Dispatcher to put a call out to all units in the vicinity of Ozark Valley on State Highway 86 to head over there, Code 3.

After strapping the holster carrying his Glock 19 pistol around his waist, he began walking towards the motor pool.

"Ernie, if you want something to help keep you busy today, why not ride along with me over to Ozark Valley," he offered. "Good chance we are going to find us a real live fugitive today."

Lieutenant Mize was more than eager to ride along with the man who was his partner for his first five years on the force.

"Of course I will come along," he said. "Someone has to protect you when you go after the bad guys."

They reached Captain Wolf's car before Ernie stopped abruptly.

"Holland, I had to come in today because the sheriff wants me to find the driver of the black Lexus that was chasing the guy that totaled the Dodge Charger Saturday. I was able to get the identity off the plates on the Dodge and won some brownie points with the sheriff. Now, where do you suggest I look to get help about the Lexus driver?"

Captain Wolf was already inside the car and looked over at Ernie who had opened the passenger side door but was only leaning in while he asked his question.

"Come on, Ernie" Wolf urged. "Time is a-wasting, and our little lost fugitive needs our best efforts to bring him out of his hiding place. If those two idiots drove across Kimberling Bridge while they chased each other on highway 13, I am quite sure I will have what you need when we finish this business over at Ozark Valley."

247

43

A taste of Honey

Sunday, September 8th, 10:00 A.M.

FRANKIE VALENTI WAS NOT SURPRISED when two burley Stone County police officers showed up at his front door. However, being that it was Sunday morning when he figured cops worked only writing speeding tickets or clearing accidents off the highways, it did fall under the description of being unexpected.

His earlier interrogation was conducted by "the babe", as he secretly rated Lieutenant Honey Holcomb, and it went pretty well. He held his own until she pulled out the "I can play tough card" and pushed him to give up his old boss's identity as the person who arranged for surprising Emily where he could take Mickey to be alone with her despite the Order of Protection that had restricted such a meeting.

While that put Frankie in a tough-to-explain situation as being the last known person to be with Emily before she became a "Missing Person" for the next ten days, Frankie didn't carry any feelings of betrayal.

"What trouble could it cause his old boss," he wondered thinking about it later after Lieutenant Holcomb released him. "Mickey was beyond having any more legal problems by that time. He was dead!"

For some reason today seemed like it was going to be much tougher, he thought while waiting inside the same interrogation room he was in the last time he was brought in to answer questions. Nonetheless, he felt a bit more at ease when Lieutenant Holcomb came into the room. For whatever reason, a feeling of familiarity existed now.

Lieutenant Holcomb was with a uniformed deputy when she entered and as he moved to stand a few feet away, closer to the door, she placed a thick file on the table and pulled out the chair opposite from where Valenti was seated.

"So," she began. "We meet again."

Frankie just looked at her. An urge to wisecrack about how he thought they would have more fun if their meeting was at Mickey Flynn's bar in Branson while they each downed shots of Jack instead of this tiny, staid room that was barely bigger than his bathroom, was held in check.

"The lieutenant is one sexy chick," he thought to himself. "But somehow I am certain that she's fixing to fuck me… and not in any of my preferred ways."

"Frankie, you were almost cooperating with us that last time we had a conversation"

"Almost?"

"You told me how Mickey used you to trick his wife into listening to him and how he then frightened her so severely she went on our Missing Persons list for the next seven days."

"I don't remember the part about him frightening her…"

Honey smiled. She kept her gaze directly on Frankie's eyes as she opened the file in front of her and pulled out the top sheet.

"It seems that remembering everything is something you find quite difficult."

Valenti tried to peek at the words across the sheet that Honey had placed down on the table. Just a word here on top and then another four or five lines down farther on the paper was all he could make out, but nothing that offered a clue regarding what she had discovered since their last session.

"Frankie, I hope you have not made any plans for the rest of today because I am going to spend most of that time finding a way to help you remember everything you know."

"Everything I know about what?"

"Well, we will start with the part you did remember well enough to talk to me about last time. You and Emily in Cassville and Mickey in the back seat of your car, a Chevrolet Traverse… if memory serves me."

Honey paused, giving Valenti a few extra seconds to catch the nuance she could not resist expressing when she mentioned her memory and how it serves her.

"When you followed them to Kylie's house at Indian Point, how long were you there?"

"Lieutenant," Frankie answered trying his utmost to appear sincere. "I was hardly inside with them at all, maybe just to fetch myself a beer or use the powder room."

"Frankie, Frankie, Frankie," Honey sighed. "We know that you were involved in helping Mickey and Emily as they were struggling with various schemes to avoid the Chicago mob from foreclosing on those loans that we also know you arranged to be made to Mickey."

"How did you find out… I mean, who told you that line of bullshit?"

Honey sat back in her chair, looking stern.

"I'll tell you what bullshit is, Frankie," she said. "You are thinking that you can spread your brand of it right now is how

I would define that expression."

Frankie felt a sinking feeling. The sexy lieutenant was beginning to act more like a Doberman than a debutante.

"Okay… okay," he stammered. "I'll play ball. Just tell me what you want me to tell you so I can get out of here sometime today."

Honey pushed back her chair and stood looking down at her weakened prey.

"You can just forget about going somewhere today other than the cell I have prepared for you at County Jail."

Frankie was shocked and his expression failed to hide his depressed demeanor.

"I said I will cooperate," he pleaded.

"Okay," Honey began while returning to her seat. "Tell me all you know about the week that Mickey, Kylie, and Emily spent on the houseboat. Tell me what drugs you brought along with the supplies to them, TWICE… Tell me how Kylie died when she consumed the drugs YOU brought to them. Tell me who put her body in the abandoned rowboat. And then tell me what happened when you and Mickey and Emily went to Kylie's home at Indian Point on the day Mickey was shot and killed."

Frankie sat dumfounded. How this woman detective knew all about… all about everything… was scary.

"Oh," Honey resumed after pausing long enough to determine that her strategy of throwing all of her questions simultaneously was working. "And then try and convince me how wrong it will be when I bring charges of murder your way." It was the Shock and Destroy method that she learned at Missouri Southern State University in courses that her boss, Sheriff Lambert, designed years earlier. Frankie looked away trying to recover some of the fragile sense of self-confidence that had slipped completely into his shoes, hearing those charges of murder appear to be imminent.

* * *

Lieutenant Holcomb was surprised by all the excitement at the Dispatcher's desk when she stepped out of the interrogation room where she left Frankie Valenti. But wanting to update Travis on the interrogation she had just completed, she went looking for him.

"I did hit some pay dirt questioning Valenti," she said after finding her boss in his office. "Among other pieces of news, he mentioned some involvement by the realtor, Armand Locke, on the same day Mickey Paladino was shot."

"Did he explain what it was that brought Locke into the picture," Travis asked showing more than casual interest.

"Just that he saw him arriving at Kylie's house and that he thought it was because of something related to a phone call Mickey made to him while everybody was hiding out at her house."

"But Valenti didn't say if Locke was at one time on the houseboat?"

Honey nodded a negative response. "He could not say for sure on that point as he was only there himself when he brought the supplies out to them. And to answer your follow-up question before you even ask it, he admitted that he included all the drugs he could gather up with the supplies he delivered."

"Say where he got them and what types?" Travis asked.

"Just that Mickey gave him the keys to Kylie's house when he dropped off the supplies the first time. He just assumed that she must have agreed because Mickey knew exactly where the drugs were hidden there."

Even from his office where Honey and Travis were going over what she learned questioning Frankie Valenti they could hear the dispatcher's communications with patrol units approaching Ozark Valley."

Honey paused her review to inquire what was happening with all the excitement about the units hurrying to that location.

"It seems that Beck... or at least someone who might be Beck, was observed close to the park's entrance after they had closed after a video review of the night shift's activities by a security guard. She alerted her supervisor who called it in on 9-1-1. I know that Captain Wolf took over and he is currently engaged in a search of the park but has not reported any sign of our fugitive there yet."

Honey saw some of the old excitement returning to Travis's expression as he described the possibility of locating the man who escaped from Plyman's Point the day before.

"Long hours, desk work doing analysis, that doesn't get your juices cooking, does it?" she teased. "How about you and I take a ride with the sirens screaming down to Ozark Valley and see if we can't catch Mr. Beck before old Howling Wolf gets the bragging rights?"

Travis got up from his chair so fast that Honey thought he was planning on doing just what she mentioned.

"Babe," he said while squeezing her close to him. "You know me like a book, and for sure that is just what I am inclined to do. But I have an update meeting with the sheriff in less than an hour and I have already arranged with Alison to let Emily know I will be over there to see her this afternoon."

Honey looked disappointed. "I thought that I would be the person to question Emily about her nightmare…"

Travis released his arms from around her and returned to his desk.

"I'm sure that you would do an excellent job with that part of the interrogation… finding out which was dream and which was memory. But, since I was the detective that questioned her when she brought along Tomas Cullerton, her lawyer, it is best that I resume in that role."

Seeing that his explanation was found only partly satisfying he returned to the Ozark Valley situation.

"Why don't you hustle over there and take on that challenge of finding Beck before anyone else does?" he suggested.

Honey paused before leaving the office only long enough to respond.

"I think I will do just that, Mon Capitan," she laughed acknowledging that his superior rank afforded him the right to make the decision.

44

Ozark Valley

Sunday, September 8th, 11:00 A.M.

WHILE TRAVIS WAS DISCUSSING WITH Sheriff Lambert the various strategies in the investigations that his C.I.D., unit had working in the two murders cases he realized that it all was spreading out in tangents, all coming closer to conclusions at much the same time.

"The two deceased, Kylie Cooper and Mickey Paladino were connected via their relationship as lovers," Travis said. "We've assigned Ernie Mize to gather as much information that he could on their activities that led to the divorce proceedings with his wife, Emily."

"And you have discovered now that the two victims were connected with a handful of others, right?" Lambert added.

"That is right. Emily worked for My Missouri Homes Real Estate where the manager was Armand Locke. We do not know yet what he was doing at Kylie's house at Indian Point other than what Lieutenant Holcomb learned this morning questioning Frankie Valenti."

Sheriff Lambert was drawing a diagram while they reviewed the status of the investigation. On the top were two boxes with the names Cooper and Paladino, with arrows linking them. Under those he drew a line to the name, Valenti, which was in a box that was connected to another box to the side of it in which he printed the name, Armand Locke.

While they reviewed each item that had been discovered up to the present time, the sheriff's graph had additional lines drawn connecting Jari Abdou to the victims and to both the houseboat and to Kylie's home at Indian Point. Another line drawn downward from Paladino's name went to a box with the names of Beck and Paladino. Beck's name had an additional line connected to Valenti's.

Before they finished their review the sheriff listed the business locations that were related to the investigation: Ozark Lakes Leisure Boats; Mickey Flynn's restaurants; Worldwide Lake Boat Sales; Plyman's Point; Central States Bar Management; Westside Sportsman's Club, My Missouri Homes Real Estate; Metropolitan Life Insurance; and Southwest Missouri Homeland Security.

Each individual and business location shown on the graph had a number attached to it which served as a code showing which detective in the C.I.D. unit was the lead investigator. While many that were coded this way showed either Captain Travis Holden or Lieutenant Honey Holcomb, the box with the words Homeland Security was marked, "Sheriff Bull Lambert."

As he prepared to leave and return to his office in the C.I.D. unit Travis remembered that they were holding Frankie Valenti without yet bringing any criminal charges.

"You think we have enough yet on Valenti to run it past the District Attorney?" he asked the sheriff.

Bull Lambert gave that some extra thought.

"We might," he agreed. "But we now know that he was Beck's cell mate and that they knew each other well enough for Valenti to arrange that loan to Paladino from Beck's bosses. Let us see if we can use Valenti like a piece of cheese and set a trap to catch a rat. We might find out that they reconnect when Beck is on the loose. Let him out and have surveillance arranged. Make sure we put on someone who we are confident will not lose him.

* * *

By the time Captain Holland Wolf and his passenger Lieutenant Ernie Mize drove through the entrance to Ozark Valley they observed two empty Stone County Sheriff's patrol cars parked on each side of the roadway outside the front gate. One of the deputies was just then exiting the nearby Gift House and signaled to get Wolf's attention.

"We got here fifteen minutes ago," the deputy said, "and their security guards took us right in to see the video."

"So… tell us what you've seen," Ernie demanded.

"Well, there was someone who broke in after closing hours yesterday… they close at 8:00 P.M.… and just like they reported when they called the station, he did walk around inside the park like he was looking for something… and that was for about ten minutes or so and since then nothing."

"Nothing?"

"Yeah, right," the deputy said. "They have gone all through the videos while waiting for us and say they could not find any more signs of him."

"They never saw him leave?" Ernie asked. "Is this the only way out of the park?" he continued without waiting for a reply to his first question.

The deputy raised forward both hands indicating what he just told them was all he knew. "The female security guard says she thinks he is probably still hiding somewhere inside the park."

They were joined by two people that just walked out of the

office along with the other Stone County deputy who greeted Captain Wolf and introduced the others as the Manager of the Nature Park and his Chief of Security.

"We are expecting a larger attendance than usual today," Paul Wooley said, identifying himself as the Manager while extending a handshake to Wolf and Lieutenant Mize. "Hopefully, the prowler is not your fugitive and was only someone looking for some food or a forgotten purse or something."

"You think…?" Mize asked giving his question more of a pejorative tone.

"What Mr. Wooley means," the still nameless security chief said, "is that if the police continue to suspect that the prowler is whom they've been looking for we would hope that the Park can remain open during the period they would be searching for him."

"That is something I will determine after we get on with our search," Captain Wolf said.

"Yes, of course," Wooley said sounding conciliatory. "We will cooperate wherever you feel we can be helpful."

By then they had all walked inside the Park Administration cabin where they were led to the wall size map of the Nature Park.

"So, where would that man seen by your security cameras have likely gone?" Captain Wolf asked the Security Chief.

"Well, we have these cameras located throughout the entire park so that we can be on the lookout for anyone getting injured, or lost children, or…"

Trying to hurry along making the decision to determine if a search of the park was still necessary, Lieutenant Mize stepped around Captain Wolf and went closer to the large map.

"Just how big is this place?" he asked. "How many places could someone hide and not be likely seen by the security cameras?"

Paul Wooley sensed that Lieutenant Mize expressed some reluctance to conduct a full-blown search that might require closing the Nature Park.

"Lieutenant, our Nature Park has over ten thousand acres, much of it still as raw and wild as it has been for centuries. There are trails that are used for biking, walking, open air tram rides, et cetera that measure in distance some ten and a half miles roundtrip,"

"I wasn't meaning for you to give us a tour," Mize snapped. "Just suggest where we might begin our search, likely hiding places that could avoid security cameras."

The Security Chief came to Wooley's rescue. "If he were or would go anywhere along the trails we should have seen that on our videos. The few places where there are no cameras are in the bathrooms, the Teepee, the Wilderness Chapel, or the cabins."

Captain Wolf looked back at the large map.

"You mentioned the cabins. Show me their locations, will you?"

"They are over here," The Chief said pointing to an area close to Big Bear Bridge. "But they are all closed… and locked securely right now as they are under renovation."

"I imagine a locked cabin might be difficult for an experienced car thief and ex-convict to break into, right Captain?" Ernie mentioned, again with much implied mockery.

After another series of questions about other locations and being shown how to find them, Captain Wolf decided.

"I want you to sit inside that Security Video room with one of their guards," he said pointing at the closest deputy. "And you can get some much-needed exercise by checking the bathrooms, the chapel, and the Tee Pee," he instructed the remaining deputy.

Captain Wolf then looked at Paul Wooley and his Security Chief.

"I will let you two, and however many of your security staff you have available, get over to those cabins and check them inside and outside. If you see anything suspicious when you get to the cabin, if it appears like they have been broken into, call the deputies here. They can determine if additional police help should be requested before going inside."

Feeling confident that there was no justification for closing the park to the public, and that the minimal search needs have been ordered, Captain Wolf motioned for Lieutenant Mize to head back to their car.

"You don't think that Beck has crawled in a hole inside the park?" Ernie asked as they drove out onto State highway 86.

"Shit, Ernie," Wolf laughed. "There is no way that Beck is the guy that showed up on video after they were closed. For one thing, he did steal a boat, and no one mentioned seeing one of those on video... or anywhere else."

"Yeah. But..." Ernie stuttered.

"There's no buts about that Ernie," Wolf interrupted. "I am not going to spend another minute of... by all rights, my Sunday off, on that wild goose chase."

As they waited for traffic to allow them to turn at the intersection to highway 13 Ernie spotted a familiar car that turned on to highway 86 and sped past them.

"Well, I'll be your mother's uncle," Ernie laughed.

"My mother's... what??"

"You didn't see who just drove past headed for where we just came from?" Ernie asked. "That was pretty little Honey Holcomb... and I'll just bet that she thinks she will get there in time to catch our missing fugitive."

"Geez, Ernie, do you want to radio her that it's a zero on the search so she can just give it up and turn around?"

Ernie Mize said nothing as he pondered why she was sneaking into his part of the investigation.

"Why don't we just let her find out for herself what we already know," Ernie suggested. "I hope I am standing nearby when the sheriff asks her what she expected to accomplish since she had to know that you and your deputies oversaw the response to the 9-1-1 from Ozark Valley.

"Why you dirty dog," Wolf laughed as he pushed harder on the gas.

Ernie Mize liked Honey Holcomb… kind of, at least. Yes, it burned him when Travis moved her into his slot after he transferred him out of the Criminal Investigation Department over to the drug enforcement unit known as COMET. But that was between him and Travis Holden. As far as Honey was concerned, she always treated him with due respect.

While he wrestled with an urge to just turn the page and start treating her much nicer, he suddenly remembered a suggestion that Captain Wolf made back at the station.

"Hey Holland," he said looking over at the captain. "What did you have in mind back earlier when you suggested that you could help me on that assignment to find the other driver… the Lexus?"

Wolf said nothing for a few seconds as he struggled to recall what they were discussing when he made the offer.

"Oh yeah," he smiled. "Now I remember. You just told me about your assignment and wondered where to start looking for the identity of the Lexus. When we get back to my office come on inside it and I will hook you up to the little device we planted by the Kimberly Bridge to watch over things for us."

"The device…?"

"Right, it is an ANPR… or Automatic Number Plate Recognition. We have very few of these because the worrywarts that cry about privacy concerns fear that government tracking citizens is Orwellian… you know, the novel, 1984."

Ernie Mize sat confused by what he was listening to from Captain Wolf. For one thing, if there was such a device… and Stone County had them… why was it such a secret? Also, not much of a book enthusiast, he was at a loss about the term Orwellian, and even more in the dark about a novel known only as 1984.

"Okay… so you got this license plate reader thing," he said looking over at Holland Wolf. "Why is it that you… think…

Wait! You did say you put it on or by the Kimberling Bridge…
on highway 13… right?"

Wolf could not help himself and let out a hearty laugh.

"Ernie, old boy," he said. "Sometimes it takes a house to fall
on you before you see the light. But, to answer your question
more fully, this device can show us that fellow Beck when he
drove over the Kimberling Bridge last Saturday night and it
will identify the driver of the Lexus that followed him before
he crashed over on 86 and Trace Hollow Road."

* * *

As she turned on to State Highway 86 Honey saw some deer
preparing to cross up ahead. Rather than slowing her speed she
opted to step harder on the accelerator assuring that she would
pass the deer's location before it made a move to cross in front of
her. It occurred to her that slowing down might encourage the
deer's decision to bolt across the road and with oncoming traffic
going the speed limit, all kinds of bad results might happen.

She was surprised to learn after meeting with the Security
Chief at Ozark Valley that Captain Wolf and Lieutenant Mize
had already left.

"The Lieutenant said that it was most likely that the person
seen on the security videos was not the man that was being
sought," the chief said. "They had my staff check out the bathrooms and cabins and any places where we have no cameras but
now that we've done all that we agree that it either was not that
man or at least he's not here anymore."

Suddenly, they were interrupted by the sounds of a woman
screaming for help in the employee parking lot. The Security
Chief took off running in that direction with Lieutenant Holcomb
not far behind him.

"My car… it's been stolen!" Marie Delmar cried out. "Please. Find it… find the person who stole my Honda," she begged the Security Chief.

Honey quickly pulled out her badge informing Marie that she was a Stone County Sheriff's Police detective.

"When did you first learn that your car was not where you last parked it?" she asked.

"I just got out of work at the Café and walked over to where we are right now," she sobbed. "My car… a Honda. was gone. Someone has stolen my car!"

Honey took down a complete description of the 2010 Honda and called the dispatcher at the sheriff's office to alert all cars to be on the lookout for a car stolen from Ozark Valley off highway 86 between the hours of 7:00 A.M. and 12:00 noon.

"The stolen car is a white 2010 Honda Accord Crosstour with chrome door handles, moonroof, Missouri license plates, first three numbers 417. The car may have been stolen by Charles Beck who is wanted for questioning for Home Invasion, Boat theft, and other crimes. He is probably armed and must be considered dangerous."

Honey then began walking to the road leading into the Nature Park from state highway 86 and was soon accompanied by the Security Guard Sandra Stevens.

"If it was our suspect that you saw in the video I imagine he would have come along this route after ditching his boat," Honey explained.

"But, if he already had a boat, why would he not use it to escape?" Sandra asked.

"Could be a lot of reasons. One might be because he didn't know very much about driving a power boat; or he might have figured that with the boat being stolen from Plyman's Point that the Missouri Water Patrol would be on Table Rock Lake looking for him."

When they got to route 86 Honey asked Sandra if she might guess how Beck may have left Table Rock Lake and managed to end up in her midnight videos.

"Well, the stream that flows under 86 feeds into Little Indian Creek and eventually into Table Rock Lake from Ozark Valley," she said. "So, it's not like his boat was being pushed this direction."

They walked across the highway and then followed the narrow creek towards Table Rock Lake. When they arrived at Porter Hollow, the point where the creek widened Sandra noticed it first.

"There… pulled up over there," she said excitedly.

Honey's eyes followed the direction Sandra Pointed where she saw partially covered in the overgrowth, was the 14-foot Crestliner believed to be the one stolen from the boat slip at Plyman's Point.

Once again Honey called in, only this time to her boss, Captain Travis Holden.

"Travis, I guess you've heard already that it now looks like it was in fact our man Beck seen in the security videos," she said.

"Yes," he replied. "We have it out for all cars to be on the alert…"

"Well, one more thing," she added. "I think we have found his getaway boat… maybe a hundred yards off the lake and by the creek that I think he followed into the park."

"Good job, Honey," Travis said. "I'll send someone out there to check it out and make arrangements for what we want to do with it."

45

Emily's memory

Monday, September 9th, 7:00 A.M.

Elizabeth awoke and was surprised to discover Emily's bed already made indicating she had woken up much earlier. Putting on the robe she saw in the closet, Elizabeth went downstairs expecting to see Emily in the kitchen.

"Morning Elizabeth," Owen greeted her. "Hope you finally had a good night's sleep."

"I did, indeed," Elizabeth answered. "Even longer than Emily had."

"I know," he said. "I was awakened myself by her a half hour ago when she came downstairs and started the coffee."

"Oh? Is that where she is now… in the kitchen?"

Owen, who was standing by the patio door, motioned for Elizabeth to come closer to him.

"I have been watching her out there, by the garden. She is quite a bit on edge this morning and I thought I would just keep away and let her work it out, whatever it is that is troubling her."

Elizabeth could see what Deputy Horner was referring to as she watched Emily, now sitting on the garden bench, and looking off at the distant horizon. It may have been another dream, Elizabeth wondered, that woke her sister earlier. But whatever it was, Elizabeth decided that until Emily expressed a need for her to be with her, she would allow Emily this time alone.

After Elizabeth finished her normal morning routine, she returned downstairs to find Deputy Horner still standing guard at the patio door.

"She hasn't moved from that location on the garden bench," he said.

Elizabeth decided that it was time to see what help she might be and took a cup of coffee with her as she went out to join Emily.

"No, it wasn't another dream," Emily responded to Elizabeth's question. "I am afraid that my memory of that day has returned… when Mickey was killed…"

Emily began sobbing and turned to the hug offered by Elizabeth.

"It wasn't a dream?" Elizabeth asked. "Isn't it a good thing that your memory is returning?"

Emily pulled back and looked away from her sister.

"No. It is definitely NOT a good thing," she said still close to losing control. "I think that what happened to Mickey will be blamed on me… by the police… I remember being told that… and then hiding in Mickey's boat… Oh, Elizabeth… I might be sent to prison!"

Elizabeth comforted her sister again, hugging her close and not saying anything. She was feeling more certain now that it was another dream that her sister had that was causing all the upset that she was now experiencing.

"Emily, isn't it still possible that what you think you remember is something that comes from that nightmare you just had?"

Emily said nothing, wishing that if only it was a remnant of her nightmare could be true. After another few moments of silence, she turned back towards Elizabeth. "You recall that I told you that I was not only on the houseboat with Mickey and Kylie but that I was also working with them to figure out a way to deal with that loan Mickey got from… what turned out to be the Chicago mob."

"I do remember that's what you told Frances and me," she said. "But it seemed to us that you were confused about the part that you tried to help them. You were, like you told us then, high on various drugs and not being able to even stay awake much of the time you were on the houseboat."

Emily agreed and said all of that was how she remembered it.

"But I really did want them to get out of that loan being called back because Mickey said it would mean that our Mickey Flynn's restaurants would not be foreclosed and taken from us."

"Do you remember now what plans you were making with them to avoid that?" Elizabeth asked.

The questions being asked by Elizabeth and even her own answers seemed to stir back more of the webs in her memories of that frightening week when everything came to a head.

"I remember that Mickey and Kylie thought that they could get Jari Abdou to buy back a half million dollars' worth of the boats that Mickey bought from Worldwide Lakes Boat Sales. I even went with Kylie when she drove to Plyman's Point where Worldwide is located trying to convince Jari that he owed us that much."

"I don't understand," Elizabeth interrupted. "Why did Jari Abdou owe you or Kylie a half million dollars?"

"No, what he owed us was help. He dated Kylie for a long time and through her he became close with Mickey and me… back in our happy times. He wanted to buy Carl Cooper's property and he was using Kylie to influence her father to sell it to him. But two things happened that put that to an end."

"You told your lawyer that Carl Cooper thought Jari was bent on converting his daughter to the Islam faith and said he would never sell the family property to him because of that," Elizabeth recalled.

"Yes, exactly… that and the fact that Carl suddenly had that boating accident out on Table Rock Lake that killed him. But after the dust settled and Kylie inherited the property, she then sold it to Jari."

"So, that's when he dumped her?"

"No, he didn't dump Kylie, but she wouldn't convert, and it became too much of a wedge between them."

While the two women talked, they began walking and were soon on the street in front of Alison's house. Deputy Horner called after them but received only their assurance they would not be out of his sight and would soon come back inside.

"I guess that it was not too much after that when Kylie and your husband began…" Elizabeth stopped from finishing her thought. She wanted to hear the rest of what Emily now remembered and did not want to shift her focus back to the time that her husband and good friend began having secret liaisons.

"I was the real estate agent that listed and then sold the Cooper property at Plyman's Point to Abdou," Emily told her sister. "So, in a way he owed Kylie and me for what we did to help his company, Worldwide Lakes Boat Sales, find what he said was the perfect location.

"You said that he listened but said no when you asked him to repurchase enough boats to help Mickey pay off the mob loan, right?"

'Yes, that's correct," Emily said. "But then Mickey produced the plan to sell only his half of our restaurants to Jari for the money he needed. Jari was interested in that, and he called his people in Australia and then met with us."

"Emily," Elizabeth stopped walking and stood surprised at hearing this account. "That was the best solution… what happened? Why didn't it happen?"

Emily just shook her head back and forth.

"They were both screwing with each other," she said. When Jari showed up he said that Australia refused the deal for fifty percent. But they countered to pay one million for one hundred percent."

"You said no to a half of a million dollars for your share?" Elizabeth asked sounding astonished.

"Yes, I said no," Emily laughed. "Sure, it would have put an end to the mob loan… and threats. But we had the restaurants appraised when we finished getting our third one in Illinois and were thinking of franchising them. Our accountant set our worth in them then at two million dollars… twice the offer from Jari."

"Still… it must have been tempting to take what you could and get free of the mob problem," Elizabeth suggested.

"I never said anything. Other than telling Mickey we needed to talk about it. I just walked below deck and let them hash it out."

"Was that the end of it… with Jari?"

"Well," Emily cautioned, "I am not saying everything is perfectly clear in my mind just yet about that time. But I do remember that Jari and Mickey made plans to meet at Kylie's house later."

"Oh yeah, what did Kylie think about all of this?"

"That part is less clear," Emily said. "I remember asking Mickey later about Kylie since I had not seen much of her that day on the houseboat. He told me then that she left and went back to her house at Indian Point while I was sleeping it off. But when Mickey and I went there later I cannot recall ever seeing Kylie there…" Emily paused, and a sadness surrounded her. "Of course, I know now that poor Kylie was never there… she was where they found her body."

"But Jari? Did he show up back on the houseboat?"

"Not the houseboat, but he was at Kylie's when it looked like he and Mickey had made a deal. I found out after Jari left that he wanted to take the proposal Mickey wrote up and fax it to his superiors in Australia for their lawyers to write it up in legal terms so that they could have a contract. He promised that if all were right with the proposal he would then give Mickey the money."

"Wasn't that something that helped Mickey relax a little?" Elizabeth asked. "Couldn't he just let the mob guys know that the money he owed them was soon coming?"

"You just never knew my husband," Emily sighed. "My soon-to-be ex-husband," she corrected herself. "I wondered just what you said you thought about, why was he still so nervous?"

"He shouldn't have worried that Jari's lawyers were going to change the terms on the contract they were drawing up... he already spelled out those terms on the yellow legal pad, right?" Elizabeth suggested.

"That was just it," Emily said. "Mickey told me later that he knew I would not sign off my interest and so when he drew up his proposal, he included my shares without telling me... and then once again... Mickey forged my signature. He hoped that Jari would have the money with him when he came to Kylie's house. And, if that were the case, even if it were for only the four hundred thousand earnest money payment that Jari suggested earlier, Mickey would take that money and pay off the mob before Jari discovered the forgery that would nix the deal."

"You're right," Elizabeth said sounding more confused than when they began. "I never really got to know your ex-husband. He cheated on you. He cheated the mob. He cheated the Australians. He was one cheating prick!"

Emily looked shocked. Both women stood facing each other until Emily broke out laughing. Soon Elizabeth was laughing too as they turned back towards where Owen who, now joined by Alison, stood watching over them from the driveway.

When they got closer, Alison walked away from Owen and joined up with Emily and Elizabeth.

"I know that you are both going through a lot," she said, "But Owen and I have been assigned the responsibility of keeping you safe from whoever that was that broke into your home," she said taking hold of Emily's hand.

Elizabeth wanted desperately for her sister to keep talking about that last time she was with Mickey and why she now feared she had done something that might send her to prison. She was sure that she could not get Emily to tell her these things in the presence of either Alison or Owen.

"Alison, we know that you and Deputy Horner are responsible for us and we both really appreciate it," Elizabeth began. "But for now, there are a few things that my sister and I must discuss in private."

Alison hoped to find a way to convince them that they should come back inside where, in addition to being safer, their conversation just might be overheard. However, she could also see the determination in Elizabeth that made that alternative less likely to happen.

"Why don't you both at least return to the garden where Owen can keep a watch on things for you?" she suggested.

While Emily and Elizabeth made their way to the back yard garden, Owen put an arm around Alison and walked with her inside the house.

"Don't worry, Alison," he said. "You tried your hardest but at least they are no longer walking targets out on the public street."

The women returned to the garden bench before resuming their conversation.

"Elizabeth?" Emily whispered. "I think I have never heard you call someone a prick before. You are going to have to tell the priest you said that next time you go to confession," she laughed.

"Are you having some fun at the expense of the only Flynn

that still goes regularly to church, baby sister?" Elizabeth asked without succeeding in hiding an urge to laugh at herself.

"Well, that's not a whole truth," Emily defended herself. "I still go to Mass at Christmas… just like we did grow up in Royal Oak."

"Okay enough about our views on religion," Elizabeth said. "Tell me now why you are concerned the police might find out you did something that could mean being sent to prison."

The pale demeanor that earlier took possession over Emily showed a rapid return. Once again, a combination of sadness and fear was seen in her eyes.

"I woke from my afternoon sleep at Kylie's to find Jari gone and Mickey knocking back some Jacks straight up. He told me all now seemed lost. He had no more ideas, no plans, no way in the world to dig out of this thing alive. I asked him again about Kylie's whereabouts and got no response. Instead, he looked angry and said he would not be in this mess if I would have just signed to allow my interests in the restaurants as collateral for his loan when he bought Ozark Lake Leisure Boats."

"Sure, shift all of it on to your shoulders," Elizabeth observed.

"I know how it sounds now," Emily said. "But at the time it struck me as partly right. I mean, we were in a life and death dangerous situation with what we feared was happening with the mob being pissed at us, and I had to take some responsibility for that," she recalled.

"But what could you do about it?" Elizabeth pointed out. "You did not cause Mickey to forge your name on the loan from the mob. That was all his doings…"

"Well, still I was feeling some responsibility and then out of nowhere he looked at me like some new grand scheme was forming inside his mind," Emily said while the memory of that moment prompted a worried frown above her eyes.

Elizabeth took hold of Emily's hands and tried to comfort her.

"Suddenly, Mickey started asking me all about the escrow

funds at My Missouri Homes Real Estate office. I asked him why he needed that kind of information now and he just pushed harder for me to explain what, years ago, I told him happens when a buyer's earnest money is held by the realtor in escrow funds until the deal closes. He wondered if a real estate business that was as big as My Missouri Homes ever carried large sums in those escrow funds. I suspected where he was heading and told him they never had much above fifty thousand in those accounts."

"Are you saying you took some of that money…?" Elizabeth gasped.

"No, I would never do that," Emily assured her sister. "But Mickey figured that what he really needed now was enough money to escape from the mob for up to a year. He hoped to sell his boat, the Mist Akin 1 for quick cash and hoped that Armand could raise the amount Mickey needed fast by dipping into that account."

"But… How did you figure in that scheme?" Elizabeth asked.

"Mickey convinced me to call Armand and begin by telling him the truth… that the reason I had been missing was the whole mob loan thing and their threats. Mickey wanted me to ask Armand to help us by purchasing Mickey's catamaran."

"Is that what happened? Did Armand buy Mickey's boat?"

Emily sighed. "At first he just said that he really would like to help me but there was no way he could raise that kind of money."

"So… no deal?"

"I told Mickey what we were talking about, and he just grabbed my cell phone from me. He sounded frightened and asked Armand how much he could raise, using the boat purchase as the purpose. Armand said he had less than five thousand in ready cash, which obviously was not going to be enough."

"How much did Mickey think could be enough?" Elizabeth wondered.

"Mickey told him that he knew that My Missouri Homes carried cash in an escrow account and suggested that if Armand would just borrow from that the small sum of fifty thousand and bring it to where we were that day, he would sign over the Mist Akin 1 to him."

"Emily, I have no idea what boats like Mickey's are worth but was the difference between that and the fifty thousand worth stealing from the real estate's escrow?"

"It must have been," Emily said. "All Armand would say was that he would see what he could raise and then drive over to Kylie's house and meet with us."

"Why in the world would Mickey think your boss would ever want to do something like that?"

Emily sat silent and stared into the eyes of her sister wondering if this was how she might expect a jury to react if the police charged her with the crime.

"Well, his plan was to play on all the flirting that Armand did with me over the years. Mickey said that he was sure that Armand would do anything if it meant that I would want him to do it."

"That doesn't make sense," Elizabeth said. "You never gave him the time of day when he flirted with you. Why would you or Mickey expect him to…"

"You're right," Emily said. "That is word for word what I said… or think I said. But at any rate, I just told him to forget it and went looking for the still-missing Kylie Cooper whom I had not seen since being told she left the houseboat."

"So, since you did nothing wrong why do you now feel that you may have to worry about… prison?"

Emily turned towards Elizabeth and grabbed hold of her hand, looking for the strength to relive the memory of that day.

"For whatever reason, Armand did show up later and he brought with him a cashier's check to buy Mickey's boat. But he said that he could only raise a total of twenty thousand dollars and showed the check to Mickey."

"Was Mickey desperate enough to just take the money?" Elizabeth asked.

"I wasn't really thinking straight while they argued," Emily resumed. "I had used the last of Kylie's stash of valium just trying to calm down. Mickey was angry but I suspected he was desperate to get the twenty thousand, so he tried to turn it into a loan kind of thing with his boat being used as collateral. Armand said that would not work because he would need to sell the boat to be able to return the money into the escrow account before it was missed."

"But, like you said, Mickey was desperate. Twenty thousand would at least help him escape for a while, right?"

Emily's eyes grew more intense.

"Things began happening fast… I was in the kitchen listening to Mickey who was terribly angry saying that it was going to have to be enough… that he thought he was being taken advantage of… and reaching for the check. But Armand pulled it back saying he needed to first get a bill of sale for the boat.

"So… Armand did steal that money from his real estate's escrow account?" Elizabeth sounded astonished by what she just heard.

"No. I would have said that he borrowed it from that account. He did intend to put it all back before it was needed."

Emily was feeling weak as her memory began replaying the series of events that followed when Armand told Mickey the deal was off without a bill of sale showing the Mist Akin 1 was purchased for twenty thousand dollars… paid in full.

"They were at the kitchen table, Mickey and Armand, and I was in the doorway when Mickey pulled a gun out and took the cashier's check from a surprised Armand Locke."

"Mickey pulled out a gun?" Elizabeth also felt some weakness just listening to her sister. "But did Armand just leave when that happened?"

"Armand looked horrified when Mickey pulled out the gun and was shocked even more when the cashier's check was pulled out of his hand. I thought he was getting up to leave but suddenly he leaped over the table trying to get back the check and to take the gun away from Mickey."

"Oh my God!" Elizabeth exclaimed, sensing the horror her sister witnessed. "Where were you when they began fighting?"

"I just stood there… watching… screaming. Then I saw that Armand had Mickey's wrist in his grip and was holding that hand with the gun in it away from himself while Mickey was just trying to keep Armand from getting the gun… they twisted around and then fell off the table on to the floor right where I was standing. I could not see the gun… underneath both. Then I heard it… the noise from a gunshot… blood… lots of blood… I bent over to help… then I was holding Mickey… his head… his blood… all over me.

Emily's breathing had grown more like panting as her attempts to stop sobbing proved futile. Elizabeth was holding her and trying her best to bring a return of some sense of calmness but found it beyond her powers as she too was now openly crying.

Deputy Horner could not hear the conversation the two women on the garden bench shared but as soon as he saw Emily breaking down and her sister showing the same level of distress he bolted away from the Patio door, calling for Alison to come quick. When they arrived where the two women sat, still openly weeping, they heard Elizabeth speaking very softly to her sister.

Owen looked over at Alison who stepped back to give the women some air.

"Did you hear what she said?" Owen asked.

"Yes," Alison whispered back. "She told Emily that she did nothing wrong, and that Mickey was already dead… when she did something…"

46

The boiling pot

Monday, September 9th, 8:00 A.M.

"HORACE, THIS IS A SURPRISE," Sheriff Lambert said wondering why the Homeland Security Chief would be calling. "I figured you guys would be awfully busy today going through everything your men managed to take with them when they finally left Plyman's Point on Saturday."

"Well, you're right," the chief replied. "We hit the goldmine of hidden secrets while you were holding Abdou and his crew for questioning."

"That's good," the sheriff said. "But as long as we've known each other neither makes a wake-up call just to say thank you. Why don't you save the niceties for when we meet for lunch and just tell me what's on your mind this morning."

Horace Haywood laughed. "You should change your nickname to No-Bull," he said. "But to answer your question, yes, I am calling about that business."

The chief paused a few seconds before making sure they

were on a secure line. What he had to talk about shouldn't run any risk of being overheard.

"Horace, you called me on my direct line. You must know that is a secure line."

"Bull, I am going to need a couple of wagons and maybe three or four deputies later this morning."

"You know you can count on me," the sheriff replied. "But just to feed my curiosity, what's going down?"

"As you recall, we placed some listening bugs while we had access to their camp there and what we've been hearing leads us to suspect that they have figured us out and are making plans to shut down their operations at Plyman's Point."

"You mean… it's now USA-1 and ISIS Terrorists-zero."

"At least it's that score in Stone County, Missouri," the chief concurred. "But there is something that we found out listening in on their morning discussions within the last hour that, if we act fast… and get real lucky, can provide us with a helluva lot more reason to call Operation Plyman perhaps the most successful anti domestic terrorist victory yet."

"Real fast? And get really lucky?"

"That is right, Bull. They keep track of everyone they train after they leave Plyman's Point. They must know their current addresses, cell phone info, email stuff… everything to fund and supply them when that might be needed. All the records for the lone wolf trainees whom they trained at Abdou's camp are kept current in a very secure encrypted cloud storage service that requires the use of two encrypted passwords to upload or download. Thanks to our newly planted listening devices we've discovered that the passwords are long and virtually impossible to decipher."

"So, how do they remember them?" the sheriff asked.

"Good question, Bull," the chief answered. "The thing is, they cannot memorize them… and they know better than to write them down somewhere. Instead, they use encrypted jump drives."

"Uh… You're not going to snow me under with any computer jibe, now, are you?" Lambert interrupted.

"Not important, Bull," Horace answered. "It is a data device that can be plugged into a USB port on a laptop. We learned that there are only two of these jump drives in Abdou's camp, each with a separate encrypted password. He has one and his finance officer, Hanna Mustafo, has the other."

"Good to know, I suppose," Bull said. "So, why is that news making you so giddy this morning?"

"We overheard Hanna whispering to Callum Rasheed that it was her jump drive that she lost during the commotion that happened after someone fired those gun shots and gave you reasons to enter the camp."

"So, if I am following you, if we can get over there in time to catch up with Jari Abdou, you figure he will have one of those jump drives on him, right?"

"That's what we are definitely hoping will happen."

"And the jump drive that was lost?"

"Not real sure about that, but if we can bring them all in and then spend whatever time it might take looking for it over there, and with some lucky breaks find it…"

"Right. You will have both passwords and can retrieve all their secrets from… what did you call that?"

"The Cloud. But even if we do not find the one that Hanna lost right away, we can be sure that Jari Abdou cannot access that data either and maybe doing so change the passwords."

"I suppose that you are also figuring that as long as we hold them incommunicado when we bring them in and don't let them tell their higher-ups what happened, you will be able to buy as much time as you need to get the lost jump thing."

"Bull, we plan on meeting on Trace Hollow Road and 86 in one hour. We'll need whatever you can send us at that time."

"Horace, like I said before, you can count on me."

* * *

Honey hurried into Travis Holden's office as soon as she finished the phone call from Alison Monroe.

"Travis, we have some new problems with Emily Paladino this morning," she said after waiting for him to finish his phone call.

"Is it something that can wait a few hours?" he asked.

She was surprised by his response. She wondered if that phone call he was on concerned something big.

"Well, I thought it is something urgent enough to bring to you as soon as I heard it," she said. "I think Emily's memory has returned and Alison suspects that her sister, Elizabeth, wants them to see the lawyer… this morning."

Travis just stood listening to Honey and then sat down, motioning for her to close the door to his office.

"What's up?" Honey asked.

"Homeland Security is going to arrest the whole bunch at Jari Abdou's camp in about an hour from now. The sheriff will be there himself and has already told Captain Wolf to wrangle up all available to follow him out there."

"I don't get it," Honey said. "I thought they planted the listening devices just last Saturday so they could…"

"They did that," Travis said interrupting her. "They heard Abdou telling his people that the jig was up and that they had to hurry up and get out while they could. He mentioned that certain information that was quite secret had been moved and replaced somewhere else which led him to conclude that Homeland Security was now on to them."

Honey immediately understood that what Travis just told her was going to be his top priority this morning. Yet, somehow, it was also particularly important that Emily be questioned about the information that Alison was able to overhear… and before the lawyer, Tomas Cullerton, was called upon.

"Are you involved in the Homeland Security raid this morning?" she asked. "Because if you are, perhaps I can drive over to Alison's and see if I can get alone with Emily long enough to find out what it is, or was, that she remembers now."

Travis stood up again and prepared to get going.

"Yes, the sheriff wanted me to bring along a few of the C.I.D. guys and be there for whatever comes up," he said. "And yes, I agree. You should head over to question Emily."

As they left the office Travis saw Ernie Mize was waiting to see him.

"What is it?" Travis asked without stopping to hear what Ernie had on his mind.

"I just wanted to bring you up to speed on that mystery car that was following Piles Beck before he crashed," the lieutenant said almost running to catch up with Travis.

"The mystery car?" Travis slowed to a halt and turned to face Ernie.

"Yes. I was able to use our ANPR device that Captain Wolf set up by Kimberling Bridge. It showed Beck's car first and shortly afterwards came the black Lexus. I was able to make out the plates and you will not believe..."

Travis knew that this was something important... at least to Ernie. But he simply did not have the extra time that Lieutenant Mize seemed bent on requiring before telling who... or what it was he discovered at Kimberling Bridge that night.

"Ernie... Just say it," Travis demanded. "What won't I believe?"

Ernie hoped that his extra work and the fact that it produced a huge surprise in the investigation of the two murder cases would be welcomed in a much more appreciative way than was happening.

"The second car... the black Lexus," Ernie said in a hurried but more subdued voice. "It belongs to a Mrs. Estelle Locke... whom I believe is the wife or mother of Armand Locke from My Missouri Home Real Estate."

47

Armond and Mickey and Emily too!

Monday, September 9ᵗʰ, 8:30 A.M.

AFTER A SMALL BREAKFAST THAT ALISON prepared for everyone, Elizabeth insisted that she and her sister, Emily, do the clean-up chores and that Alison and Owen should relax in another area of the house.

Feeling that they could continue their earlier conversation without being overheard, Elizabeth moved close to her sister and whispered that she wondered if she felt composed enough to finish talking about what happened when Mickey was shot.

"Like I told you, I do not know how it happened, only that it was Mickey who pulled out a gun and that after they fought and fell down onto the floor, Armand was on top of Mickey, but the gun was somewhere between them when it went off."

"But then, why do you now think that you did something that would lead the police to think it was you that fired the gun?"

Emily just looked at her sister wondering what it was that she did not understand.

"I was there when it… whatever… happened. I was the person that Armand came to help. I was the person who was the real reason that Armand took money out of the escrow account… something that if it was found out might either send him to prison or, at the very least, cost him to lose his realtor's license."

Elizabeth could see that her sister was still highly agitated. She led her back to the table and pulled out a chair for Emily to be seated in, hoping that doing so would prompt a break in the anxiety that was revving up inside her. As she sat alongside her, Elizabeth felt that so far, from what Emily told her, she could not see what action her sister took that was in any way a criminal offense.

"What you've said are only reasons that Armand did something," Elizabeth pointed out. "You were just in the same room when they fought and somehow the gun was fired that killed Mickey. But that was limited to just the two of them. All that blood that you remember on him… and on you when you tried to help after he was shot… none of that is criminal."

"Well… there's more," Emily said.

"You mean, besides what you remember doing to help…?" Elizabeth's voice could not hide the undercurrent of frustration that she felt.

"When Armand freed himself from being entangled with Mickey, the first thing he did was to look after me," Emily said. "He worried that I was injured and only after being sure that I was okay did he see that Mickey was actually dead."

"You mean he checked for a heartbeat or something like that?"

"No. He just saw what I saw. Mickey was shot in his head and after that he… there was no movement. He was not breathing."

"But… Couldn't you… or Armand call for an ambulance? Elizabeth hoped not to sound accusing but could not understand that both her sister and the man that was fighting with Mickey were the right people to decide he was just... dead!"

"I tried to call for help," Emily said defending herself. "I went to get my cell phone but Armand chased me down. He said that with all that blood on my clothes that the police would suspect that it was me that shot Mickey."

"But you had no reason..."

"Armand said that the divorce problems that I was having could cause that suspicion. He told me to clean up and change out of the bloody clothes and that while I was doing that he would make the 911 call."

"So, is that what happened? Elizabeth asked.

"I really am not sure," Emily sighed. Again, the effort to remember every detail seemed just out of reach.

"That's okay baby," Elizabeth said knowing that Emily was close to losing it.

"I gave Armand the bloody clothes and he took them out to his car to hide them before the police or ambulance arrived. When I finished showering away the blood from my body and got dressed, I saw someone park on the street by the neighbor's house and then sneak along the side of Kylie's and then... he stopped suddenly."

"What did he want? Was he a detective?" Elizabeth had questions being followed by more questions.

"I could not tell who he was, but I was worried it could be that mob guy that Mickey said could appear at any time. He stopped suddenly when there was a loud noise... Armand was backing out of the driveway and upon entering the street he floored it... heading out of Indian Point."

Elizabeth gasped. "Armand took off... leaving you there alone... with some stranger sneaking around the house... and poor Mickey's bloody body on the kitchen floor???"

"I was just as confused as you are now. I did not know what to do so I ran out the side door farthest away from where I saw the stranger… and kept running until I was at the lake. I was by the boat slips and saw Mickey's catamaran. I ran inside it and down the steps below and hid… for hours."

"Emily, we have to find some way to go and see your lawyer, Mr. Cullerton," Elizabeth said, surer of that decision now after listening to what her sister finally remembered and had not told to anyone before.

Outside, below the open kitchen window, Alison looked at Deputy Horner and motioned for them to sneak away towards his car that was parked in the driveway.

"Radio into the station and tell Captain Travis what we've just heard," she whispered. "I will try to distract them if I can from calling the lawyer. I am sure he is going to want to take Emily away from us."

48

Emily moves back home

Monday, September 9th, 10:00 A.M.

TWYLA TURNER WAS BUSY POSTING the sales appointments on the My Missouri Homes web page when she was signaled to answer a phone call that their receptionist described as urgent.

"Oh, it's you Mr. Sutcliffe," she greeted him. "Don't we usually have these accounting discussions on the FIRST Monday each month?"

"Yes, we do,", Sherman Sutcliffe agreed. "But as you remember, Labor Day was the first Monday."

Twyla always found these chats with the accountant for My Missouri Homes more tedious than of any value. There was no doubt that his questions and nit-picking rehashing of the previous month's ledger activities was necessary. And Sutcliffe himself was as good as there was available in all of Springfield regarding knowledge of the rules and regulations that real estate firms had to follow. But it was not something Twyla found enjoyable.

"I have many of the same points that seem to come up often enough to be a part of our usual monthly back and forth," Sherman said. "But for today, there is one that probably needs an answer more urgently than the others."

"Yes, our receptionist said that you wanted to let me know that this was to be an urgent call," Twyla said, delighted to be able to throw that word around and right back at him.

"Well, let me tell you what it is then and let you decide if it has any urgency," he said sounding annoyed by the lack of importance being given to the reason for his call. "SFN is one of the banks that My Missouri Homes uses for escrow accounts that are for medium term durations."

"Yes, that I already know,' said Twyla. "What is it, specifically, that you are referencing today? Did we miss a comma somewhere between numbers on one of my Escrow Amount Analysis worksheets?" This was exactly the type of picayune procedure that Sutcliffe's accounting firm put her through at the end of most reporting periods.

"Twyla, let me come right to the point. I was called soon after I came to work this morning by Herman Cushner, VP at Springfield First National Bank and Trust, concerned about a disbursement from the My Missouri Homes escrow in the amount of $20,000 on August 16th."

"I do not recall such a disbursement," Twyla said, only this time indicating some new concern with her response.

"Right. That could be because this disbursement was made to Armand while he was present at the bank, and he requested that it be in the form of a cashier's check. No specific line item in the escrow general account was tabbed to show the deficiency."

Twyla was busy pulling down the August business summaries on her desktop computer and did not immediately respond.

"I told Mr. Cushner that I was certain that information was not purposely withheld and that I would get that line item's identity known to SFN, specifically to him by close of business today. Can you investigate this and get back as soon as you can?...... Twyla?"

* * *

Travis was disappointed to discover that his presence during the raid at Plyman's Point was merely to be there in a back-up role. If that were made clearer, he might have begged off so that he could have turned his attention to the interview with Emily Paladino. He stood alongside Sheriff Bull Lambert and the two C.I.D. detectives he brought with him as they watched from outside the camp while Horace Haywood and five of his Homeland Security agents executed a search warrant.

One by one the DHS agents brought out members of Jari Abdou's team and turned them over to Captain Holland Wolf who secured them in waiting squad cars.

"What's the plan, sheriff, after they are brought into the station?" Travis asked.

"Horace and his agents are coordinating that with the FBI. From the briefing that Horace gave before we set out this morning, I was led to believe that Abdou and his team will be flown to Fort Leavenworth in Kansas within a few hours after they are brought to our Stone County jail.

Travis stepped aside to answer his cell phone as federal agents carried out boxes of files and laptop computers placing them into large U-Hall rental trucks.

"What's up Honey?" he asked seeing the call was coming from his second in command.

"Travis," she began. "Sorry to be interrupting what is going on out there but I have to return a phone call to Emily's lawyer who said he has spoken with her this morning and has instructed her to stop talking with us until he meets with her."

That bit of news surprised him as he wondered what had occurred that caused Emily to contact her lawyer.

"I was hoping that you would have got to her before that happened," he said.

"I was also hoping that" Honey replied. "But something set off Emily after she regained some of her memories of the day when her husband was killed. Alison overheard much of what Emily told her sister and then called me. But before I could get to them, I was called by Tomas Cullerton saying he advised her to hold back from more police questions."

"Is he planning on going to Alison's to talk with Emily?" Travis asked.

"No, it's worse than that," Honey replied. "He wants Alison or Deputy Horner to drive Emily back to her home where he is more assured that their conversation would be as private as he felt it has to be."

Travis paused and considered what moving Emily back to her home would do to the need to provide her safety.

"Did you tell Cullerton that Beck is out on the loose right now and what that could mean to his client's safety?"

"I did,' Honey said. "It did not seem to change his mind. I think that if we let Alison drive Emily back to her house that she will be allowed to stay… at least close by when Emily meets with her lawyer."

"Well, that will help address our need to provide for Emily's protection," Travis considered. "But we are losing the advantage of having Emily answer our questions more freely than she might if the lawyer wasn't sitting next to her."

Travis turned back to where the sheriff stood talking with an FBI agent and told him that he needed to drive into Kimberling City and organize a security plan around the vicinity of Emily Paladino's home.

"Honey," he began after returning to his cell phone. "I am leaving here right now and can meet you in the parking lot outside of Harter House Supermarket. See if Cullerton will have no objection to Deputy Horner accommodating Alison and Emily back to her home. Otherwise, tell Horner to meet with us there."

49

Beck knows now

September 9th, 1:00 P.M.

FRANKIE VALENTI LIKED THE SIMPLE things in life and one of those was a foot long turkey sandwich with tomato, red onion, mayo, on a whole wheat bun prepared at his favorite restaurant, the Subway in Kimberling City. The people who worked the counter were always knowledgeable and happy. It led Frankie to think that Subway must be a good employer who paid their employees good wages.

There was never a problem finding a Subway anywhere around the Table Rock Lake area. When he was in Branson, he had his pick of three of them. Nearby Reed Springs even had two Subway sandwich locations. But, given his choice he always preferred the one along state highway 13 located down at the end of the shopping center where the RT Restaurant was in Kimberling City. The food was the same in all the Subways but only this one had Marnie Coyne waiting on customers. For Frankie, that was all it took to drive past the other ones.

When Frankie was released by Lieutenant Honey Holcomb, he was not surprised to see that he was being tailed by someone in a deep brown Chevrolet Equinox. He knew that the gorgeous detective who interrogated him was not completely taken in by his responses to her questions and that she suspected that he would meet up soon with Piles Beck, who escaped from the cops earlier at Plyman's Point.

Of course, she was correct in making that assumption but there was no way that he would lead them to finding their fugitive. Instead, after Piles managed to steal a car in the parking lot at Ozark Valley and purchased a prepaid cell phone at a gas station to make contact, the plan was that they would not meet.

Frankie was happy to be off the hook from being expected to help Piles make his escape. Doing anything like that would mean a return trip to some prison for him once it became curtains for Piles. Either Piles would squeal and give him up or some cop would figure that out all by himself.

But Piles was not about to leave Frankie completely out of his life. He still had to find a way to get to Emily Paladino and fulfill the contract that Lucas Paladino sent him into the Ozarks to do. The mob needed Emily to be as dead as her husband Mickey was so they could foreclose on the loan and take over the three Mickey Flynn's Restaurants. Frankie's job was to find out where the cops were hiding her and tell Piles. After he managed that he would be free of having any further connection with him.

After Marnie prepared his sandwich, Frankie paid at the cash register and was on his way back to flirt with the attractive server when something caught his eye in the large parking lot. The brown Chevy which had been tailing him throughout most of the morning was backing up and driving towards three other vehicles that were parked with their driver's side doors open.

A woman was outside one of the cars and signaled the driver of the Chevy to hurry and join them. Frankie recognized that it was Lieutenant Honey Holcomb and he slid away from the window lest she see him there.

The four cars that assembled directly across from the RT Restaurant were quickly emptied as their drivers gathered around one who was holding a map and making pointed gestures to it. Each person there nodded that they understood whatever it was he was pointing to when he singled them out. After less than a few minutes had passed they each hurried back to their own cars and drove out on to state highway 13.

Frankie's immediate thought was that he was now free to go anywhere he wished as his tail, the brown Chevy, left with the other cars. But then he suddenly wondered if this group, which was obviously detectives from Stone County, were part of the task force assigned to guard Emily Paladino. Her house was only ten short minutes away, he recalled, in the direction they all drove towards after departing from the parking lot.

Frankie hustled out to his Chevy Traverse and climbed inside where he could use his cell phone without fear of being overheard.

"It's me," was all Frankie said when he heard Piles Beck's voice.

"Good, I thought you were in county jail."

"I'm in Kimberling City and I just saw something that makes me believe that the chicken is back in the hen house."

There was a long pause on the other end of the line before Piles came back on.

"You been reading those gangster comic books you used to love back when we roomed together in the Joint," Beck sneered. "Or you are speaking some kind of code. Which is it?"

"No… I am saying I found Emily and if I am guessing correctly, she is back home."

Another pause, this one longer before Piles spoke again.

"Okay. I have been thinking this would happen, just thought it would be more like a week from now."

"A week?"

"Yeah, they would hide her for a while and then... like in a week, you know... back to normal."

"So... you got all you're going to get from me," Frankie boldly exclaimed. "What you do now is your business. I am clean. So, let us say goodbye and hope we do not meet up again."

"If she is there, like you just said... then, yes. I will do what is necessary and be back in Chicago by this time tomorrow."

*   *   *

After Tomas Cullerton had finished meeting with Emily at her house, he was convinced that her fears that she did something that could eventually lead to criminal charges were totally exaggerated. He knew that the police would not find it worth their while to go after her on any drug charges. And, regarding the events surrounding the death of her husband, the only thing she was guilty of was failing to call the police afterwards.

Cullerton decided that Emily's only concern now should be regarding her own safety. The worry about the mob having a hit on her life now had the most urgent priority. And the man that the police said who was sent to do it was still on the loose, meant that continued police protection was mandatory.

"If I am made to answer Captain Holden's questions again, I'm sure he will ask me to tell what happened when Mickey was killed," Emily complained to her lawyer.

"Then, I think you should tell him exactly what you have told me now and your sister earlier," Cullerton advised.

"But that might make them suspect that Armand Locke killed Mickey. All he did was try to help us and the way it has ended he might lose his real estate broker's license for breaking the law and taking money out of the escrow account... and he might even be charged with Mickey's murder!"

Cullerton listened to Emily's reasons for not wanting to go back to the Stone County Sheriff's office and face the tough questions that she enumerated. But, as her lawyer, he made it clear that she needed to do just that.

"Mr. Locke will probably be picked up and questioned," he told Emily, whether you tell your story to the police or not. I am sure he will first be given an opportunity to consult with his lawyer and, providing everything happened just as you have now remembered it, he will not face murder charges."

When he was satisfied that Emily understood and agreed with his advice to cooperate fully with the police, Cullerton waved to Travis, who was waiting outside in his car, indicating that he and Emily were coming out and would follow him back to the Stone County Sheriff's office.

Taking every precaution possible, when they departed from Emily's subdivision and drove back to state highway 13, Captain Holden's car was followed by Lieutenant Honey Holcomb. Tomas Cullerton with Emily in his car was tucked safely next in line. A third plainclothes detective stayed a few car lengths behind them and was followed by the detective in the brown Chevrolet that earlier was assigned to tail Frankie Valenti.

As the parade of five cars drove along state highway 13 and passed the parking lot out front of Harter House Super Market a woman with a full cart of groceries and a panicked expression on her face stood looking in all directions from a vacant parking space where she earlier left her white 2012 Ford Explorer.

50

Officer Vague

Monday, 7:30 P.M.

ELIZABETH ATTEMPTED TO ASSURE HER sister Frances that she was not in danger now. "If you saw how many police cars that were here earlier before Emily and her lawyer agreed to answer more questions and returned with them to their headquarters…"

"But that was earlier," Frances interrupted. "They are all back at the Stone County Sheriff's office in Galena now and you are all alone sitting in Emily's house. Don't you worry that the person who was sent to murder her will come looking for her right where you are?"

Elizabeth paused as a feeling of having overlooked that possibility prompted a surge of anxiety to overtake her. Elizabeth's mind raced back to four hours earlier when she watched her sister get into the car with her lawyer. A string of four police cars waited as the car Emily was in was motioned to slot in behind the front two. Elizabeth remembered how her only thought at that time was that the police were leaving no stone unturned in providing protection for her sister. The observation that Frances just made about how that left herself completely alone was likely not on anyone's mind at that time.

Frances, waiting for a response, realized that what she had just meant to be merely a part of their conversation was now causing an emotional concern for her sister. Elizabeth forgot to mention any steps that the police also took to provide her with some protection.

"Surely the police have thought about this, don't you think," Frances asked hoping to diffuse the unintended scare she felt was her responsibility. Again, there was a prolonged silence while Elizabeth was searching her memory for being told anything by either the police or Emily's lawyer before they left regarding what was being done to protect her until they returned.

"I don't remember anything being said," Elizabeth finally responded. "But, around an hour after they had all left, I remember seeing a car that drove slowly past the front yard, like someone looking for the address. He kept driving so I thought it was just someone who was a bit lost. But since then, I have seen that car a few more times. It was a plainclothes police officer they sent to keep a watch on me."

Frances suddenly felt afraid for her sister. Still, not wanting to burden Elizabeth with the suspicions that now rushed into her own mind, she decided to take charge of things, at least as much that she could, being that she was far away at her own home in Tampa.

"Sweetie," Frances began. "I am going to call Captain Holden and find out what he can tell me about assigning anyone to protect you while you are all alone. What I want you to do is first tell me where you are right now in the house."

Elizabeth immediately was relieved hearing her big sister's words indicating her determination to take charge of things. It was just as it had always been while they were growing up.

Frances was always the sibling who had the capacity for clear thinking in any crisis. Her own anxiety was just an overreaction and now Frances was going to guide her past the problems that overwhelmed her.

"Elizabeth…??"

"Yes, I'm here… I heard you," Elizabeth answered. "Right now, I am just sitting out here in the lanai. I was preparing to read a bit to pass the time when you just called."

"Elizabeth, listen to me carefully," Frances tried to hide the fears that were building within her with each of her sister's responses. "You do not want to be out there in the lanai with only the screen walls for protection. First, lock that door that leads from the lanai to the back yard. Will you do that right now for me?"

Elizabeth ignored the way she was being talked to as a child and decided to follow her sister's instructions. It was all in letting Frances play the welcomed role of being in charge.

"Okay, the screen door is locked," she said.

"Now, go inside the house and lock the back door as you pass it and then do the same at the front door."

These were things that Elizabeth was going to do without being told but now was not the time to challenge her sister's authority.

"Alright sweetie," Frances comforted her. "I'm sure that you are fine but what I will do now is to call Captain Holden and be sure. Just tell me as much as you can about that car you noticed that was driving by Emily's house."

Elizabeth was feeling much more relaxed, and the memory of that passing car came easily in vivid recollection.

"Well, I am not sure of the make… or the year…… just that it was white… all white… and, wait… it was not a sedan… more like a SUV."

*   *   *

Monday, 7:30 P.M.

The job as a police officer on the Kimberling City Police force seemed to be one step above his previous job as a bank guard. Both jobs required wearing a uniform and each was permitted to wear a holstered side arm. But each understood the limitations under which they served their local law enforcement role. Guards were required to prevent stick-ups inside the bank that employed them. If a bank robber was not stopped or apprehended inside their bank, the guard's role ended and the crime became the responsibility of the next higher up link in that chain, the City Police force.

Eugene Vague understood the system as well as anybody could, having begun his career right after returning to his hometown after completing a three-year hitch in the Coast Guard. His grandfather pulled some strings at Table Rock Bank and Trust to get him selected to replace him when he retired as their bank guard. Eugene worked hard at that job to impress not only his boss, but the bank customers as well and when there later became an opening at the Kimberling City Police Department, Eugene was the unanimous recommendation from the Police and Fire Commission to fill that vacancy.

The prestige, excitement, and pure joy that Eugene felt during the first five years he served on the force slowly gave way to the realization that his job as a police officer was as high up the career ladder that he could expect to achieve in Kimberling City. The entire force was made up of only six other uniformed police officers, two detectives, a clerk, and the Chief of Police. Just as pull from a family member got him his first job, Eugene suspected that each of the positions above him used some form of influence to get their positions.

He was still the most recently hired officer even after five years which meant that Eugene's seniority for bidding on assignments always resulted in him getting the least desired one known as the

Night Shift, the one that worked between 6:00 P.M. and 3:00 A.M. While it was true that these hours were normally thought to be when most of the action takes place, for a city police officer whose domain was limited to only those streets within the City's boundaries, the complete opposite was the case. Most of the roads into or out of Kimberling City were designated as either county or state highways. They were patrolled by Stone County Deputies or Missouri State Highway Police and all crimes that occurred were left to be investigated by the Stone County detectives too as they had the required advanced technology and workforce.

When he reported to work this evening and stood for roll call his sergeant listed several items for the shift to be on the alert. The Chief had received a tip that a drinking party was being planned by vacationing teenagers for that evening at Kimberling Airways, the private airport out on Bonanza Drive. Also mentioned was that a white Ford Explorer was reported stolen while a vacationer was shopping at Harter House earlier that afternoon and that all cars on patrol should be on the lookout for it. Before he could get any more details a 9-1-1 call came in reporting that a man was seen walking between houses on Skipper Drive and the caller worried that he could be a potential Peeping Tom.

Sergeant Dooley dismissed Officer Vague from Roll Call and instructed him to proceed to the area and patrol Skipper Drive and the surrounding streets and report any findings. Eugene was so excited to hurry toward the peninsula on which the airport and those streets were located that he turned on the squad's siren until he heard the voice of his sergeant coming across the car radio commanding him to proceed in a less obvious fashion.

"If someone is snooping around out there you don't need to inform him that you're on your way to catch him, right Officer Vague?"

"OH? I mean, Roger that, Sergeant," Vague responded and immediately turned off the siren.

As he left highway 13 and drove on to James River Road, he clicked on his cell phone and called his wife.

"I'm on a hot one, Rosie," he told her. "There's a Peeping Tom… or maybe just a burglar… prowling around down by those houses around the airport and Sergeant Dooley sent me out to investigate it."

"Oh. Honey, be careful," his wife cautioned. "I know you want to show them you are someone they should consider for that opening when Detective Hunt retires, but maybe whoever that is that's snooping around might have a gun…"

"Baby, I'm not going to worry about anything like that," Eugene interrupted. "If I find him and capture him while he's looking in someone's window it should go a long way to putting me in the spotlight when Selection time arrives."

His direction after leaving highway 13 was down towards the homes on Skipper Drive near the bottom of the peninsula where it began at James River Road and continued along Joe Bald and then into neighborhoods along quiet streets. When he reached Hoot Owl Point, he turned on Kimberling Airways Drive where it leads into Bonanza Drive. Eugene slowed while he was passing by the airport and decided to cruise over to the gate and search out the places the teens would choose inside the fenced off airfield for their party after it was dark. The runway and hangars, used only by the people who leased them for their privately owned aircraft, were closed and looked deserted.

Sergeant Dooley mentioned that the Chief previously checked after receiving the tip and learned that the privately owned airport had no planned uses for the evening which explained the absence of anyone being seen inside there now. Sunset had started but it seemed logical that the drinking party would not begin for at least another hour when the night's darkness would assist their plans to sneak inside the area around the hangars. He decided to resume his patrol looking for the man suspected to be a peeper for now but, if he were unable to spot a suspect, he would return and pick out a good place to hide and catch the partygoers.

Eugene pulled out of the airport's parking lot intending to travel towards where the 9-1-1 caller reported last seeing the prowler without alerting him. He decided to circle back to Hoot Owl Point and take it a few blocks west of Bonanza and the street that ran parallel to it, Skipper Drive. That way he could catch sight of anyone sneaking around the houses there. When he reached Breezy Point Lane, he noticed that both streets ran at an angle into it and from that point where he could observe anyone that might be seen along either of the two streets. He decided to wait there and parked across from a house with a For Sale sign in the front yard and a Ford Explorer parked in the driveway.

Eugene mentioned the house and the Ford Explorer when he radioed in his position and was surprised that it prompted a quick response call-back from Sergeant Dooley.

"That Ford Explorer you mentioned," Dooley began. "You remember that we are looking for just such a vehicle that was reported stolen this afternoon, right?"

Eugene turned back and took another hard look at the SUV that was parked not more than ten feet from his location.

"Roger that, Sergeant," Eugene responded. "I thought about that too. But this one does not look to be our stolen Explorer, more like one that belongs to the people who live in the house where they parked it in their driveway."

After a moment of radio silence, Dooley came back on and asked if it was a white Explorer.

"Uh, yes… I would say it is a white one okay. But like I just told you it belongs to those people inside the house."

"Okay, you're probably right," Dooley said. "The woman who reported the stolen Explorer hasn't got back to us yet with the plate numbers so why don't you read them from the Explorer there and we can run them just to be sure."

Upon checking, Officer Vague was surprised to discover that the Explorer in the driveway had no tags and hurried back to report this to his waiting sergeant.

"Perhaps you should just go up to that house and ring the doorbell and ask them about this," Dooley said sounding a bit irritated.

Less than a minute later Office Vague was calling in that no one answered the door after he rang the bell and knocked very loudly on the storm door.

"I looked inside, and it is all empty. No one lives there," he reported. "Why would they leave their nice white Ford Explorer in the driveway of a house that they already moved away from?"

A full moment passed before Sergeant Dooley gave out a sigh and then responded. "Perhaps someone else parked the Explorer in that driveway."

51

The trip home for Emily

Monday, 7:45 P.M.

AFTER LOCKING THE SCREEN DOOR on the lanai, Elizabeth hurried back inside the house and following each of her sister's instructions, began locking all windows and doors. Noticing that the door to the utility room was ajar she pushed it closed on her way to the Master Bedroom which had sliding doors that opened to a Walkout Patio. She was surprised to find them opened halfway and hurriedly closed and locked them. To be sure that the lock was properly set in place, Elizabeth tried pulling the doors open and was relieved when she found they remained locked.

She had earlier locked the front door after saying goodbye to Emily when she, and Captain Holden, left. But unable to ignore the nagging suspicion that the storm door was unlocked, she turned back into the living room to make sure it too was shut. She had taken only a few more steps when she heard someone behind her. Suddenly she was in the grips of a man who put his hands over her mouth and wrestled her to the floor.

The intruder held her face down on the carpet and straddled her back, while asking questions too fast to allow her to respond.

"Where is Emily Paladino… How long will she be gone… and who the fuck are you? I will kill everybody inside this house, lock, stock, and barrel if you start playing any games with me."

When he loosened his grip to allow her enough room to lift her head to answer him, Elizabeth twisted on to her side and bucked him partially off her.

The intruder swung a punch towards the back of her head and in so doing lost his balance, falling headfirst against the nearby stone hearth fireplace. The injury caused much bleeding and left him dazed long enough to allow Elizabeth to escape from under him. She managed to get as far as the front door but no farther before he was upon her again. She turned just in time to see the shadow of his arm swinging the butt of the Ruger 380 caliber pistol in his hand. The blow knocked her unconscious with such force that she bounced against the front door and collapsed to the floor.

* * *

8:00 P.M.

Alison Monroe laughed as she drove behind Tomas Cullerton who was taking Emily back to her house in Kimberling City. She radioed to Deputy Horner in the car behind her sharing how it seemed like Times Square on New Year's Eve earlier that afternoon at the Stone County Sheriff's Office.

"We could have lit the No Vacancy sign," he laughed in agreement.

"We started the afternoon off holding the Jari Abdou foursome that Homeland Security brought in," Alison recalled.

"Don't forget we were already holding the three who trained under them at Plyman's Point," Owen said. "All of them were waiting to be transported to the Federal Prison at Leavenworth, Kansas."

"Then Captain Holden brought in Emily Paladino for questioning, along with her lawyer. Sergeant Platt brought in Armand Locke just a few minutes later," Alison sighed. "Almost at that same time Lieutenant Mize brought in Frankie Valenti."

"Except for Valenti, who waived counsel, and for Jari Abdou, Rais Azari, Hanna Mustafo, and Callum Rasheed, who would not need an attorney until they were questioned after they arrived in Leavenworth, the others had at least one attorney who was present during their interrogations which added to the crowding," Deputy Horner pointed out.

"Horace Haywood was also inside the station busily directing the movements of his Homeland Security agents who were coordinating the transportation of their prisoners to the Springfield airport," Alison remembered. "Using any of our two Interrogation Rooms almost required making a reservation," She laughed.

"Right," Owen explained. "Captain Holden had gone inside one room to question Emily Paladino who was with her attorney Tomas Cullerton. Inside another Interrogation room Lieutenant Honey Holcomb and Sergeant Platt questioned Armand Locke who was accompanied by his lawyer. Meanwhile, Frankie Valenti was in a holding cell waiting for his turn inside an Interrogation room."

"Kind of leaves me winded just recounting how busy it got," Alison laughed.

Access to the subdivision where Emily lived was mostly limited to the intersection off Route 13 at James River Road. As she followed the lead of Tomas Cullerton who had switched on his turn signals, Alison prepared to say good-by to Owen.

"So, you're going to leave us here, right?" she asked.

"Roger that," Owen answered. "After I pick up my prescription I'll hurry back and help you stand guard at Emily's tonight."

Turning on to James River Road, Alison waved good-bye out her side window as Deputy Horner continued into town on route 13. Although it was just past 8:00 P.M. sunset arrived almost thirty minutes earlier and she could not be sure that Owen saw her sending a kiss along with her wave.

While it was less than a five-mile drive remaining to Emily's home on Bonanza Drive, still it took almost nine minutes to get there as the road changed directions and merged with Joe Bald Road and then into two other streets as it snaked through a dense residential area.

After Alison pulled into the driveway alongside where Tomas Cullerton had parked, she watched as Emily hurried towards the front door. Her lawyer did not accompany Emily and instead walked back to meet with Alison as she got out of her car.

"I'm leaving you all for the evening," he said. "I just want a minute to review with you what I worked out with Captain Holden for this protection detail. I'm sure that Emily has told him everything she knows regarding the week she spent with Mickey and Kylie, on his houseboat and at her home at Indian Point. But I do not want her to face any more questions without me present from you or anyone else on that subject."

"Yes," Alison assured the lawyer. "Captain Holden is only concerned now with making certain that there is protection for Emily until we catch up with Piles Beck."

"That's fine," Cullerton answered before suddenly stepping back indicating he had one last question. "That fellow, Beck. I know that gangsters get pegged with various nicknames like Mad Dog… or Bugsy. Did any of you detectives ever find out why… or how he got that nickname, Piles?"

"If someone has looked into that they sure as heck have not clued me in," Alison laughed as she stepped around Cullerton and proceeded towards the house.

52

And so it must end!

Monday, 8:00 P.M.

CAPTAIN HOLDEN HAD JUST FINISHED the phone call from Emily's sister, Frances, when Honey walked into his office looking genuinely concerned.

"Travis, did you hear that earlier today, about the same time we were escorting Emily and her lawyer back to headquarters that a SUV was being reported stolen outside a supermarket in Kimberling City? I am wondering if our missing suspect has found another mode of transportation..."

Travis looked startled by Honey's news. "I think we may have left Elizabeth Lane all alone at Emily's home earlier... completely unprotected," he said. "That stolen SUV... Did you get a make on it... the color?"

"It was a white Explorer," Honey responded. "The Kimberling City cops are handling the stolen car investigation," she added. "I'll contact them to see if it's still an open case."

"That's good," Travis said. "But I'm still concerned about Elizabeth"

"Well, she won't be alone for much longer," Honey said. "I assigned Alison to stay with her for protection until we get an opportunity to bring in Piles Beck. And Lieutenant Wolf has generously provided Deputy Horner to the protection detail," she added. "He will be outside covering the perimeter while Alison is inside with Emily… and her sister."

"Sounds like you have everything covered," Travis said sounding much relieved. "After you talk with the Kimberling City Police pass that info along to Deputy Horner."

Monday, 8:10 P.M.

After finishing her conversation with Tomas Cullerton, Alison approached the front door to follow where Emily had walked into the house when suddenly she heard a terrifying scream from inside.

"ELIZABETH???"

Alison recognized that it was Emily who had just screamed and guessed that what she saw was not only shocking but meant that something bad was happening or had happened to her sister. Rather than charging into the house Alison withdrew her pistol and went into a crouch position just off to the left side of the now open door. Peeking inside she saw the body of a woman on the floor and then heard Emily screaming again…

"OH… NO… PLEASE… NO…"

Suddenly… a gunshot… and in the same instant… a woman simultaneously fell out on to the porch as if she had just been thrown, facedown alongside of her. Alison saw that it was Emily, and she was bleeding… and at best, unconscious.

Again, Alison peeked from her crouched position into the house. This time she saw someone… a man… running through the kitchen towards the lanai at the back of the house. Not knowing if he was alone, Alison did not immediately change her position. She heard the door in the lanai slam shut and guessed that the man had left and was either running away through the back yards or was circling around to come up from behind her. As she looked around to guard against a surprise attack, Alison caught sight again of Emily, who had just made a quiet moan. There was a small pool of blood under her that Alison guessed was coming from a wound to her chest or stomach.

Another gunshot… this one coming from the front yard… Alison turned in time to see Tomas Cullerton, bleeding, and being pulled away from the open front door of his car. The man who had just pulled him out of the car quickly got behind the wheel and began driving toward where Alison and Emily were, unprotected, on the front stoop. Alison fired one shot through the windshield and the car swerved. The driver appeared to have been struck by the bullet and slumped lower to avoid another round of fire. With the direction of the car changed away from the house he gave it more gas and sped across the yard and onto Bonanza Drive.

Alison immediately pushed on her PTT Chest Mic and called for ambulances and additional police help.

"At least three persons have been shot and need emergency medical assistance," she reported. "The shooter is believed to be the fugitive Piles Beck and is escaping at high speed on Bonanza Drive in the direction of highway 13. He is armed and dangerous.

*　*　*

Office Vague stepped away from his squad car to further inspect the white Ford Explorer when he heard what sounded like a gunshot. He turned reflectively to where the sound seemed to originate from a nearby house around the corner on Bonanza

Drive. As he hurried back inside his squad car he heard another shot, then another and the sound of broken glass.

He had just reported over his radio that multiple shots had been fired at a house on Bonanza Drive when he observed a car being driven across a front lawn and onto the street at a high speed. Guessing that the offender was looking to get over to highway 13 to affect an escape, Officer Vague used Hoot Owl Point to head in that same direction knowing that he would arrive at Kimberling Airways Drive at the same time as the fleeing car and would engage him there.

As they raced together, the Kimberling City squad car on Hoot Owl Point and the desperate, fleeing shooter on the parallel street, Bonanza Drive, the timing was perfect. Officer Vague's squad car met up with the car being driven by Piles Beck when both turned on to Kimberling Airways Drive at full speed. Neither had time to swerve and avoid the head-on crash that resulted.

53

BREAKING NEWS OZRK24
BREAKING NEWS

Monday, 9:00 P.M.

The camera is pointed where the regular NEWS AT NINE anchor, Elaine Valley, is seen hurrying to her usual position at the news desk.

"Good evening, Springfield! We are interrupting our regularly scheduled MONDAY MOVIE, *They Died with Their Boots On*, to bring you this on-the-scene BREAKING NEWS Report. My co-anchor, Steve Gardner, is at the scene in Kimberling City where earlier this evening there were reports of a Home Invasion, multiple gun shots that has resulted in three or more persons seriously injured, and a police chase that ended in a head-on crash."

The director switches to the camera crew at the crash scene, with their mobile camera on Steve Gardner who is waiting anxiously for the signal to begin talking. It is after dark and the lighting is limited to only the headlights from emergency vehicles that are positioned to illuminate the accident scene. Alongside the reporter is a police sergeant.

"Elaine, I am at the corner of Kimberling Airways Drive and Hoot Owl Point where less than an hour ago there was a terrific head-on crash involving two cars, one a police squad car. I have with me Sergeant Dooley from the Kimberling City Police. Sergeant Dooley, what can you tell our viewers about the crash and the related shootings down on Bonanza Drive?"

"Earlier this evening Officer Eugene Vague was investigating a report of a stolen car when gunshots rang out at a nearby residence on Bonanza Drive," he began. "Officer Vague saw a vehicle exiting that location at high speed and he gave pursuit by circling around on Hoot Owl Point to head him off. When both vehicles turned on to Kimberling Airwaves Drive where it links Bonanza Drive with Hoot Owl Point their vehicles collided."

"Sergeant," Steve Gardner began asking. "When I arrived here with our camera crew we observed fire trucks, tow trucks, and ambulances at the crash site and shortly afterwards, at least three more ambulances speeding away on Hoot Owl Point heading back to Highway 13.'

"The shooting victims are being transported to Mercy Hospital in Springfield," Dooley responded. "Their condition is not at present known to us."

"And the crash victims?" Gardner asked. "I see those two ambulances are still here?"

"Yes, both the drivers were pinned and remain inside their vehicle," the sergeant answered. "The crew are using the Jaws of Life to help us get to them." His voice revealed much sadness and concern. "We have not yet been advised if either has survived…"

54

One week later

Monday, September 16th, 8:00 A.M.

Captain Travis Holden was the first one to arrive at the C.I.D.'s Case Review Session followed closely by Sheriff Cole "Bull" Lambert. As each member of the Stone County Criminal Investigation Department walked in, the Sheriff and the Captain shook their hands as they passed by and thanked them for the part they played in the successful murder investigations.

"This better not be one of those ass-chewing events that we've grown so accustomed to whenever the Bull is in here," Lieutenant Ernie Mize joked to Sergeant Arnie Platt after he settled in the chair next to him.

"Are you talking to me?" Platt deadpanned without turning to look at Ernie.

The lieutenant's jaw sagged to his chest, weighed down with the severe disappointment he felt at that response.

After the last of the detectives arrived and took their usual places at chairs around the table facing the Whiteboards that still had the photos and evidence comments posted on them, Lieutenant Honey Holcomb entered and followed the sheriff and captain to the front of the room.

Bull Lambert looked toward the doorway where everyone just passed through and waved-in to an unseen person.

"Deputy Alison Monroe views this room as nothing short of being an inner sanctum, where only the few who have made it to the rank of detective are admitted," he told everyone. "While she was… and remains, just another deputy," he said, trying hard to retain the straight-faced demeanor most often associated with him. "It turns out that she performed as an important role as anyone in this room during the two murder investigations we've just completed."

At that point, the sheriff stopped what he was saying and waved more vigorously for her to come in and be seated with the detectives.

Alison did as she was instructed, unable to hide the one joyful teardrop that spilled onto her cheek.

"Alison's hobby is writing novels," the sheriff told those in the room. "She has been writing about the recent investigations… with my permission since she is changing names, et cetera, to protect both the innocent and the guilty."

The other detectives laughed and gave Alison a round of polite applause.

"Before I leave and let you all begin the Case Review for the Cooper-Paladino death investigation, let me bring you up to date," Sheriff Lambert said. "Attorney Tomas Cullerton suffered a bullet wound to his chest when Piles Beck pulled him out of his car while trying to escape. He was transported by ambulance to Mercy Hospital where he was declared D.O.A."

The sheriff stole a look back at where Travis and Honey were standing. He knew that both had formed a relationship with the attorney and that his death left its effect on them.

Turning back to the seated detectives the sheriff allowed himself to swallow before continuing.

"Mr. Beck's attempted escape was thwarted by the heroic efforts of a Kimberling City Officer, Eugene Vague." Once again, the sheriff paused. He coughed once, then looked away hoping to curb the emotional pull now taking hold inside of him.

"I received word just before joining with you today that Officer Vague passed away this morning while in surgery at Mercy Hospital."

The news was completely unexpected and the shocked responses from the seasoned detectives were immediate. "Oh no…; Oh my… God!"

The mood of sadness in the room was followed by one of almost unanimous anger.

"I have not yet received anything regarding plans for Officer Vague's funeral, but I fully expect that there will be a large contingent of fellow police who will want to be in attendance," Lambert resumed.

"Piles Beck, as you know, was pronounced deceased at the crash scene," the sheriff pointed out hoping to address the anger he felt and saw in most all the detectives in the room. "The woman who Beck attacked inside the house, Elizabeth Lane, suffered a head injury that caused a concussion. She is expected to make a full recovery."

Once again, the sheriff took note of where his detectives were in the room paying particular attention to Alison Monroe.

"Emily Paladino remains in the hospital where she was transported after Beck shot her. She was shot in the upper chest where the bullet tore through a part of her lung. She lost a lot of blood at the crime scene and her wound required a pulmonary tractotomy. She remains in the hospital only because there are sometimes complications that need to be guarded against."

As the sheriff exited the meeting, he turned it back to Travis and Honey.

"As you all know, we conduct these sessions known as Case Reviews to consolidate all of the evidence we collected, the facts that we suspected, and the conclusions we detected, before Lieutenant Holcomb and I meet with the state's attorney," Travis began.

"What we want to do today is… dot the." Travis paused, noticing that something was happening behind his back.

While he was talking, Honey had begun writing on one of the Whiteboards… Dot the Eyes and Cross the Tees.

It was a play on spelling the words Captain Travis preached throughout every investigation and was timed perfectly with his predictable opening remarks. It drew the expected laughter from the other detectives.

"Yes," Travis smiled. "I know you have heard me say those words a few times before. But the words I will use right now come right out of the Detection for Dummies handbook that I plan to write when I retire," he joked. "To solve the crime, you must eliminate the suspects one by one."

Travis nodded to Honey who began writing on the Whiteboard the names after Travis called them out.

"The death of Kylie Cooper occurred on a houseboat where she, Mickey Paladino, and Emily Paladino were hiding after being told that the Chicago mob had ordered a hit on them," Travis explained.

The detectives watched as Honey wrote those two names under each other.

"Another person was also on that houseboat by the name of Frankie Valenti, an employee of the company owned by Mickey."

Honey wrote Valenti's name on the Whiteboard. Without being told she wrote Jari Abdou's name next.

Travis paused, examining the names on the board.

"Write one more name," he insisted. "Write Kylie Cooper and next to it write Cause of death: Accidental Overdose of drugs and alcohol."

Travis then approached the Whiteboard and erased the names of Emily Paladino and Jari Abdou.

"The Medical Examiner said that Kylie's death was from the drugs and alcohol, but we needed to investigate that to see if it was accidental, deliberate, or was this fatal combination sneaked into something she consumed by someone else? All evidence concludes it was accidentally consumed."

Honey Holcomb then approached the board and drew a line under the names of Frankie Valenti and Mickey Paladino.

"These men concealed the death of Kylie Cooper," she said. "Of course, Mickey is beyond the law now, but our Frankie Valenti has been charged with that crime."

On the adjacent Whiteboard Honey printed the name of Mickey Paladino and then stepped back indicating it was again the turn of Captain Holden.

"Regarding the death of Mickey Paladino, we began our investigations employing the teachings of Sheriff Cole 'Bull' Lambert. Come on, anyone?" Travis threw the challenge out to everyone.

"I believe you are now referencing… MOM," answered Lieutenant Ernie Mize.

Again, those seated all gave a mild applause to his answer.

"That's it exactly!" Travis said congratulating Ernie. "Motive, Opportunity, and the Means. Find them and solve any crime."

Travis walked toward the center of where the group of detectives were seated.

"The Chicago mob put out a hit order on Mickey because he deceived them when he put up collateral for a loan from them. The loan came through Lucas Juliano. So, we have someone who has a motive for murdering Mr. Paladino"

Honey wrote that name under Mickey's.

"Juliano sent Piles Beck to carry out the hit on Mickey and added the name of Emily which the mob consigliere, Guy

Chevron, thought would expedite the foreclosure on the restaurants used as collateral. Here, we have someone with a motive, and the means, and he next had to search for an opportunity to make the hit on Mickey."

Honey wrote each of those names next on the Whiteboard.

"Beck needed an insider to get at Mickey and Emily and lucked out when his old roomie at Stateville, Frankie Valenti, was in that position. Through contacting Valenti, Beck would find the opportunity needed to commit the crime."

The name of Frankie Valenti was written under the others.

"Emily Paladino was present when Mickey was shot," Travis resumed. "She was in the final stages of a divorce proceeding with Mickey. She had discovered he cheated on her with Kylie Cooper. She discovered that he forged her name for the collateral used to get the mob loan. And she would eventually receive the recently purchased life insurance payouts first, when Kylie died, and then after Mickey died while he was still Emily's husband. Emily Paladino hit the jackpot, scoring three for three having the Means, the Motive, and the opportunity. However, someone else was present and he also scored perfect in the MOM test."

Honey wrote Emily Paladino under Valenti's name.

"Armand Locke was not only present when Mickey suffered fatal wounds from being shot," Travis told everyone. "He was struggling with him, trying to take back a cashier's check in the amount of twenty thousand dollars which was funded by his theft from the real estate firm's escrow Account."

Honey wrote that name next to Emily's and under Piles Beck.

Travis said nothing as he walked across the front of the room and then behind the seated detectives, before circling back to where Honey Holcomb was standing. He put his hands on his hips and let a disappointed expression reveal the frustration he felt before resuming with the results of the investigation into the death of Mickey Paladino.

"Mickey Paladino died from a bullet fired from a .333 mm with a silencer… a gun that he owned… that he was using to steal money from Armand Locke… and that never left his hand during a struggle with that person. In short, Mickey Paladino's death was accidentally self-inflicted."

Almost immediately, Lieutenant Ernie Mize jumped up from his chair.

"Wait a minute!" he demanded. "That Emily woman had all those reasons… and you say that she just stood there while it was all going down… and did… NOTTA?"

Captain Travis just shook his head.

"And that real estate person, Locke, who stole the money from the escrow accounts and… and was actually fighting with the victim… he gets off Scott free too?" Ernie was beside himself.

"I didn't say anything about anyone getting off," Travis said when Ernie took a breath.

"Ernie," Travis said using a tone which he hoped would calm down the angry but misguided lieutenant. "I want to discuss these concerns you've just enumerated but perhaps it will work best if you finish with whatever questions that you still have now."

Lieutenant Mize realized he was off base the way he attacked the C.I.D. Captain with his questions. He paused and then apologized saying that he was just frustrated because the bad guys were not being made to pay for all they had done when breaking the law.

"Captain," he began sounding more in control of his emotions than earlier. "I just figured that we had at least one murder charge that would come out of our investigations. But, yes, I do have one final question."

Mize waited as the other detectives all let out a Bronx cheer when Ernie said he had one final question.

"On that night… or early morning… when Piles Beck broke into Emily Paladino's house the first time," Ernie began his question. "He was followed when he escaped down Bonanza Drive and out onto route 13 by someone in a black Lexus."

"Yes," Travis acknowledged. "And you did one whale of a fine job in later identifying the owner of that Lexus... Mrs. Estelle Locke."

Ernie was surprised that the captain was complimenting him now in front of his fellow detectives, especially after he had just angrily asked the other questions.

"Uh, yes... and thanks," Ernie said still quite surprised. "I am just wondering now if we turned up why... whoever it was that was driving that car... chased after Beck and then took off when Piles rolled his Dodge Charger off route 86 and Trace Hollow Road?"

Travis answered that they did investigate that situation.

"When we brought Armand Locke in for questioning, we focused on his fight with Mickey Paladino. We were able to corroborate his statements with other witnesses later," Travis said. "He was there because Mickey and Emily said that they were hiding from the Chicago mob and feared for their lives and needed his help."

Travis motioned towards Lieutenant Holcomb and asked if she would summarize her interrogation of Armand Locke.

"We already knew about the twenty-thousand-dollar illegal dip into the firm's escrow account," Honey explained. "Sergeant Arnie Platt managed to find that information from two sources, Twyla Turner, and Sherman Sutcliffe. And Captain Holden also was able to confirm that during his questioning of Emily."

Honey moved away from the Whiteboard, closer to where Ernie Mize was standing before resuming.

"Even with his lawyer present, Armand admitted that he took... he called it borrowed... the money saying it was to purchase the catamaran that Mickey owned. He first made a telephone call to a client who assured him that he would be interested in buying it from Armand at a ceiling price of $100,000.

But when he arrived at Kylie's he discovered that Mickey did not have a bill of sale ready or any assurance that he could get a clear title to the boat. Trying to leave, he was stopped when Mickey pulled a gun out and took the check from him. When he fought with Mickey, he said it was to keep from being shot."

"Self-defense?" asked Sergeant Ben Hedges sitting in the front row of chairs.

"That was the argument suggested by his lawyer who was present during the questioning," Honey responded. "So, I put that down as just something to run by the district attorney later. Instead, I switched to the night that Ernie just mentioned, and asked what he was doing over at Emily's home on Bonanza Drive. I told him that we had identified him driving behind the car driven by Beck when they crossed the Kimberling Bridge."

"So, did he try to deny?" Ernie rhymed his question, drawing a few whistles by fellow detectives.

"First, he just sat dumbfounded. His lawyer was already prepared for this line of questioning and leaned over and whispered that he should just tell me what he was doing there that night."

Honey paused and waited to continue until she took a sip from the water bottle next to her.

"He said he was drunk!"

"Drunk?" The whole room asked that one simultaneously.

"He told me that by then his entire world was crashing around him. His secretary, his accountant, the MREC... which I had to ask, stands for Missouri Real Estate Commission... and that very night even his wife, Estelle... all had found out about the escrow account misuses."

"Okay, but why was he getting drunk in Emily Paladino's neighborhood that first night when Beck broke into her house?" Ernie asked.

"He said he played poker with friends who rented space for their planes in a hangar at the Kimberling Airways, the private airport not far away from Emily's on Bonanza Drive. Around midnight, he left to drive back home, realized he was too drunk and pulled over to sleep it off. He awoke just when all hell was breaking loose. He said he was confused and thought that the car Beck was driving was his wife driving it… and that she always suspected he was cheating on her with Emily Paladino and, still in a drunken stupor, imagined that she must have been there looking to catch him. So, he took off following, whom he thought was his wife, until Beck crashed. He said it shocked him enough that he became more sober, saw it was not his wife, and drove home."

The whole room was groaning after hearing that explanation and Travis moved back to center stage to rescue his second-in-command.

"We will give the information we have on Armand Locke regarding the money he took from the escrow fund to the district attorney and let him decide if criminal charges or civil charges are in order."

Sheriff Lambert came back inside the room accompanied by the Homeland Security Chief.

"By now, most all of you know my good friend, Horace Haywood," the sheriff said while placing his hand on the shoulder of the DHS's top man. "He has completed his agency's interrogations of the people you helped capture over at Plyman's Point. "I'll let him take over now."

"Homeland Security was tipped some time ago to suspicious activities involving the purchase and use of the property over at Table Rock Lake known as Plyman's Point," the chief began. "Looking back now, I am reminded of another saying that was originated by your sheriff."

The chief paused to see if Bull Lambert guessed his reference.

"Things are always going to be connected," Bull Lambert beamed while reciting his observation. "People, Places, and Things can seem completely unrelated to each other until something happens that bring each into focus… Then, after discovering their connections you wonder why that had gone unnoticed until now."

The room remained quiet, slowly going over the message contained in the sheriff's observation. A few heads were seen nodding to their understanding of it, then a few more.

"I'll let you all give that more thought," Haywood laughed. "But I asked your sheriff if I could address you with the results of our investigation. First, none of the people we took into custody have been willing to talk with us. That is their right. But the fact that they were engaged in training American citizens to become domestic terrorists is now more than a mere suspicion. The evidence we obtained in our raid there provides that proof."

That news was met with a loud, appreciative cheer.

"The last link," Haywood resumed, "was finding out how they have managed to hide within our state, within our country. We previously learned they kept records of not only everyone who was trained at Plyman's Point by the ISIS connected team under Jari Abdou but also their current plans and, even better, their current locations."

The room was quiet as everyone listened intently, knowing that what they were hearing was something more serious than being a threat confined to Stone County or even the state of Missouri. It was a plot to destroy America.

"They did not have such valuable information printed and secretly stored somewhere. It always had to be accessible on short notice but could prove their undoing if our government found it. So, they kept this data in encrypted files stored in password protected cloud services requiring two passwords to retrieve it."

The Homeland Security Chief paused and glanced over at Sheriff Lambert before continuing.

"Jari Abdou had one of the passwords and his finance minister in their camp, Hanna Mustafo had the other. Both passwords were required and one by itself was useless. When we surprised Abdou during our raid on his camp we discovered that he had on his person a flash drive disguised as a tool in a pocketknife. The other that was assigned to Hanna Mustafo was missing. She had lost it when your deputies responded to rifle shots and chased inside their camp."

The DHS Chief suddenly began smiling.

"We took possession of all that was Piles Beck after he died in the crash and discovered the missing password. It was also inside an encrypted flash drive disguised as a locket which by fate alone, Piles came into possession of while he was hiding from you at Plyman's Point on that morning of the rifle shots. I am sure that he had no idea what it was but, I suspect that he thought it might make a nice gift for someone. We were able to use the flash drive passwords to gather complete dossiers and have everyone that was trained there now in federal custody."

Even Sheriff Lambert joined in the spontaneous outburst of cheers.

An investigation into one murder that turned out to be connected to a second murder which turned out to be no murders at all but was connected to a fraudulent loan application that led to a mob ordered hit that connected two former inmates that connected three loving sisters with one County Sheriff and an entire police force in Stone County, Missouri who connected with one government agency that ended the connections of thirty-two ISIS domestic terrorists.

Epilogue: One year anniversary

Monday, September 7th, 2025, 6:00 P.M.

"WE'RE EASILY THE THREE OLDEST GALS in this bar," Elizabeth laughed as she and Frances found Emily making last minute arrangements for when the others would arrive at her Branson Mickey Flynn's Restaurant and Bar.

"We are for now anyway," Emily agreed as she looked over the assembled crowd of persons in their early twenties that were drinking, dancing, singing, or making plans to link up while at the bar and at tables around the dance floor. "In another hour or so, Sheriff Lambert and the others will be joining us to celebrate our first anniversary since all that trouble we went through, and that should advance the average age inside this place."

"How many RSVP'd," Frances asked.

"I was surprised," Emily said smiling. "Everyone that we invited will be here."

Two large tables, each having seats for six people, were reserved, and set up for the special invitees.

Emily began pointing at empty chairs picturing the people who would soon be sitting there.

"I see Sheriff Lambert sitting next to Horace Haywood, then Travis Holden and Honey Holcomb, Arnie Platt, and Ernie Mize," as she circled the table. "At this table," Emily continued, "we have Alison Monroe and Owen Horner, Twyla Turner, and the three of us."

Labor Day at Mickey Flynn's restaurants was an annual custom for those celebrating the end of their summer break. The bars and dance floors were taken over by college-aged people looking to end their summers in any way that would produce party memories that would last, if not a lifetime, then at least until the following summer. It happened that way since the first year at the bar that Emily and Mickey Paladino opened in Branson and became a ritual in each of their restaurants ever since.

Emily recalled how Mickey's idea was that first Labor Day when they only had the Branson Mickey Flynn's. He called it "Summer Bye-Bye Baby Time" and he filled the bar with drinks that stayed below three-dollar levels; Jello shots for a dollar; four-liter jugs of wine for less than fifteen dollars; bottled Busch Beers at a dollar and Blue Moons for a dollar and a half. The bar served beers by the pitcher and Old Crow bourbon for young adults looking to move it on up.

"Were you as surprised as Frances and I were when you learned that the mob decided to recover the money Mickey owed on the loan by taking ownership of Ozark Lake Leisure Boats instead of going after your restaurants?" Elizabeth asked.

Emily breathed out a sigh of relief.

"It was their lawyer, Bronson Cummings, who came up with that strategy," she said. "He convinced Lucas Juliano that trying to foreclose on the restaurants would fail in court and in the long run could lead to him being criminally linked with the murder charges that Piles Beck would have faced if he survived the crash."

That night, Mickey's memory was welcomed in Emily's thoughts more than it had been since the troubles in their marriage began.

"You're off in space tonight," Elizabeth said. "Lots of memories, I guess."

"Yes," Emily turned and looked at Elizabeth. "I was thinking that my marriage to Mickey Paladino was both at the top and the bottom on my list of things that should happen in my lifetime. I believe now that ours was one that seemed to travel only on rocky roads and down twisted trails. But looking back, every bump and all those turns only made the ride... ever more special!"

THE END

Acknowledgments

The idea for my story began on a warm morning while I was in a boat fishing for bluegills with my dad and his buddy Johnny Ahern. The night before we hosted a cookout with neighbors, listening to tales of long-gone times. The stories fascinated me, including names and places that gave origin to the wonders they inspired. It was about a time that preceded Dogwood Canyon and when the bowling alley in Kimberling City was the favorite restaurant and bar in the area. Branson was going through some growing pains but still attracted some of the biggest stars in Country and Hillbilly music. The story took root when I was later sidelined from surgeries for stage four colon and liver cancer. I am presently five years free of any cancer and thankful for the prayers that were offered for my recovery. Publishing my novel would not have likely been possible without the help I received from Joel and Laura Pitney's Launch My Book team. They did so much but nothing near as important as providing Sayde Walker who steered me through the learning process. She is a godsend.

About the author

Tom Wood became a reporter and byline journalist at four newspapers in suburban Chicago after retiring from the U.S. Postal service. After *Alone Along Writers' Roads* (2024), *A Table Rock Mystery* is his second published novel.

Tom is available for select readings and locations. To inquire about a possible appearance email rightermi@gmail.com.